SAVAGE HORIZONS

Visit us at www.boldstrokesbooks.com

By the Author

Unknown Horizons

Savage Horizons

SAVAGE HORIZONS

by
CJ Birch

2018

SAVAGE HORIZONS

ISBN 13: 978-1-63555-250-8

This Trade Paperback Original Is Published By
Bold Strokes Books, Inc.
P.O. Box 249
Valley Falls, NY 12185

First Edition: August 2018

CREDITS
Editor: Ashley Tillman
Production Design: Susan Ramundo
Cover Design By W.E. Percival

Acknowledgments

First of all, I'd like to thank everyone at Bold Strokes for being the amazing people they are. I'd also like to thank my editor, Ashley Tillman, for her relentless attention to detail and also for asking the very important question: are there puppies in space (there are). You've made this a better book for it.

Setting a book in space doesn't really give you the opportunity to do firsthand research. Maybe I'll write a book set in coffee shops so I can do some hard research while doing my second favorite thing in the world (drinking coffee). Instead I had to get my knowledge from the internet. So thanks, Google. Any errors understanding said internet are mine alone.

And last but not least, I want to thank all my readers for continuing the journey with me.

CHAPTER ONE

I wake with a raging headache and my cheek plastered to the floor with spit. The ship's alarms are blaring, the ringing bounces between my ears. The contents of my shelves lie scattered across the floor. I choke as tequila fumes float up from the damp carpet. The shards of my prized bottle litter the desktop.

I stumble to my bed, hoping what little I've eaten in the last twenty-four hours stays in my stomach. I plop on the firm mattress and take a calming breath to assess the situation. The last thing I remember was watching Sarka leave with Ash.

And then, nothing.

Just Ash, promising me she wouldn't do anything foolish. Judging by the disarray around me, I have to assume she did. Goddamn her. For once I wish she'd think things through before jumping headfirst into every situation.

I run through all the facts. There was an explosion. Not aboard the *Persephone*. We wouldn't have survived an explosion that big. It must have happened on board the *Posterus*.

As soon as I stand, the ship lists. I collapse back onto the bed. Glass and debris careen off my desk. Out the window, the stars move in a sickening arc. We've lost control of the stabilizers.

Eight months and eleven days. The total sum of my captaincy. I've been in charge less than a year and I've already destroyed the ship. And this on the brink of embarking on the most prestigious mission of my career, hell, of any captain's career.

Eight months ago, I walked onto the bridge for the first time gripped with a strange mixture of fear and elation. There was no one else, only me, in charge of one hundred and eighteen individual lives. My choices were no longer for me. I needed to be selfless. A trait prized by every Belter but achieved by few. It doesn't matter where you're from. The mines on Epsilon, the farms on Delta, the factories on Beta, or the government on Alpha. It's the same across the Belt. There's a saying on Delta: feed the cows first. It's the farming capital for a reason. They're not too bright when it comes to articulation.

You don't come first. There isn't a single person who hasn't felt the sting of that lesson. Even on Alpha where they're taught to serve the people. Life isn't easy.

Where I grew up on Delta, things aren't so bad. If you like farming. At least there's work. On Beta, too many jobs are becoming automated, leaving workers no choice but to head to Epsilon. And on Delta the work takes years to kill you. Not like on Epsilon where working the mines has a life expectancy of months not decades.

And if you don't want to farm, mine, or slog away in a factory, you can join Union fleet. The life expectancy isn't much better than Epsilon. But who wouldn't trade in the mines for a ship? Most of the time we're hauling cargo from one asteroid to another. But when you compare it to working the mines or farms, it's freedom.

When I imagined finally docking at the *Posterus,* this is not what my mind pictured. I had no idea I would show up in a burning wreck, reeking of failure and feeling like crap.

I march, with as much dignity as my wobbly legs will allow, to the bridge. I need to see what that bastard did to my ship. I need to find out if Ash is okay.

It's chaos.

As soon as the doors slide open, the acrid smell of burning solder and copper slaps me in the face. It's followed by a heat so scary, my pulse skips a couple times before kicking into high gear. We're on fire.

"Vasa!" I shout to my comms officer, who has his head stuffed behind a console. "What's our status?"

The ship lists again. Seven crew members in various positions of panic, grab for a bulkhead. I, on the other hand, flail about until my feet skid to a halt in the doorjamb.

"Captain." Vasa lurches toward me, but I wave him off. I don't need his help. What I need is to get this situation under control. The bridge tips again, sending us all starboard. My head glances off the helm controls and I land on my hands and knees.

"What's wrong with the stabilizers? Why are we listing so goddamned much, Vasa?" I pull myself up, crawling along the starboard controls until I reach comms up front.

"The docking clamps blew, too much strain from the reverberation and now we're drifting. I haven't assessed the damage. But I'm going to be honest, Captain, the stabilizers are the least of our problems." He waves toward the surface in front of him with its blinking lights and swallows hard before continuing. "We've got a hull breach and fires on four different decks, including engineering." His dull brown hair coats his forehead in a sticky mess. Sweat runs down his pasty face.

Fuck.

That's my first thought. Too many first priorities. That's my second.

Vasa stares up at me like a trusting puppy, as if now that I'm here, I'll have all the answers. The truth about being in charge, and this is the part that sucks, is that most of the time you're faking. Most of the time you sound like you know what you're talking about. But you don't. You're guessing and hoping your guess doesn't kill people.

As I stare into the wan face of my third in command, I can't decide which is the worse of our two problems. Getting sucked into space by a hull breach or the fires sucking up all our oxygen. Either choice I make will kill someone.

"Where is the hull breach?"

"Deck four. There are twelve people on that deck as far as I can tell. But there could be more. The fires are messing with some of the sensors."

"And where are the fires?

"Med deck, engineering, officer's mess, and the forward shield compartment." He traces the blinking lights on the console. Julianna Olczyk, my helms officer, slides up beside us, eager to hear my plan. Her thick blond curls escape her tight bun. I look at the hard faces staring up at me from various stations around the bridge. All with those same hopeful eyes. I know they're waiting for orders. Waiting for me to take charge.

Fuck. Fuck. Fuck. Fuck.

"Get a team down to deck four to seal the breach."

"Comms are down."

"Christ, Vasa. Is anything working?"

"Emergency life support."

"Fantastic." I pace toward the helm to buy myself time. The movement helps keep the panic at bay. I rub my forehead. That helps a bit too. Think of something, and make it fast. I press the heal of my palm into an eye socket, bright blinding pain and light follows. I know what I have to do. I just don't like it.

"Okay," I say. Everyone's attention snaps even tighter, a thread pulled taught. "Vasa, I need you to work on restoring comms. When you get it working, let me know, then contact the *Posterus* and get a report from them. Olczyk, stay and help him out and see if you can figure out what's wrong with the stabilizers." I point to the five other crew members. "You guys, follow me, we're going to split into groups to tackle the fires and the hull breach."

Four chutes and ten minutes later, we're standing in the landing on deck four, suited up. Two sets of eyes, panicked, await my orders. We're trained for emergencies, but in truth, these guys aren't prepared for this. They're bridge officers. The chances of us finding anyone alive are remote. Our real goal when we enter the deck, is to plug the gapping hole in our hull. I'm unsure if I should prepare them for it. I know none of them will back out now and I'd rather no one throws up with their helmet on.

"Okay, keep your eyes peeled for survivors. There's a good possibility that no one survived. We all know the textbook description of space exposure, but the reality is much, much worse. Trust me. If you feel sick, don't play the hero. Head back here." Nods from both of them. Good. I hope they actually listen. "We need to make it to the starboard side, section fifteen. That's where the breach is."

I sent the other three to engineering to get control of that fire first. Without engineering we'd be dead in the water. After that, we're all headed to the med deck. I have a feeling it'll be filling up real soon.

I wave my hand over the door sensor and it opens to a silent hallway. The atmosphere is eerie. The emergency lights flash red above and the LEDs blink green along the floor. Each pointing the direction to safety. Opposite the direction we're heading.

As soon as the door closes behind us, the ship lists again and we stumble along the corridor. I lose my footing and slide face-first onto the floor, inches from a wide-eyed Fukui. His skin is a dull gray, his expression frozen in a horrified grimace. I stagger back. The ship swings aft and my knee slams down on his hand.

It shatters.

In an instant, pieces of the engineer are falling through the metal grate at my feet. With my palm braced on the wall, I take deep, calming breaths, willing my heart to slow and my mind to focus on our task.

The hole, when we reach it, is no bigger than my head. Through the opening the *Posterus* spins into view as we drift further away. It looks undamaged except for the patch we tore off. Debris streams from the breach like water trickling from a tap.

I'm amazed by our sheer dumb luck. As the vastness of space spreads out before us, the silence is so powerful it's almost deafening. Our insignificance and fragility has never been so clear. It's indescribable, this feeling that washes over me. As I stand on the edge, I'm humbled and awed and at an utter loss as the stars, so numerous, swarm my senses. We should be dead. So many moments in our evolution, in our history, should have aided in our extinction.

Yet here we are, a misplaced comma in a line of code, so small and yet still capable of wreaking havoc all the same.

In moments, the sight is gone as we place a panel over the hole and apply welding tape to bind it in place. As soon as the weld is complete, a whoosh of sound breaks free and surrounds us.

"Come on guys, let's go put out some fires."

The intercom crackles in my helmet and I hear Vasa's voice make contact.

"Do you copy, Captain?"

"Status report."

"Well, I've got good news and bad news."

I huff at him. "Get to the point. What's happening on the *Posterus*? Do they know what happened? What the casualties are?" Is Ash alive?

"That would be part of the bad news."

"Only part?"

"You should come up to hear this, Captain."

"I'm a little busy right now. I'm about to rendezvous with the fire teams."

"Fire teams just checked in. All but one have been neutralized. We need you on the bridge."

"Was that the good news?"

He hesitates. "No, I've got comms back up and working."

"Shut those goddamn alarms off, Vasa." I growl as I step onto the bridge. I turn, startled to see Sarka leaning against the wall. Olczyk's got a gun pointed at his stomach and there's an insouciant grin on the bastard's face.

I jerk a thumb at him as I stomp toward the helm. "Part of the bad news?" Vasa only nods. He's focused on the chart in front of us.

"The *Posterus* isn't much better off than us. Sensors are down, but they were able to launch a probe." He transfers the chart to the front holo. It darkens to become a mass of stars and ping times running up along the side.

"What is that?" I ask, stepping closer to examine the chart.

"That's where we are." Our call sign pulses lost—along with the *Posterus*'s—amid various colored dots. Each represents a different type of star. I don't recognize a single configuration.

"That can't be. The probe must be malfunctioning."

Vasa shifts, running his hand along the front of his tunic. "They sent out three, all came back with these results."

"What does that mean?"

"It means this ain't Kansas." Still leaning against the wall, Sarka grins. It's wolfish and mean.

Vasa frowns. "Um, I'm not sure what Kansas is, but we're definitely not in our solar system anymore."

CHAPTER TWO

"Why can't we go back?"

The room, which a second ago had been full of screeching representatives, goes deadly silent at this question. The question comes from a short man with bristly eyebrows too large for his forehead. His light green uniform holds the insignia of the wellness division. It's a lie that there are no stupid questions. And judging by the reaction of Captain Harrios sitting next to him, he agrees.

Two days have passed and we still have no better understanding about what's happened. Somehow we've traveled to another galaxy. We have no idea how, or even the distance from our own. It's as if some giant hand has lifted us from one pond and plopped us down in another.

I'm not a religious person. I've never believed in a higher power. Yet, I'm always intrigued by the theories we are either dust in the grooves of someone's floor or a simulation. These theories explain when science can't. They're like the gods of our past. There's always a scientific answer and I know there must be for what's happened to us. We have to be patient.

"Go back?" Amit, the *Posterus*'s head of engineering stands, an incredulous look on his face. "How? We don't even know where we are. It would be like blindfolding you in a maze, leading you to the middle, and asking you to make your way out the way you came." The giant man spits as he talks. He peers around the table, silently asking for confirmation that this man is stupid and should leave.

The room stays silent. A few of the members, bored already, gaze out the window onto the enormous concourse of the *Posterus*. Everything is shiny and new. Compared to the *Persephone*, which has years of smells, the *Posterus* is sterile. Every dent, scorch mark, burn and stain on my ship comes with a story. This place feels like the packaging hasn't even come off yet.

Captain Harrios—our representative for Union fleet—clears his throat. While I agree finding a way to get back is the wrong focus for this meeting and our immediate goals, I keep quiet. As Captain Harrios reminded me before the meeting, I'm a side note. I'm only here to give a brief on the events that occurred with Davis Sarka.

Having to explain how the leader of the Burrs hijacked my ship was not how I wanted to spend my morning. Never mind trying to explain the logistics of turning a human being into a bomb.

Call him what you want, a terrorist, space pirate, pain in the ass, his involvement is the reason we're here, stuck in this unknown system. We're in this mess because of his ideals about humans and interstellar space travel.

Harrios opens his mouth to speak but Amit interrupts him. "We aren't going anywhere, not until we repair the engine. And that's going to take months." Amit flops back in his seat. It groans from the weight. "Months." He throws his hands in the air to emphasize his statement in case anyone thinks he's exaggerating.

The room explodes again. Politicians, engineers, doctors, even the chef and botanist have opinions. I lean back and observe as each screams louder. Each hoping their voice will be the one to rise above the din, even though they refuse to listen. I watch as Ash's great hope disintegrates into ego and rhetoric. Our first chance to prove we can govern better than the Commons and here we are, no better. Each section thinks they know best. Each representative bullies for their opinion to matter. It makes me sick to think how right Vasa is.

When we began the planning stages of this journey, we also created a new way to govern. We formed committees with one representative from each of the sixteen departments. No one is in charge, everyone has equal say. Each section votes on their representative.

"Correct me if I'm wrong, but isn't the point of this whole mission to find a suitable planet to colonize? So what if our starting position has changed, why does the mission? Why can't we continue from here?" It isn't very loud. I say it more to myself than anyone else, perhaps that's why it gets noticed. Everyone stops and turns to me. Captain Harrios's nostrils flare as he shoots me a venomous look. There is a clear warning in his eyes: keep quiet.

Harrios stands. His six foot four inches tower over the table. He runs his hands down the front of his uniform, emphasizing the medals displayed at his breast. What an ass. "I suggest that while the engine is being repaired we use this time to assess how we got here. Figure out how, if possible, we make it back. If we have no idea where we are, there's no possible way we can find Kepler 980f from here." His build and stature remind me of my father when he was a young lieutenant. From the pictures I've seen, they both have that same cocky attitude pouring out of every orifice. Only Harrios isn't so young and it's beginning to show. His cheeks are drooping off his face like pudding sliding down a wall and it's getting harder for his uniform to hold in his paunch. It protrudes out the bottom when he forgets to keep it sucked in.

Captain Harrios is the epitome of career officer. He was born into a family of generals leading back to several world wars. He's made a name for himself by stepping on anyone willing to bend over enough for him to get a foothold. While I don't deny my own similar ambitions, I doubt I've left the same wake as Harrios. There are several rumors flying around that he bribed his way onto the mission. It's the only way to explain why someone ten years older than the age cap made it onto the mission roster. Only a select few in extraordinary circumstances have been able to bypass the age cap. I almost didn't make the cut myself. At thirty-four I slipped in with one year in my favor.

"I'm not suggesting we do. I'm suggesting we find a different planet, one that's closer. I've been studying the information sent back by the probes. It's clear there are planets in the sweet spot within a hundred light years of us. And while we're waiting, instead of sitting on our as—sitting around, why not send out the fleet ships? We can mine from some of the surrounding asteroids." I'm not about to sit around for six months waiting for other people to decide my future. I'd rather be in charge of that myself.

I didn't choose the best career path if I wanted to be in charge of my own life. Maybe that's why I've spent the last fifteen years doing everything I could to get where I am today. Granted, lost in an unknown galaxy fighting over who's in charge is not the end goal. But I'm captain of my own ship. I at least have command over my own officers. With the Union fleet commanders a distant speck, I can steer myself and my ship with more say. Harrios may be our representative, but he doesn't command me. We're the same rank. I'm not going to let him take charge and decide what the *Persephone* does for the next six months.

There are nods around the table as my idea takes hold. We started this mission with the knowledge that none of us would make it to our final destination. Our estimate is that it would take us over a hundred years to make it to Kepler 980f, the planet we've chosen for colonization. But any number of things can set us back. There's even the possibility we'll get there and it won't be suitable after all. This mission is a big risk. The asteroid belt can't sustain our species forever. It was only a temporary solution until we could find something more permanent.

The exodus from Earth to the Belt wasn't something that happened overnight. It took decades. Over fifty years of planning. Fifty years of knowing there was nothing to do but watch a planet die around you. The ecosystem that humans once fit so perfectly in was disintegrating around them. I can't imagine what it would be like to know your children wouldn't grow up in the same world you did. Millions of others before you destroyed that for them because of ignorance and laziness and greed. Those fifty years were the worst.

There was poverty and death like nothing the world had ever seen. The wars were over, leaving nations devoid of resources and money. The only way to survive was to pool together and start fresh. That's how the Commons started. The dregs of the world's nations banded together and created the rudimentary council that became the Belt's government.

They constructed ships and made plans. They built modules to transport up to the asteroids in the Belt and constructed the first cities. They started on Ceres, which was the largest of the asteroids, a dwarf planet which became Alpha. They established the first colonies and the Commons to oversee the rest of the settlements. There were five. Alpha, Beta, Gamma, Delta, and Epsilon. A stray asteroid destroyed Gamma over fifteen years ago. Few survived.

But before all that, before even the last wars, humans had pipe dreams of terraforming Mars. They spent almost a quintillion on the project. The last three countries with space programs sent up five ships with a different purpose. The Frontier missions. Robots manned the first four and established the settlement. Each dropped off a set of supplies for the fifth and final mission. The last one, manned by five astronauts.

But the ship never made it to Mars and no one knows what happened. The ship didn't explode. It didn't crash. It disappeared into the unknown. The program bottomed out after that. And then the resource wars started and all thoughts of building settlements on distant planets vanished.

After Gamma's destruction, the Commons proposed our current mission. We needed to think bigger, think long-term. They designed and built the *Posterus* over the next twenty years. A generational ship carrying over 45,000 people to begin a new life on a new planet. Only now, those 45,000 people are stranded in an unknown galaxy with no clue how we got here.

"How long would it take to send a ship to one of these asteroids?" The captain of the *Posterus* is a squat woman with short, stylish white hair. I'd only met Captain Wells one time before, but she struck me as someone you didn't want to cross or piss off. I get the impression that Harrios is coming close to doing both.

"A couple of weeks—"

"Depends on the asteroids' orbitational position—"

Harrios and I both speak at the same time. Before Harrios can commandeer the discussion, I stand and launch into my proposal.

"There are two asteroids within easy reach. I propose we send each of our ships out, the *Persephone* and the *Brimley* and investigate. It would only take a few weeks, a month at most, to get to each, mine resources, and get back. We could be there and back in under six months, easy."

Sixteen people focus on me. I'm leaning forward, my palms pressed into the hard metal surface of the table, my heart thumping hard. Before anyone can reject the idea, I push forward. "It's the reason they included our ships in the mission. We're faster and more maneuverable than the *Posterus*. It's better we spend our time on something productive."

"You'd want the ships to investigate together?" Someone at the far end asks.

"No." Both Harrios and I speak at the same time. He looks at me. It's a brief glimpse, but I see his disdain. He hides it as he turns to Captain Wells. "No. It will be faster if we travel separately."

"The asteroids are in opposite directions. It's better if we split," I say. Even if they were close together, I'd find another asteroid. I don't need Harrios micromanaging my day to day.

Amit snorts from his seat. "And of course you'll want to take Hartley with you?"

"Of course. He's my head of engineering. I'm not going to leave him behind."

"We need him for the repairs to the engine. It's his engine."

This is true, but I suspect Amit wants Hartley to make the work easier for himself. There's no reason they can't rebuild the engine without him. "You don't need Hartley. He may have designed the *Posterus*'s engine, but he didn't build it. He'll be more use to me on my ship."

"Is this true?" Captain Wells asks.

I nod. "We're still making repairs."

"What if he'd rather stay here? Hartley's a scientist, not an adventurer." Amit raises his eyebrows at me.

I don't know if that's true or not. It's Ash, my first officer, who knows Hartley best. But it doesn't matter. I'm going on this mission with Hartley or not at all. I have to find the diplomatic way to make this clear. "If you need help with the engine rebuild I have no problem transferring crew from my ship. Fukui has been working under Hartley for the past month, he would be as good…" I trail off, remembering Fukui's blank stare. The weight of it crushes me. We knew starting out there would be casualties. Space travel, even in this century, is dangerous. But we've barely begun, and already our death toll is at sixteen, eight of whom are from the *Persephone*. I try to think of Fukui as a number, one among many, but it isn't possible. I can see all eight faces as if they're standing in front of me.

I look up to see everyone staring at me. "Um, Fukui was one of our casualties." I take a deep breath, I need to be strong about this. "But you can have your pick. Not Hartley. I need someone who knows my ship. And it's not a good time to introduce a new head of engineering to my crew. Not with everything else that's happened." I let that thought sink in. Everyone knows we've had the greatest loss. I'm sure many see it as a failing on my part, but that's not something in my control, so I let it wash away. I have too many other things to worry about.

"That's a reasonable request," Captain Wells says, pulling everyone back to the situation at hand. "If no one else has any other questions why don't we take a vote?" There will be seventeen votes. Because this is a Union fleet matter, Harrios's will count as two. I have a feeling he's going to shoot down the idea, knowing him, he'd rather play it safe. And sure enough, when it comes his turn, he votes no, so does Amit for obvious reasons. But Captain Wells, the man from the wellness division and eight others vote yes. That means in a couple of days, once we finish repairs, the *Persephone* is going exploring.

CHAPTER THREE

The meeting breaks up shortly after the vote. I elbow my way through the crowd formed at the door, searching out Captain Wells. I keep at least three people between Harrios and me at all times. The scowl on his face has hardened and I don't want to get in front of that.

I catch up with Captain Wells near the lifts. It amazes me, still, the sheer size of the *Posterus* stretching before us. We stand on an upper deck overlooking the main concourse two kilometers in length. I can hardly make out the details at the other end. Above us, the ceiling towers. It's covered by metallic glass, projecting a constant night sky.

I found a book once, among my father's things, called *Jonathan Livingston Seagull*. And it always struck me, that he never once thought of the sky, only the ocean below and the way it felt to dive toward it. The air through his feathers, land rushing to meet him. I remember wondering how something so much a part of the sky could take it for granted. I felt let down that he didn't spend more time describing the sky. If I had the chance, I would never take the shades of blue and the clouds and the lightness of it for granted.

"Captain Wells, may I have a word?" She turns, her head at breast level, and stares up at me with dark, expectant eyes. "As you know, we have Davis Sarka in our brig. I don't want to take him with us on our exploration. When can we arrange transfer to the *Posterus*'s brig?"

Of course he survived. The man is indestructible. When my crew found him wedged under a bulkhead, there wasn't a scratch on him. Both members of his crew weren't so lucky. We still haven't found them.

She blinks a couple of times, her eyes, if possible, going darker, then says, "Our brig?" She shakes her head. Her white hair moves with it like it's sculpted. She takes my arm and pulls me aside and, from her expression, I know what she's about to say will not make me happy. "I know it will be an inconvenience, but it's best if you keep Sarka with you. Union fleet has training to deal with the Burrs that we don't." She gestures to a man standing a few feet away. He's so thin, his stomach is concave. His pale face searches the crowd, watching, but it's only cursory. Behind those eyes, no one's home. His mind is miles away.

"That's Brian. He's our security on board the *Posterus*. He won't be much use if we have to deal with Sarka."

"That's your security?" I'm stunned. I look out again at the vastness of the station.

"He's not our only security, but he's a good representation. We're a small community, Captain Kellow. Yes, the ship is big, but the settlement itself is small, especially if this were the Belt. Both the *Persephone* and the *Brimley* have brigs and ample security. We don't foresee the need to have more than that." Someone beside me snorts.

Harrios, who has maneuvered his way through the crowd, says, "We'll see how long that lasts." For once we actually agree, but I keep my mouth shut.

"But what am I supposed to do with him? I can't keep him in my brig forever. It's tempting, believe me, but inhumane."

Captain Wells shrugs. "I'm afraid I can't help you with that. The jurisdiction is clear. He's Union fleet's problem." My mouth falls open and I close it. Harrios raises his hands like it's not his problem either. Great. What the hell am I supposed to do now?

Her attitude is understandable. Sarka has a reputation for being brutal and dangerous. If I were in her position, I would do the same. He's a problem no one wants. Most of all me. A large part of me

SAVAGE HORIZONS

wishes he'd died in the explosion. It would serve him right after he tried to blow us all up.

Captain Wells steps into the lift, and I move to follow, but Harrios taps my arm. I suppress a sigh, hold back, and watch as all hope of offloading Sarka disappears behind two metal doors.

I turn toward the stairs instead of sticking around to hear what Harrios has to say in front of a dozen or so strangers. The meeting has dispersed, but there're still a lot of people milling about. Every few seconds I have to squeeze between one person or another. Behind me the captain huffs and snorts, like he's walking up the stairs instead of down.

He catches up to me at the bottom, matching my stride. It's getting on my last nerve the way he stomps after me. I stop and turn and he almost rams into me.

"What?" I put my hands on my hips. "Is there a reason you're following me?"

I don't like his expression. His face is so pinched the skin between his brows has almost swallowed his eyes.

"I don't know what the hell you're up to, Kellow. If you want my position on the council, you're going to have one hell of a fight ahead of you." Again, his hands slide down the front of his tunic. His fingers caress the medals like they're announcing he's better. My uniform is bare compared to his, especially today. The only pin above my breast is my captain's insignia.

With everything that's happened, I've had no time to think let alone worry about my appearance. Harrios plays the career officer well. If he hadn't joined this mission, he would've done well in the Commons. I was surprised when I heard his was the other fleet ship selected because we all assumed he'd go into politics.

I huff and turn to leave. I don't need any of his posturing bullshit. Not today. But I know he'll stalk me all the way to the med center. So instead I say, "The idea of laying up for half a year when we have one of the greatest opportunities human exploration has ever known, is shortsighted. But if that's your thing, by all means, have at it. But I'll be damned if I give up this chance to see what's out there." You can keep your fucking council position. I don't say the last part. Letting it loose in my mind makes me feel better.

"You expect me to believe that show was so that you didn't have to sit around for the next couple months?" He smirks, as if I couldn't be telling the truth. His tone and that look gets my back up like nothing else. I can actually feel my nostrils expanding like a bull ready to charge.

But I hold it in. I tuck the anger deep, like always. "To be honest, I don't care what you think." I stomp off and leave him standing in the middle of the hallway, dwarfed by the soaring concourse.

It's a good hike from the command center to the med center, and as always, the exercise helps calm my mind. It feels almost like walking through one of the major avenues on Alpha. Only this is more—I don't want to say rustic, because it's not. But there's a pioneer vibe to the whole thing, as if they've channeled Earth's early settlers.

Some of the stores are still boarded up, having sustained damage during the explosion. But others, like the food stalls and cafes, are packed with customers. There's a party vibe floating around. And why not? We all survived our first test. Space is a dangerous place. If you don't have the balls to hack it, you shouldn't be out here.

Most of the *Posterus*, the ones who will make up the majority of our population, are looking for a better life. They're from places like Epsilon and Delta. I don't blame them. Who would want to stick around for a job mining or farming? I sure as hell didn't. Others are adventurers. They're looking to explore without having to join Union fleet or become an asteroid miner. And others still are looking to get around the one child law. Out here, it's encouraged to procreate. Back on the Belt, pregnant women are viewed with equal parts envy and wariness. Resources are scarce.

After humans fled Earth to colonize the asteroid belt, food was less a privilege and more a luxury. I've heard of kids starving to death, especially in the group homes on Epsilon. There are a lot of accidents in the mines. If you're unlucky enough to be born on Epsilon and your parents die in the mines, they put you in a group home where one day you'll take their place. Every child, once cherished, is now seen as another mouth to feed. It's no wonder thousands signed up. Everyone here will be dead long before we reach our destination, but it's still a hell of a lot better for some than life on the Belt.

I enter the med center located on the *Posterus*'s lower decks, looking for Ash. With everything that's happened, I haven't had a chance to see her. I've been going nonstop since I woke up in my cabin two days ago. Every time I tried to come see her something else would come up. I haven't even had a chance to sleep. I only have the doctor's word she's alive. But I need to see it for myself. I need to make sure she's all right.

I still don't know how it's possible. No one does. Even Hartley said she should be dead. We all should. I spoke to him yesterday evening. He said he grabbed her so she wouldn't fall into the engine pit. As soon as he touched her his hand felt heavy like it had become the weight of her and himself combined. And then there was this sense of lightness like they were floating and everything went white. That's all he'll say. He can't remember anything else, and I can tell it's infuriating him not knowing.

He woke up on the floor in the engine bay with Ash next to him. His grip was still fused to her forearm. He wasn't hurt.

But Ash was.

The doctor said she had burns on most of her body and a dislocated shoulder. Her right hand gripped some device of Hartley's. He removed it along with most of the skin on her palm.

I hear her before I even reach her room. She laughs at something someone's said and I walk a little faster.

I stop before I enter and stare. From where I stand, I can see her, but she can't see me. A blue sling holds her arm tight against her chest, keeping it immobile. She's in a hospital gown, her leg flung on top of the blanket. There's a deep purple bruise along her calf and grafting bandages on most of her left side. She looks so small sitting in the hospital bed, I have an urge to encase her in protective foam.

Her face is still lit up from laughter, acting as if she were sitting in the mess not the hospital covered in burns. She doesn't look like she almost died two days earlier. She's pulled her auburn hair back into a messy ponytail. Her pale skin has a healthy flush to it.

There's someone sitting on the bed in front of her. I can't see who it is, but when I hear that booming laugh, I realize it's Hartley.

"I guess I should be happy, even if I don't get a school named after me. You think the captain will let me name the incident after myself? That is, when I figure out what and how it happened. The Hartley incident sounds pretty cool, right?" he says.

Ash's face drops a little. She picks at a piece of lint on the bed. "Have you seen her?"

"The captain? Yeah, I briefed her on what happened in the engine room earlier. She has a meeting with the council today. I didn't tell her it was your idea to eject the core. She seemed kind of mad at you, so I let her think it was my idea." I roll my eyes at this, like I thought for a second anyone but Ash would be behind such a self-destructive idea.

"Thanks, Hartley." She reaches out and grabs his hand. "But I doubt she bought it." There's silence for a few moments and then she asks, "How did she look? She didn't get hurt or anything did she?" I feel guilty now. I shouldn't be eavesdropping on such a personal conversation. I begin to move away to come back later, but Hartley's next question stops me.

"Is it true then? You and the captain?"

I'm surprised as hell to learn this has been a topic of conversation. Not that much happened. One night. But I thought we'd been discreet.

"What's that supposed to mean?" She scowls, pulling her hand back.

"Oh come on, everyone's heard the rumors. Well, I guess you haven't since no one ever talks to you except me and the captain. And also the rumor's about you, so I guess they wouldn't tell you even if they did like you." He takes a breath, then continues, "But there's a rumor going around about you and the captain." He lets the sentence trail off and everyone's imagination goes places it shouldn't.

But what she says next tears at my insides more than anything. "Do I look like I'd be dumb enough to get involved with my commanding officer?" He doesn't say anything. Ash huffs and turns away from him, her free arm coming up awkwardly to cross at her chest. "Well, I'm not, Hartley. There's nothing going on between us. And I don't care who thinks there is, they can go to hell."

I lean my head back against the wall. I close my eyes and breathe for a few seconds. Of course, she's right. There isn't anything going on between us. There can't be. But if I'm being honest with myself, there's more there. Our relationship goes beyond command and friendship. The way she says it though, like it's nothing to her, fills me with shame. Shame at the way I behaved, shame at my own constant selfishness. Always that.

I push off from the wall and rush toward the exit, almost laughing at my own unerring selfishness. If I see something I want, it doesn't matter what I have to do, who I have to hurt, I'll get it in the end.

CHAPTER FOUR

I drift through the concourse, no longer awed by its grandeur. I don't know how long I roam. My thoughts are a jumble of regrets and resolve. I find myself standing in front of the brig waiting for Corporal Wyatt Fossick to open the door.

"Me, finally me." Sarka sits on a thin cot. He grins, taunting me. It's a smile I remember well. When I was a child I used to love it. That smile meant he was paying attention to me, even if he was teasing. It made me feel wanted, loved. Now it infuriates me. It stirs the rage deep inside, like hydrogen feeds a star, keeping it burning.

If he has to come with us, I'd rather he stay in the brig. But I can't keep him here forever. There's a brief moment when I contemplate proposing the reinstatement of capital punishment, but push that out immediately. I'm not a murderer, and I don't want my crew to be either.

"So this is how it's going to be." I lean against the door. "I'm taking you to quarters with a twenty-four hour guard. If you try to escape, I'll bring you back here. If you so much as lift a finger to one of my guards, I'll bring you back here. If you even step out of line or bad-mouth my crew—"

"Yeah, yeah, I get it, brought back here." Teeth flashing, he says, "Here's nice, though," and looks about the room as if it's a grand place with a view. "What if I want to stay here?"

I shrug and move off the door. "Fine with me." I turn and knock for Fossick to open up.

"Although, you know me. I've always been a bit of a gossip, and this place is kinda echoey. Who knows what I could let slip out."

If I hadn't seen the crew's reaction to Ash, to the fact she has a piece of the Burr's technology in her, I wouldn't care. I'd tell the crew myself. But if they're willing to hurt Ash for that? What would they do if they found out I had twenty-three chromosomes from Davis Sarka? What would they do if they knew I was one half of the nightmare?

I lean my forehead against the door. The cold metal spreads across my hot skin. I knew, before I even walked in, he'd be difficult. This is what he does. He plays head games, always those same twisting mazes to confuse you, to make you reveal your secrets. He'll play with me, holding it over my head, and each time I give, he'll take more than I'm willing. He'll toy with my fears until he knows them all and has all the control.

I can't let him win. Not like this. Not again.

"Go ahead. Tell them. But the second you do, I'll slit your throat." I turn back to show I'm not bluffing. I want him to see how much I mean it.

The door opens behind me, and I nod to Fossick, then look back at Sarka, a question and challenge on my face. He doesn't say anything, just unfurls from the cot and stalks toward the doors.

"Cuff him," I say.

He stands and holds his hands out to Fossick. "If it'll make you feel safer, you can cuff me to one of your security officers." He says this without sarcasm. He's rearranged his face to be expressionless. It smooths out the skin and doesn't look as stretched. I push him through the door. I'm not in the mood for any of his bullshit today.

Fossick steals looks at Sarka's face as he places the cuffs around his wrists. This is the closest any of my crew have ever been to a Burr. It must be unsettling, to see up close what we only talk about in hushed voices. I wish I knew what he was thinking. Is Sarka worse or better than what he has worried about his whole life?

Once a handsome man, Sarka is now a plastic version of himself. During the resource wars Ethan Burr developed a special type of soldier. He engineered them to be the last soldier any army would need. He implanted mind knots—tiny bots to control their actions—and programmed them to act without question.

What most people don't know is that he also rewrote some of their DNA, like opening a computer program and rearranging some of the code to get a different result. This was, of course, before they banned genetic manipulation. As a result, Burrs are almost impossible to kill. It isn't so much that they can't die, it's that you usually only have one try. Their reflexes were improved and their pain receptors dulled, which makes them more like robots trained to kill than human beings let to live.

We're led by two security guards down the corridor. I'm in back, Sarka is in the middle and Quinn Yakovich, my head of security, and Fossick are in the lead. They make a strange pair side by side. Fossick is short and stocky and Yakovich is tall and lean. Her muscular shoulders fill out her tunic in a way Fossick must envy. The only thing they have in common is a lack of hair on top. Fossick's bald head is not by choice. The ring of stubble around the nape of his neck shows he hasn't shaved it in a few days. The rest of his head is very shiny, so much so that it reflects the LEDs that line the hallway. It's a shame, that bulbous head of his would look a hell of a lot better hidden under hair.

Yakovich's head is the perfect shape for bald. Hers isn't shiny like Fossick's. She keeps it short on purpose. Only a few millimeters of hair coats the surface. The blond stubble frames large brown eyes and a pointy chin.

A few of her tattoos peek out the back of her tunic. One of them is the unmistakable mark of the Dirt Demons, a guild of miners who work stray asteroids for specialty minerals. From the time she was six until she was sixteen, she grew up in one of those group homes on Epsilon. I wonder if she even remembers her parents, or if the only thing she knew was the dirt and grime of the mines. I've heard rumors that the tougher ones start working as early as ten. It's against the law, but out there it's hard to police. And sometimes working in the mines is better than starving in the homes. At least if you're working, you're guaranteed rations.

Mining the strays is a hundred times more dangerous than mining asteroids in the belt. It's why they pay more. Stray miners are like the rock stars of the mining world. If you can last a year on one of those crews, you're set for life. The problem is most don't make it past ten months. If you're not killed when you land the ship on the asteroid—which happens more often than you'd think— you're killed in the explosion when they open a new seam. Or the Burrs get you when they raid your ship for the minerals you've risked your life to get.

Not only was I impressed to learn she worked with the Dirt Demons, but she spent two years with them. Why the hell she joined Union fleet after is beyond me.

Fossick is going on about some mahjong game from the other night. Yakovich is doing her best to ignore him.

We round a blind corner on deck five and run into a crowd streaming out of the crew mess. I grab Sarka, pulling him tight against the wall. Yakovich moves to the other side gripping his arm. Her eyes never leave him. I cringe in horror as Fossick steps away from us to high-five someone in the group. I make a mental note to switch Fossick off guard detail. That's the last thing I need, Sarka discovering the weak points in my security. Finally the crowd disperses, I hear a few, "Hey, Captains," as they pass.

A few more stare when they see who we're escorting. Yakovich pushes them off. I nod to Yakovich to keep going. I don't need a bunch of gawkers hanging about.

I'll post two guards in front of his door that he knows about and two more on either end of the hall by the chutes. Those he won't know about. That way, if he does make it past the first two, there are still four more. What it also means is that I'm going to have to enlist crew from other departments to make the rotations fair. Six crew sitting around, scratching their asses all for the sake of one man is going to grate on my nerves real quick.

I leave the guards at the door and enter. Sarka is already getting comfortable on the bed. He clasps his shackled hands behind his head and crosses his feet at the ankle. His eyes close like he's about to take a nap. It's strange, he hasn't changed much since I was a child, but I suppose that's the point. They corrupted the Burrs's physiology to enhance their natural abilities. It also makes them age slower than the rest of us. Davis Sarka is one hundred and sixty-eight years old and doesn't look a day over fifty. But there's an artificiality to him. His hair is too black and skin too taut, his lips too red and eyes too blue. He almost looks like those early twenty-first century versions of robots. They look real, but something's still off.

He turns those blue eyes on me now. And like that, I'm eight years old begging him to take me on his next raid.

"Hold out your hands," I say.

He sits up. "You know, it's a mistake letting your crew get so chummy with you." I roll my eyes as I grab the cuffs and enter the passcode. I knew he was going to latch onto that.

"Not everyone leads with a heavy hand."

His eyes are hard and he answers immediately. "If you're lax on respect, soft on the rules, they'll replace you faster than you can slit their abdomen open." I step back but he grabs my arm tight and yanks me so close I can taste his breath. "You have to keep them afraid of you. But you can't play at it. Can't pretend. They'll see through you, like children, and when you turn your back, they'll gut you." I pull away and the movement makes me stumble. I grab the desk chair, placing it between us. "I'm not going to hurt you. What do you take me for? A monster?"

"Oh, you're human. But human nature is dark. You taught me that." The heat in my belly builds until it's a small fire burning.

I glance around the room, taking in the bed, the empty desk, the shelves, searching for anything he might use to escape. When I'm satisfied there isn't anything, I turn, ready to leave.

In a voice so innocent, I know it's trouble, he asks, "Will you come visit me?"

I stop and pivot, not sure I heard him correctly. "No one's going to visit you."

"What if Alison comes to visit me?" He props himself up on his elbows, his eyes dance with suggestion.

I take the two steps to the bed and stand over him. "She won't."

He's goading me. It's what he does. He's testing his limits and I'm at the top of the stairs, teetering. "Oh, she might. I made quite an impression on her."

And like that, I'm toppling down the stairs, speeding to the bottom. I lean in, getting close enough to see the brown flecks in his irises. "I will fuck you up if you so much as look at her." My voice is low, calm, but I'm seething inside.

"There's my girl." He chuckles.

I grit my teeth, the rage now a warm ball of hate in the pit of my stomach. "What you did to her, you don't deserve to even talk about her."

"Oh, please. It was only a bit of light torture. It was entertaining, actually." He grins, stretching the skin around his cheekbones. "I was sorry she broke so quickly. I had a lot more fun planned for her."

He's trying to make me mad that Ash broke, that she wasn't strong enough to take it. But I'm happy knowing it was quick, knowing for once, her stubbornness gave way to good sense. Then my insides drop. He's lying. Ash would never give in that easy. I watched her endure an excruciating medical procedure because she was too stubborn to let the doctor sedate her. No, Ash didn't break. She would've gritted against anything he tried to take from her by force.

"If you mention Ash again, I'll cut your throat."

"If I thought you meant it, I'd actually be proud."

I reach into my cargo pocket and unsheathe a Bowie knife. It's his. I relieved him of it when we escorted him to the brig. I don't know why I still have it, but I've been carrying it around with me for the last two days. I guess it felt safer with me.

"You may think you know me." I stare into his dark blue eyes, so much like my own. "But twenty years is a long time. You don't know me any better than you knew Mom." I grip the knife's handle, feel the smooth hilt against my palm. At first it was bravado, a way to show who's in charge. Then an image of Ash strapped down, made to endure God knows what, flits through my mind and I grip tighter. She wouldn't tell me what he did, but it only makes it worse because I've seen what he does to people who don't cooperate. And in that instant, I know it's not bravado. I will gut him if he so much as gets within a meter of Ash.

He moves so fast, I didn't think it was possible to cause a blur just by moving. But he's in front of me in a flash, slamming me against the wall. His hand grips my wrist, driving his fingers into my tendons. I release the knife and he turns the point of the blade toward me and strikes. It all happens so quick, I'm left breathless.

CHAPTER FIVE

My breath lodges in my throat. I stare down at the knife. It sticks out of the wall inches from my abdomen. Adrenaline surges, rage, with its all consuming power, shame that after all these years he can still provoke me, and fear because one day I might not be able to pull back in time. All of it boils to the surface. I shove Sarka. A low growl, from deep in my throat, escapes through gritted teeth. I knock him onto the bed, giving him what I hope is a deadly stare. Based on the smirk curling the edges of his lips and my heavy breathing, I somehow doubt it.

I run a hand over my face, trying to calm down. I turn back and tug the knife from the wall. My hand shakes as I grip the handle, my fingers tingle.

"Don't pull a weapon unless you intend to use it," he says.

How can he be so calm? I'm about ready to burst through my skin. "You made your point." I fumble the knife back into its sheath and take a moment to compose myself. I have nothing to focus on except the plain desk jutting from the wall. I use a breathing exercise, taught to me by Kate, the woman who took me in after my mom died. I haven't had to use it in years. Now there are two people in my life who drive me mad enough to need diaphragmatic breathing.

"Jordan, I'd never intentionally hurt you."

"You couldn't if you tried." I storm out of his cabin.

❖

I spend the rest of the week overseeing repairs and readying the ship for our exploration of this galaxy. Any initial trepidation gives way to excitement. This is a chance to see what's out there. We're actually going to discover something new. After a millennia of hiding out in our own galaxy, never venturing further than our own solar system.

As I walk the decks, running my fingers along new panels, I'm gripped by a sudden surge of pride. She isn't much, the *Persephone*, but she's got spunk. In a few more days, we should be ready to launch.

The only thing left is the outside repairs to the hull near the breach. I don't want to leave on such an unknown mission without having the ship one hundred percent ready.

I'm in the mess the day before we launch. Meals don't feel the same without Ash. Even Hartley, who hasn't stopped talking the whole time, can't keep my mind off her. I blink and look up at him when I notice the quiet. He's stopped talking.

"What?" I ask.

"Didn't you hear the intercom?"

I cock my head, even though there's nothing coming over the speaker. "No. Was it for me?"

He shovels spaghetti into his mouth and speaks around the noodles dangling from between his teeth. "The doctor wants you to report to the med center." A glob of tomato sauce rolls down his chin as he sucks up the noodles.

"Dammit." I jump up and dump my food, shoving the tray in a stack near the door, and rush out.

My first thought is Ash. What if there's been a complication with her treatment? Then I remember her harsh words the other day. She didn't sound all that infirm to me. My next thought is probably more on the mark. Sarka.

When I enter, Yakovich is lounging on one of the beds, confirming this thought. Her legs hang over the edge, swinging. Her shoulder is wrapped in a white bandage. The tattoos from her neck are visible now. They run from the nape of her neck all the way down her shoulder to her back and branch out along her arm. It's clear what she spent most of her wealth on. Body art. The bandage is obscuring a hawk. Its wings span her back, the beak and head angle along her other shoulder. The detail and shading is astounding. She must have had it done on Alpha. That's not something you'd get on one of the mining ships or even one of the mining cities on Epsilon.

"What happened?" I ask. I scan for any other damage, but she appears fine otherwise.

She leans back, but stops and sits up again when the movement puts pressure on her shoulder. "Wrestling match didn't quite go my way. I'll be fine, Captain. It's a scratch."

"Wrestling is with hands, not sharp pointy objects," says Dr. Prashad. He lifts a tablet from the counter and thumbs through her chart. The top of his dark brown scalp peeks through the hair at the top of his head. There's a lot more gray now.

I look over and see Ash sitting on a similar bed next to the doctor and my heart lurches. This is the first time we've been face to face since Sarka pulled her out of my cabin. And then the shame hits me full force. Shame that I never had the nerve to visit her, shame at what she said to Hartley.

Instead of dealing with it head on, I turn back to Yakovich. "I thought Sarka…"

She shakes her head. "He's been as quiet as a cucumber." She hops off the bed, careful of her shoulder. "Am I good to go, Doc?"

Dr. Prashad waves her off. "Stay away from sharp objects for the next couple of days. And it's as cold as a cucumber, not quiet."

"As far as I remember, cucumbers don't make noises." She smirks and ambles away, turning back to gaze at Ash. "Take care, Ash." She nods at me as she passes. "Captain."

I turn back to Dr. Prashad. When I first met him, I didn't think much of the short, opinionated man. That changed real quick the first time I had to go see him. Back then, I was only a second lieutenant, helming on a small cutter. And, as the doctor put it, I'd bitten off more than I could chew. I was dating this woman in botany, who among other things, was running me ragged with her stamina. One night, she had the idea of sneaking into the hydroponics hold where they grew the wheat grass. It turns out I'm allergic to wheat grass. I'm indebted to Dr. Prashad for his discretion, even if it did come with unsolicited advice.

Ash is in uniform pants and a tank top, her tunic folded over the table beside her. She's no longer wearing the brace, but her arms are still covered in grafting bandages. There are less of them, but they plaster the majority of her body. Her skin is so pale the freckles on her face stand out, making her appear younger and vulnerable.

"Is she fit for duty?" I ask Dr. Prashad.

"I'm fine."

I stare at the doctor, knowing Ash's version of fine and mine aren't the same in the least. Even if she'd lost a hand, she'd still say she was fine.

"I don't want her on any space walks until the grafts are healed, but I'm clearing her for light duties." He hands me the tablet with her workup. I scroll through trying, and failing, to stay neutral. But seeing it here, her injuries stacked in list form, is overwhelming.

"What are light duties? The grafts aren't going to give her any problems are they?"

"Despite my injuries, sudden deafness wasn't one of them. I'm right here, you can talk to me, you know." She glares at me from the exam bed. Her face is flushed. It happens often. Always a good indicator when she's mad. Those green eyes flash dark, which means she's ready for a fight.

"You want to tone down that attitude, Lieutenant?"

Her shoulders slump, but her eyes stay hard. "I'm sorry, Captain." She sighs and looks down at her stilled legs. "I don't think I can take another day sitting around doing nothing."

Classic Ash. I swear they invented the motto "it's easier to beg forgiveness than to ask permission" for Ash. Her stance suggests she's ready to beg forgiveness, but I'm not falling for it this time. Those eyes are still on fire.

I touch Dr. Prashad's arm, stealing his attention from a set of test results in his hand. "Can you give us a moment?" Startled, he looks around the empty med center and frowns.

Sarka was right. My commands are more like requests. It's a humiliating thought.

I raise my eyebrows in question when he still doesn't move. He makes a big show of taking his time. He purses his lips. He huffs. He unhooks the sensors covering Ash's upper chest, then leaves.

Christ. Am I that lax? Or did it start to unravel with Ash?

Once we're alone, I retreat to the counter a few feet away and lean against it. This is the first time we've been alone since my cabin. A million and one emotions slice through me. I want to explain to her how different it has to be. I want to scream at her for being reckless and scaring me to death. And at the same time I want to close the space between us and soothe the pain I see in her eyes. But I resist those things. Instead, I fold my arms across my chest and say, "I'm still your commanding officer."

"I don't appreciate being ignored." She's quiet as she says this. I'd almost prefer if she yelled it at me. It would give me a chance to yell back and get rid of some of this pent up energy.

"I wasn't ignoring you. I was asking someone a little more objective about your condition. You'd jump back into work with missing limbs if I let you."

She shakes her head, like I've misunderstood her. "Are you going to let me resume my duties?" She looks equal parts angry and scared and confused. And beautiful. Even her bandages and bruises can't take away from the innate fire deep inside her.

I take a little too long to answer. I'm staring and it makes her self-conscious. She tucks stray hairs into the band keeping her hair up, trying to tame it. The red is darker in this light. It's probably been days since she's washed it.

Before I can answer her she says, "I promise I'll only work one shift. And I won't overwork myself or the crew. I can't sit around any longer."

"And if I order you to take it easy if you're pushing yourself too hard?"

She grabs her tunic and pulls it on, mindful of the grafting bandages on her arms. My fingers itch to reach out and help her with it, but I don't. "Then I'll pull back."

I snort. "You disobeyed a direct order, two if I remember correctly."

"I was trying to save people's lives."

"It's not up to you to decide that. I'm the captain. I make those choices." I clamp down and take a few calming breaths before I go too far. It would be so easy to let go, for once, and get dark and furious. Usually I have no problem controlling it, but since my father's been on board, it's getting harder. I haven't even dealt with the fact that she injected me with a drug to knock me unconscious so she could attempt suicide in an escape pod. "Ash, I need to be able to trust you, and right now, I don't."

She sighs. It affects her whole body, lifting her shoulders. I know the choices she made were, in her mind, for the greater good. But if I let her get away with disobeying orders, she's going to keep making those choices. I have no idea how to punish her. Usually I add an extra shift or confine them to quarters. If this was any other crew member I would assign them extra guard duty, but I don't want her anywhere near Sarka.

"What do you suggest I do? I mean, the amount of rules you've broken is staggering. I can't let that go."

She laughs. It's flat and angry. "I'm not the only one who broke rules."

"True. And we can both see why those rules are in place to begin with."

She hops off the bed and stalks toward me. "And I'm the one who gets punished for it?"

And that's all it takes. I let loose all the worry and frustration and anger I've been holding onto for the last couple of days. I barely stop myself from pushing her back onto the bed. I lean in close enough to smell the laundry detergent on her uniform. "Don't you dare. Up until now, I've been so lenient with you. I've let you get away with more than I would any other crew member. I stupidly, stupidly thought you were worth the benefit of the doubt."

Ash's face drains of all color except for two flecks of pink on her cheeks. She pulls away, but stumbles on the bed behind her. Her reaction isn't enough to slow my diatribe.

"I told you not to do anything stupid. And instead of listening to me for once, you go and do the opposite by ejecting the engine core. What did you think was going to happen?" I clench my fists so hard by my side, my muscles ache from the effort. "And what's worse is that you knew you were going to do it even as you were promising me you wouldn't. That whole time I was pouring my heart out, you were thinking, 'What's next?'" I turn away because I can't look at her any longer. There's so much more I want to say, but some of it I can never take back.

I take several long breaths and wait for the calm to descend. It doesn't help. I'm still furious at her. More than anything, I feel used, like a jackass for letting her play me. She could give two shits about me. All she cares about is herself and it hurts that I didn't see it earlier. No wonder everyone on this ship thinks they can treat me like I'm nothing more than a fellow officer.

It stops now.

I turn back. Ash shoves her fists onto her hips. "Two days in the brig then," she says.

"What?"

"That's what you should do to punish me. Put me in the brig for two days." She stares up at me with such challenge behind those fierce eyes.

"I'm not going to put you in the brig." If I did that, the crew would lose any respect they still had for her. As much as I want to put her in the brig, I can't. It would certainly help me keep control of my crew. But I have to consider both of our reputations. There's only one punishment that'll work. "I'm putting you on medical leave."

Her whole body sinks. "No."

I hold up my hand to stop any argument. "You have two choices. Take medical leave, stay in your cabin, run on the track, but stay out of the way. Or, if you don't like it, I'll ask the *Posterus* to keep you and tell them you're not well enough to come. That way, there won't be a mark on your record. And that's being generous."

If I thought she'd paled before, I was wrong. Her whole face has gone deathly white. She knows I mean it. I'm kicking myself for not doing this earlier. Maybe we wouldn't be in this mess in the first place. But as I march toward the door a small voice reminds me that we'd all be dead if I had. When I get to the door I say, "You don't have to decide right now." I can't look at her. I'm too sick with emotion. It's all too much. Instead of making me feel better, my outburst has made me feel worse about it all. "But I need to know before we disembark in two days." I leave before she has a chance to respond.

Chapter Six

I hear the intercom go off a few times before it registers that someone's trying to get ahold of me. I check my clock. It's a little after five in the morning. I groan and whip the covers back. This had better be important.

"What?" It's a little gruffer than I intend.

"I'm sorry to wake you, Captain, but we have a situation in the forward storcell." It's Tekada, my operations officer. Damn. He's probably having an anxiety attack. He hates to be the bearer of bad news. And if he's calling at five a.m., it's bad news.

If I had to choose one thing I hate about being captain, it's being on call twenty-four seven.

"I'm on my way." I debate for two seconds if I should half-ass it and throw on anything, or actually take the time to look the part. I decide on the latter and rush out of my cabin, still fastening my tunic.

I still haven't woken up by the time I climb down five decks to the storcell, but as soon as I open the doors, I'm wide awake. What started off as the most boring send-off in human history has become the week from hell.

We launched from the *Posterus* eight days ago and since then, nothing has gone right. It all started when one of our matter sails came loose and lodged in a bank of solar panels. It ripped the sail, destroying four panels. It forced us to cut systems to save energy.

That was day one.

I'd like to say I've never been one for superstitions or bad omens, but I'd be lying. It's like that old sailor's saying "you should never start a journey on a Friday." As luck would have it, we launched on a fucking Friday. Of course, they also once said it was bad luck to have women on board a vessel. If that were the case, Union fleet would never have gotten out of dry dock.

A few days after the matter sail disaster, we had a fire in the crew mess. We've had to close it down and outfit one of the cargo holds to handle the runoff from the officer's mess. We now have only one kitchen with two ovens to feed over a hundred people. To keep everyone happy I've had the cooks prepare prepackaged protein meals the crew can grab off-hours. It also means keeping the officer's mess open twenty-four seven. But so far I only have four cooks threatening to mutiny if they don't get their kitchens back.

Ash has become a stranger. It's for the best and I don't blame her, but I notice her absence more than I'd like to admit. I spend all my meals watching Hartley slurp his way through our menu, hoping Ash will join us. But she avoids regular mess hours.

One day, Hartley surprises me by asking, "Would you like to have dinner with me sometime, Captain?"

I hope he isn't asking what I think he is. "We're having dinner right now."

"I don't mean like this." He waves his hand around, indicating the crew surrounding us, or the mess itself. "I mean like you and me."

"Are you asking me out on a date, Hartley?"

He nods and spears his fork into some pasta on his plate. It wobbles for a second before breaking off a hunk and falling on the table. "Is that a yes?"

I look around. It's empty now. Most of the crew prefer to eat at the larger tables in the cargo hold. But there's still enough to overhear our conversation. "Did someone put you up to this?"

He picks up his fork as he shakes his head. "No, why would you think that?" He mashes his potatoes flat with the tines of his fork. "Ash is teaching me to pick up women. And I thought since you're a woman and I already spend time with you."

I try not to smile. I don't think he'd appreciate it. "She's teaching you to pick up women?" This is what she's decided to do with her time?

"She calls it, 'talking to women,'" he says with air quotes. "But I know how to talk to women. I don't know how to make them continue talking with me after the first few minutes."

"Well, Hartley, I'm flattered you chose me as your guinea pig, but—"

"I asked Olczyk first, but she turned me down. And then I asked Quinn, but I didn't push my luck because I'm pretty sure she could kick my ass."

"So I'm your third choice?"

For once, Hartley picks up on the social etiquette of the matter. He shoves a clump of potatoes into his mouth and mumbles, "Something like that."

As far as disasters go, being asked out by Hartley doesn't even rank.

Tekada jumps out from behind one of the gel vats used to store excess energy from the solar panels. His face is covered in sweat and grime. His uniform, which is a little on the small side, bulges where it buttons at the front. His brown doe-eyes blink rapidly. For some reason he always looks like he's startled. Perhaps it's because his eyebrows start halfway up his forehead.

"Oh good, Captain." He steps through some yellow sludge oozing out one of the vents in the wall.

"What's the situation?"

He points down a shaft opening in the wall. It's at hip height and about the size of a basket ball. "The filter cover is stuck again. There's a lid that filters the gel through the vats, keeping it active by moving it around the system. If the lid doesn't shut properly, for safety reasons, it shuts down the whole system." The warm orange glow from the canisters illuminates his face. The vats look like giant containers of honey, lit from the bottom. Ambient light bathes the whole room.

"Safety reasons?"

He flutters his hands around, indicating the floor. "We'd be knee-deep in gelatin if it didn't."

I nod and wait, not sure what he needs me for. We stand for a few seconds, me trying hard not to yawn, him rubbing the tips of his fingers together. The dried crud flakes off onto the floor.

"And?"

"It's happened a couple of times now. We don't know what's wrong or why it keeps happening. The only thing to do is crawl through the shaft and unstick the door manually."

Who the hell would be stupid enough to squeeze down there head first? "What's your normal procedure?"

"Umm, Ash usually takes care of it. I mean, I would." He holds his hands to his pudgy chest, his fingers dig into the flesh around his rubbery pecks. "If I could. You know?" He waves at the small opening. "And since Ash is still on medical leave, we don't have anyone brave enough to go down there."

Brave? I have a different word for the person who would squeeze into a hazardous hole in the side of the wall.

"When is she coming back? Usually I call her up and she's like, 'no problem, be right there.'" He shuffles his feet in the flecks that have fallen from his hands.

"I'm not sure. It depends on Dr. Prashad."

"He said it was up to you." His face flattens and his eyebrows, if possible, climb higher. "I didn't want to bother you with this, Captain. And no one but Ash will do it."

"So you're calling me to do what?"

"Give permission to call in Ash."

I'm unsure if I'm relieved he didn't call me here to dig around a dark hole, or angry he asked me to reverse a punishment. To be fair to Tekada, he doesn't know I relieved Ash of duty. As far as the crew know, she's still not well enough to resume her post. So my options are to do it myself, or to call Ash in to help. Neither of those sound good.

"How far down is the flap?"

"Six or seven feet? We usually tie off one of Ash's legs and lower her in."

Christ.

He pushes a button next to the opening and the hatch hisses open. All I see is a deep, dark hole. "It might have gotten out of line after the explosion and we didn't notice it with all the other repairs."

Defeated, I turn toward the door. "All right, see if Ash'll do it." I'll let Dr. Prashad know she's not cleared for duty yet. This is a one time event.

Before I leave him, I turn back and ask, "What did you guys do before Ash signed on?"

He shrugs. "It never happened before."

"Never?"

He shakes his head. "It's only happened, like, twice."

"Have you tried changing the flap out? Do we have a spare on board?"

"I don't know, but I can check. If we don't, I'll see if we can make one."

"Good. I don't like the idea of having to rely so heavily on one crew member to fix a part of this ship."

"Does this mean Ash is coming back for good?" There's a hopeful note in his voice and not for the first time this week, I'm surprised at how engrained Ash has become.

"I don't want to get your hopes up, Tekada." Has everyone forgotten she was in the middle of the explosion that caused so much damage to the ship?

As I head back to my cabin and bed, I get a summons from Vasa.

"Captain, when you have a moment I'd like to go over some of the data we collected from the probes. There are a few curious anomalies that we should give our attention to." I debate putting him off. I'm scheduled to have a briefing with security staff later this morning, which will push the rest of my day back.

I sigh.

The bridge is silent when I enter. Only Vasa is there. He's taken hell shift—midnight to eight to oversee repairs.

I take my seat at the back and rest my head against the back rest. You'd think with the amount of time we spend in these things, they'd have the decency to design them with comfort in mind. But they're more like something you'd install in a public space as a loitering deterrent.

Vasa is off to the side at his console. He has several screens up, which he throws to the holo screen at the front. It activates and the whole bridge dims by a quarter.

It's a lot of data, charts, star trajectories, and some things I don't understand.

"So what am I looking at?"

He brushes his hair off to the side. It looks lank and a little greasy after having worked the night shift. I notice he doesn't do well on this shift, even though he requested it. For some reason he always looks like a zombie after a few days. I don't think he sleeps during the day. By the fifth day of hell shift, he starts to get jittery, jumping at odd noises and talking too fast.

By the look of him, he's been on this shift for two days. He's only halfway zombified.

"I sent out a second probe after we departed the *Posterus*. There are some strange gravitational waves in this quadrant." He zooms in on a map of the system and points to an area that doesn't seem to have anything in it.

"What do you think it is?"

"I don't know, but there's definitely something unusual there, and I recommend we investigate. It's on the way. We'd only have to adjust our course a little. We would only miss a few days." His talking has sped up and he's started to blink a lot. I wonder if I've misjudged how many days he's been on the hell shift.

He shrugs. It's up to me to decide. Vasa doesn't usually give much. He keeps to himself. I know he comes from Delta and that his parents work a farm near the capital. But that's about all I know about him. Other than his love of arguing against the possibility of universal cooperation.

I give him the go ahead to inform helm to make the corrections.

Later that day I enter the officer's mess—we're still all jammed into it—and spot Ash sitting with Vasa. I'm about to approach when I see her laugh at something he's said. She throws her head back, eyes alight, and I'm slammed with jealousy. It bites into my heart so fast I forget what I'm doing. In a daze, I place my tray back on the rack and leave the mess, ashamed I can't even function like a normal human being. Or, I'm embarrassed I'm being too human at the moment.

I spend the rest of the day distracting myself with mundane tasks. It isn't like me to evade a problem, and that's what I'm doing.

I've started avoiding Ash.

I climbed up two extra decks and circled half the ship to keep from bumping into her.

I go back to my cabin and spend a whole ten minutes with my forehead pressed against the wall, mad I'm such a coward. It was only in that moment that I understood what Ash meant about my position being isolating. I'm not an extrovert like Ash. I have to force myself to be social. I much prefer my own company after a long day. And rarely do I need someone to confide in. The only person on the ship I'm comfortable with, besides Ash, is Len Prashad. But I would never go to him with something like this. This is too much.

When I was younger, I used to hide out for hours on the farm, avoiding everyone, even Kate. I'd grab a tablet filled with books, a couple boxes of rations, and hike into the fields.

We grew corn on our farm. It was easy to get lost and stay lost in the giant stalks. They would stretch up high, holding me in like a cocoon. No sound from the roads or transports could penetrate.

When I first arrived on Delta, everything was so different. On the station growing up, they tacked additions on when needed. It was a maze in there, closed in and claustrophobic, noisy too. There were always dozens of voices within hearing, yelling, laughing, fighting. It was constant.

That first moment I stepped between the boundary stalks was a balm. I'd never known such calm before and it soon became addictive. Whenever I'd had a bad day or got into a fight at school, I'd hide in the corn with my books.

Sometimes, instead of reading, I would lie back on the ground with my hands behind my head and look up at the stars. They looked like tiny specks of dust from underneath the metallic glass. I remember thinking one day I would take a closer look.

That isolation and comfort is a hard habit to break.

My first night at the Academy was the second worst night of my life. That first night spent on Delta at Kate's farm after my mom died was the worst. Being at the Academy was like being back on the space station again with its noise and chaos. I worried I'd made a mistake. But the truth is, if I'd stayed on Delta, I'd have been miserable. Being trapped on a farm for the rest of my life and missing out on the adventure was no way for me to live.

Now I have the benefit of both. If I need calm, I can come up to my cabin, turn off all the lights and stare out at the stars. Sometimes, running on the track gives me that peace. But I don't have to give up my adventures to have that. For the first time Ash has me questioning my need for isolation. She has me questioning everything.

Chapter Seven

The night before we start our second week out, I spend an hour on the track getting my mind in order. Olczyk says we're six or seven days away from our target asteroid. That's another week to get the ship back up to one hundred percent.

The kitchens are almost repaired. Another day or two, according to Hartley, and we'll have our matter sails working again. I put Candace Ito in charge. Next to Ash, she has the most space time logged.

"How's Ash doing? I heard she's still on medical leave. We'd get this done in half the time if she were back." Ito, who works with Tekada in operations, runs a hand through her rail straight hair. She looks up at me, her dark eyes filled with adoration. "I wish I could glide around the hull of the ship as fast as she does. She says it takes practice, but…I mean, I'm pretty decent, so please don't mistake me, Captain. We'll get the job done." She shrugs. "Ash is all about efficiency. I once saw her leap from one side of the docking hatch to the other."

I shut my eyes at the thought. I'm going to have nightmares because of that image.

"Oh, don't worry. She ties off. Everything's by the book." Ito bites her lip, worried she's gotten Ash in trouble.

"I'm not sure when Ash will be back. Please promise me, no acrobatics."

Ito nods and bounces out of my cabin. She's not the first or the last crew member to enquire about Ash. Whatever animosity the crew had for Ash when she first signed on has slowly evaporated.

I'm not sure if that's because of her work ethic or because they respect all this badass daredevil shit.

Just when I'm beginning to suspect this whole Ash debacle is behind us, I get a call in the middle of the night. It's Yakovich. I throw on my uniform and make my way down to the officer's mess.

When I enter, I stagger to a halt. I'm in shock, but only at first. It gives way to rage in an instant. Ash is bound to one of the support beams, her toes barely scrapping the ground. She's naked except for the rigging tape securing her to the pole. It snakes around her ankles, waist, breasts, and mouth. And I can see by the red welt on her right cheek that Yakovich tried to pry some of the tape off and removed skin with it. There's even tiny specks of beaded blood. We use rigging tape to repair the matter sails, solar panels, and various equipment on the ship. It's made to withstand radiation and all sorts of disasters. You're not meant to apply it to skin. Ever.

I take a step forward, then stop. Ash's focus is on the ground near her feet. She hasn't looked at anything else since I entered. Her skin is flushed from the tip of her hair line to above the swell of her breasts.

This is all very familiar. It takes me a moment before it hits me. One of my father's crew was strung up in the mess like this. I was only eleven, but I'll never forget the stench. He'd died in the middle of the night and his bowels had opened, dribbling down his pant leg and pooling at his feet.

His crime? He'd tried to claim treasure that wasn't his. That's what they called it. Treasure. It didn't matter if it was a shipment of soap or an engine from a cargo ship, it was all the same.

He'd tried to lay claim to a woman he'd found aboard a freighter heading toward Alpha. I don't remember her. I wasn't ever allowed to watch the parade of goods as they arrived back on the station. I wouldn't have even remembered the man if it hadn't been for this incident. He was a warning to the others. What came on that station belonged to my father first. Only after he decided he didn't want it could others claim it.

Mostly I remember his face, forever frozen in death. It's the same look on Ash's, the look of abject mortification.

"Has anyone else been in here?" I don't want anyone seeing Ash like this, like she's broken.

Yakovich shakes her head. "The doctor's on his way." She stuffs her hands in her pockets, keeping her gaze on me. "I came in after shift to grab one of the dinner packs and found her like this."

"Stand guard outside and make sure no one but the doctor enters."

"Yes, Captain."

I wait until Yakovich is out before I approach.

"Who did this?" It takes her a moment before she finally shakes her head as much as the tape will allow. "You're not saying that because you want to go after them yourself, are you?" Her eyes, when she finally looks up at me, are two green flames, fierce with fury.

I hold up both hands in surrender. "Okay, but it was a valid question." There isn't a spot on her body that looks safe to touch right now, so instead of comforting her physically, I make her a promise. "We'll find who did this. Whatever it takes."

I begin to ask if they did anything besides tape her to the beam, but if her answer is yes, it will need more than a nod. I realize most of my questions will need more then a yes or no response. The silence that fills the mess is absolute.

There's only one crew member I know who doesn't like Ash. Fossick, and he wouldn't have the balls to do this. Then there's Chloe. But she's more afraid of stupid folk tales than anything that's real. And she wouldn't do this. Fear is a great motivation, but I don't believe she's capable of this, even if she were strong enough to lift Ash onto the beam.

I'm about to go after the doctor myself when Prashad finally enters, carrying his medical case and a stretcher. He stops as soon as he catches sight of her, and I have the sensation of seeing her again for the first time. The initial shock passes and the professional veneer slides over his face.

A few years ago we were on a mission to rescue a crew of miners who got stranded on a stray. Some of them were still stuck in one of the shafts they'd created and couldn't get out. He insisted on getting suited up and joining the team that went down. Even after two tremors threatened to collapse the tunnel, he refused to leave. He could've waited on the ship for casualties to arrive. But because he didn't, we were able to triage on site and saved more lives. He's a small quiet man, but I learned a long time ago not to underestimate him.

"Can you remove the tape without taking skin with it?" I ask as soon as he enters.

He steps closer and places a soft hand on Ash's waist. He tests the bond between her skin and the tape and shakes his head. I don't miss it, but neither does Ash. Her eyes fill and she averts her gaze, steeling herself against the oncoming pain.

"You're going to sedate her before you remove the tape."

"I had planned on it." He removes a syringe from his case.

I put up my hand before Ash can even begin to protest. "I'm pulling rank. There's no way I'm going to let you endure that kind of pain because you're stubborn." I step close, placing a calming hand on her arm. "I'll be here the whole time. The mind knot has no control over you anymore." At least I hope that's true. The doctor said it was dormant, but he also said it could, at anytime, become active again.

It only takes a moment for the sedative to take effect. Ash's eyes and head droop at the same time and as they do, it's as if a veil lifts. My calm and control leave. I sink onto one of the benches and rest my head in my hands, hoping for the calm to return. I have this rage building deep inside, ready to strike out at anything or anyone that comes near Ash. My breathing becomes ragged and as I gulp in air, I grip the bench. My knuckles go white.

"Am I going to have to sedate you as well?"

After a moment of mindful breathing, I shake my head and stand. "Let's get this done before we have a corridor full of hungry crew."

He hands me a vial and cloth. "The acetone should help weaken the adhesive. But it may not be enough, especially around the grafts on her arm. Work slowly. Roll or peel, don't pull."

We work in silence. We cut her from the beam first and lower her onto the stretcher. We cover her and transport her to the med center to finish the procedure. It's a long process of soaking, rubbing, and peeling. Every time I pull skin back, another spark ignites.

I will find who did this.

❖

"I won't do it, Captain. I won't. It's unethical and dangerous." You'd think I'd asked him to implant mind knots in each of the crew the way he's going on about it.

"I get why you think it's unethical, but telling the crew that we're implanting trackers would create chaos. I couldn't order them to do it without facing mutiny. But I can order them to be vaccinated."

The doctor paces in front of my desk, his hands stuffed into his lab coat pockets. It's been two days since we cut Ash down from the beam in the officer's mess. Two days of knowing I have a serious problem on board, and that I have to solve it immediately. I've stressed over every possible solution and this is the best I can think of until Vasa gets back to me about the mess security footage. This whole thing screams Sarka. He might not be the one who acted, but he planted the thought.

I need another way to see who's coming and going from Sarka's cabin and who's interacting with Ash. I don't care if it's unethical to invade my crew's privacy if it will save a life.

If I don't put a stop to the mutinous crew members, they'll only get worse. And if no one but myself and the doctor knows about the trackers, no one can hack them.

While the majority of my rage is on behalf of Ash, a significant part is for myself. I can't believe my own crew could hate so much they would turn to violence. This isn't tearing up a mattress and ransacking a room. This is bodily harm. I'd like to say it's the first time, but things have been getting worse. Someone has it in for Ash. And I have to discover who they are before they tear this ship and crew apart with their prejudice.

"I understand you have a ship to run, but I don't want any part of this. Putting things in places they don't belong is what got us into this mess."

I'm almost left speechless by his comment. He's so wrapped up in his world sometimes, he lives on a molecular level. Doesn't he realize this is going to get so much worse if we don't do something immediately? It's going to spread like a disease.

"Having mutinous crew members on board is dangerous. For everyone." I need to put it in a way he'll understand and overlook the more than dubious methods. "Please sit down, your pacing is giving me a headache." I motion for the chair across from me and wait until he sits before I continue. "This isn't about being dishonest to the crew, which is how you're choosing to look at it. I get that, I do, because in a way we are. But a crew isn't about individuality, it's not about one person, it's a living, breathing whole. And right now, that whole has a disease. It's attacking itself, and what do we do when organisms attack themselves?"

It takes him a moment before he realizes it wasn't a rhetorical question. "Oh. We find the cause and treat it by removing the attacking cells." Even though he's stopped moving, his leg is still bobbing up and down.

"And that's all we're doing, we're in that first stage, we're finding the cause. Once we do, we'll remove it."

"You're sure the individual doesn't matter? It feels very much to me that you're willing to break more than a few rules when it comes to Ash." It's not said with any malice, instead he speaks in the same reasonable tone as always. I can't help but worry there's more behind the statement. Then again, Len has never been one to play games, which is one of the reasons I appreciate him so much. And of course, he's right. Even if I won't admit it to him, I need to admit it to myself.

"In part. Yes. Ash is the symptom, but she's only an indicator that the disease exists. If it wasn't her, it could be someone else."

I stand and move to the window. Staring out at the expanse. Nothing looks familiar. We're millions of lightyears from our own galaxy, from our home, and yet our problems follow. Is this what makes us human? Our inclination toward conflict? Were we delusional to think if we found a new planet, a new home, we wouldn't follow the same path as before? Or are we condemned to repeat the same cycle again and again?

"It'll destroy us from within if we don't stop it before it goes too far. If something happens to Ash, nothing we do can pull us back from that," I say.

When he answers his voice is close. He has followed me to the window. The blackness beyond plays off his dark skin, making it darker. "I'll concede that, in a way, this is like a vaccination. We are treating an underlying problem."

"If it makes you feel better you can put a real vaccine in the serum."

"It won't. But if I'm going to inoculate the crew, then I might as well do some good."

Even though it's a victory, I don't smile because I know how much it cost. "Thank you, Len."

I'm sitting on the track, legs crossed, lost in thought. I've dimmed the lights which gives me an unparalleled panorama of stars. It's been four days since the incident with Ash in the officer's mess. The doctor has vaccinated most of the crew. He and I are the only ones who know about it and I'd like to keep it that way. I'll keep a tablet on me to watch and set my cabin computer to display the crew. Anyone who enters a one meter area around Ash will ping on the monitor. One meter doesn't seem very far, but this is a small ship. Crew in the adjacent cabin can be less than a meter away from each other.

Once I've set it up, I have to wait it out. I'm not exactly sure what I'm looking for. But I hope I know when I see it.

The intercom interrupts my thoughts. It's Olczyk. I sigh and make my way to the bridge, prepared for the worst.

Chapter Eight

Wwhat about Hades?" The table erupts at Hartley's suggestion, most against the idea. Their voices echo in the empty crew mess.

Three days ago, we discovered a planet. It was the strangest thing, one minute empty space, the next, an entire planet. Hartley has yet to explain how an object the size of Mars could hide from our sensors. But here it is.

"You want to name the new planet after the Greek god of hell? Doesn't that seem a bit negative?" This from Yakovich who's spent most of the meeting glaring off into the distance like a sullen teenager.

It's been three days and we're still debating what to name it. Well, they're debating names. I'm trying to decide whether we should land on the surface and investigate or report back.

"We should hold off naming it for now." I try to steer the meeting back before Hartley takes us off course.

The probe we sent out to the planet came back with promising data, but even more so are the pictures. Not only does this planet have water and rock formations, but it has oxygen and plant life, in abundance. I've put us into a high orbit to observe until I can decide what to do.

"We can't keep calling it LLB78596i." Hartley looks around the table, hoping for some support. "We need to come up with something fitting for the occasion, you know." His eyes are wide and excited as he takes an uncommon pause to think. "Something historic."

I refrain from rolling my eyes. The last thing I want is to waste time debating something so inconsequential. We haven't even discussed whether it will be possible to land on the planet. Instead my department heads have spent the last forty-five minutes discussing shore leave, hunting, and what to name the damn thing.

I wish I could share my crew's buoyant state, but all my thoughts have been on Ash. I've only seen her in passing, mostly on the track. Since she isn't working a shift, her visits are sporadic. She's changed, more subdued. It's almost like the moment she woke up tied to that post, she boxed up who she is for safe keeping. Hartley said he hasn't seen her either, which, from the way he said it, is unusual. I only understand about two thirds of what he's saying. Either because it's too fast or is so Hartley, it goes right over my head.

The room explodes in a philosophical debate about naming planets after gods.

"Enough." I slam my hand down on the table. "It doesn't matter what we call it. Let's figure out if we can actually land on it first." Sometimes it's like I'm looking after a bunch of children. The room becomes silent as six people turn toward me.

"Okay, that's better. Hartley, are we going to have any issues landing on the planet?"

"The only advice I can give is to land on igneous or metamorphic rock formations, something like granite, basalt, gneiss or obsidian. That way we're less likely to risk the ship being too heavy and sinking. Everything else is a bit up in the air, so to speak." He smiles like he's made a joke. When no one laughs, he continues, "We've had a chance to analyze the atmosphere. It appears similar to Earth, but there are a million other factors at play we won't know even exist until we try to land."

"So what you're saying is we have to hope for the best?" asks Vasa, shaking his head. "That's your advice?"

"Let's plan for the worst, though. Hartley, come up with contingency plans in case anything goes wrong. I want to know at what altitude our point of no return is." I scan through the agenda on my tablet. My palm still stings from slapping the table, but I resist the urge to rub it on my pant leg. "All right, so let's say we do land, will we have enough power to break free of the planet's gravitational pull when we take off again?"

"They designed the ships to exceed the escape velocity needed to launch from Jupiter—if it had a surface—so unless there's something unique about this planet, my guess is it'll have a lower gravity than Earth."

"Is that a yes?" I ask.

"There is no definite answer to that question, Captain." He strains, like he's trying to understand what I'm asking. I've noticed he does this a lot, almost like our questions are too dumb for him to contemplate.

I try asking a different way. "In your opinion, if we land this ship, what are the chances of us taking off again?"

"I wouldn't know the exact odds off the top of my head, but if you give me a day I can get those for you."

Finally, Yakovich takes pity on me and leans toward Hartley. "She wants to know if we'll end up stuck on the planet if we land." I have no idea how that statement is any different than the last two I've asked. But somehow she breaks through the mantel of Hartley's brain.

He perks ups. "Oh, no. We'll make it off the planet, don't worry, Captain."

Christ.

I ask each department to submit two names for planetary teams. Then, I dismiss everyone except Hartley who I keep back to discuss a few side projects.

I decide to throw myself into planning our exploration of the planet. It would take too long to inform the *Posterus* and the *Brimley* of what we've discovered and wait for a response. If I'm being honest with myself, I know they'll demand I wait for the *Brimley*. I don't want Harrios to have any part of this discovery. So I'm taking a page out of Ash's playbook. I'll ask for forgiveness later.

Since none of us have ever been on a planet, it will take a lot of work and imagination to predict what supplies we'll need. I've been working closely with the crew, building endless lists. Together we'll assemble our kits. There's a lot to consider. Owen Mani, our botanist, Hartley and Dan Foer, one of his engineers, have spent most of today debating whether we'll need flashlights or not. I don't plan on us being out there after it gets dark, but Mani makes a good case. The forests might be dark or, and Foer pipes up at this, there might be caves. He's almost giddy at the thought.

We'll be on foot so we don't want our packs to be too heavy. We'll weigh less on this planet than we do on the *Persephone* or the Belt—their artificial gravity is modeled after Earth's gravity—but we still don't want to bring too much.

Anything can happen. There could be hostile fauna on the planet so we don't want to pack too light and be defenseless.

"I propose we modify the space packs to bring with us," Mani says. His mop of curls falls forward, obscuring his baby face until he flips it back and continues. "They're lightweight and we can bring sample cases with us to grab—"

"No. We leave what we find on site. I don't want anyone picking up anything, no matter how innocent or pretty it looks. We have no idea how it'll interact once it leaves the planet's atmosphere. We are there to observe only." I look around the table, locking on each person in turn until I end on Hartley. He gives me a thumbs up. I make a mental note to have everyone go through an inspection before coming back on board.

"It's too bad we couldn't send a smaller team ahead to get a feel for what it's like on the surface. This is a little like building a house in the dark. I have no idea what we're going to need." Mani looks back down at the selection of tools in front of him.

Foer, one of the few engineers who breaks the scrawny nerd stereotype, grins. Two dimples appear on his cheeks. "Did you guys ever read those *Choose Your Own Adventure*, books growing up? They had a lot of safaris in them for some reason. But they always packed food rations and things to make a fire."

"We don't have anything on board that can make a fire. Not as its first intention." Thank God. "But food rations are a good idea. I'll have the kitchen figure out a way to make them lightweight and airtight."

"Is Ash going to be well enough to join the mission?" Hartley looks around at everyone as he asks this, gauging their reaction.

Mani and Foer are busy comparing lists. Foer leans on the table, supporting his considerable girth with his massive arms. Next to Mani—who can't be much over five feet—Foer looks like a giant.

Yakovich is off in her own world, studying a list of onboard weapons. We don't have a huge weapons locker, just enough to defend ourselves in case of a Burr attack. Nothing we have to worry about out here. But as Yakovich points out, any animals down there will be a hell of a lot scarier than a bunch of stinking space pirates.

"I'm not sure if the doctor will release Ash for that kind of mission. She did almost blow up after all." As I say this, I start to wonder if Ash bribed Dr. Prashad. With all those injuries, I'm shocked he was so willing to let her resume her duties. I guess he knows a lost cause when he sees one. Trying to get Ash to take sick leave is like inviting a cat to take a bath. We haven't released the information about Ash's attack in the mess. I give it a day before the rumor mill is turning out scenarios.

"How many weapons can we bring?" Yakovich asks.

I'm thrown for a moment. "How many do you think we'll need?"

She places her tablet on the table and leans back in her chair, giving it some thought. "Well, we should equip everyone with a handheld gun. Nothing too large. They should be able to draw fast if an animal approaches. Plus, at least one person should have a shoulder mounted rifle, in case of flying predators. Have you ever read about pterodactyls? And for hand-to-hand combat, or in case someone loses a weapon." She gives us a look that says this is a crime worthy of death. "Everyone should have a good kni—"

"No." I'm already shaking my head before she's finished. I do not want a bunch of science nerds running around the forest, armed. The thought of it is giving me heart palpitations. "No. We do not need to be that heavily armed. No knives, and only the group leader and the security details have weapons."

She's about to protest when Hartley cuts her off. "Captain, I've been working on this awesome—"

"No."

"But, Captain—"

"I don't care if you've invented a giant bubble gun that carries the prey into the atmosphere. There will be only two guns per team."

Yakovich nods, but even in that simple gesture she manages to convey her disapproval.

After the meeting breaks up, Yakovich sticks around. She hands me a stack of tablets. "You've seen the footage?"

"I did. Was Vasa able to see how they manipulated the recording?"

She rubs a knuckle along her bottom lip, thinking. "He did, though you're not going to like it."

"Nothing about this is likable. What did he say?"

She pauses, finding the best way to say her next sentence. I'm on edge. "He said someone shuffled the footage's timestamp." She uses her hands to explain, forming them into shapes and exclamations as she goes. "He explained it like an operation. Someone removed the time stamp from the real video and substituted it with another. So to find that footage, we'd have to search through all the footage."

"And how long until we figure out where the footage is?"

There's a long pause as she stares at her boots. I hope she's calculating. She isn't. "That's the thing. This is an old ship, and we don't delete anything, we archive it to a smaller format. There are millions of minutes of footage on our servers. It would take months, years to view all the footage, that's if I had all my staff working on it day and night. The hack impressed Vasa, actually. He said he couldn't have done better if he tried."

My heart sinks. "So what you're saying is…"

"That avenue of investigation won't help us. But that doesn't mean there aren't others. We'll find who did this, Captain."

I can't understand why someone would go to so much trouble. When I find the culprits they will spend the rest of their lives in the brig. Possibly shot out into space in an escape pod. "Why not erase it?"

"Because that would've alerted the system there was something missing. This way, everything appears in order, but isn't."

This is starting to feel more sophisticated than a hate crime toward a crew member. "Thanks. Keep me posted."

CHAPTER NINE

Yakovich and Fossick are positioned outside Sarka's door. Yakovich notices me first and I wave her over. "Has he given you any problems?" I ask. I've postponed this next visit long enough. I needed to get my emotions in check. I don't want a repeat of last time.

She shakes her head. "He's been quiet."

"Who brings him his food?"

Yakovich frowns, marring what is usually smooth and flawless. She's dedicated and far more serious than the other officers her age. The week before we launched from Alpha I watched her break up a bar fight with nothing more than words. At six foot two she's as tall as most men. Her broad shoulders and calf muscles strain against her uniform. She's got a natural confidence, not something forced. She has this way of leaning in, like she's telling you something important. The first time I had her in my office I asked her what she'd said to the guy to calm him down. She told him he had two choices, a punch in the face and a night in the brig or another pint on her. She gets what most people don't, if given a choice to avoid a fight and still save face, most people will take it. I like that she understands that.

"It depends on the shift, Captain. When I'm on watch, I do. I can give you a list of the other guards."

I nod toward Fossick. He crosses his arms behind his back as if he's standing at ease, but I can see the tablet he's trying to hide.

I keep my voice low. "I thought I asked you to keep Fossick out of rotation."

For the first time, Yakovich appears worried. "I'm sorry, Captain. We're short crew. This is his first shift since you asked me to reassign him. I didn't want to bother you with this. I've kept him here so I can keep an eye on him. He's had no interaction with the Burr."

I hold up my hand. "It's fine. When I leave, I'd like you to move Sarka back to the brig. And from now on, I want you to be the only one he interacts with. If that means he has to wait on meals, that's fine."

"Yes, Captain. Do you want to keep the secondary posts?"

"No, it takes too many crew. We'll have more control with him in the brig. In here, we have no record of what goes on once we shut those doors." Yakovich opens her mouth and I stop her. "I trust you. But you're not the only one guarding him."

When I enter Sarka's room, he's leaning against the headboard with his feet crossed at the ankles. "How nice. A visitor." He has that same smug grin on his face. And as quick as that, my ire is up. It doesn't matter how many days I take to calm down, it only takes a second for him to stir it all up.

"I'm not here to visit."

He throws his hands in the air, like it doesn't matter. "I'm not expecting a tea party, but any company is welcome." He's taken his jacket off and folded it and placed it on the edge of the bed. His room is exactly as it was when I left him. Bed's made, desk is spotless. There isn't anything for him to do except sit and think. And plan. At least in the brig we'll have a camera in the room so we can keep a better eye on him.

"I'll keep this brief. I want to know who you've been talking to in here."

He sits up, eager. "Why, did something happen?" His eyes brighten and the skin along his forehead tightens. It's like stretching fabric between two poles.

I won't give him the satisfaction of telling him about Ash. Who else would think to tie Ash up in the mess hall? It's such a humiliating punishment. A punishment he himself has employed plenty of times. Somehow, he implanted that idea where it seeded and grew.

"You've been influencing my crew—"

"Now be reasonable, how—"

"Reasonable? Reasonable?" I kick the bed. "I've got you set up in this cushy room after you tried to kill us all with your crazy plan. I could've left you in the brig, or worse."

"I wish you'd calm down, Jordan."

"I wish you'd never boarded this ship. I wish you'd left well enough alone. But no, you had to stick your goddamned nose in where it didn't belong. Who asked you to wield your sword of—"

"Obviously something's happened to make you angry. I'm not sure what it is, but I can hazard a guess. This has to do with Alison, right?" When he says her name, I flinch. He pounces on me. "Is she seeing someone else? That butch outside, right?" He threads his hands behind his back with glee. "Aww, I'm touched. You came to me for advice on women."

"That's not why I'm here."

"Is this a fist bump moment?"

I turn to leave and he jumps off the bed. "Okay, okay. You win. We won't talk about Alison." He sits on the edge with his hands on his knees. "I haven't been talking to anyone. I've been minding my Ps and Qs right here in this mildly-more-comfortable-than-the-brig-jail-cell."

"I don't believe you."

"Why are you so against me? I could help you know. I do happen to know a thing or two about running a ship. Done it for a bit of time now."

"I don't need your help. My ship runs fine without you."

"Then why are you here?"

"To ask who you've been talking to."

"Oh, come on." He flops back on the bed plumping his pillow behind his head. "You might as well ask me what you really want to know."

I turn to leave. I'm not playing any more of his games.

As I raise my hand to knock and signal I'm ready to leave, he says, "You want to know what to expect on the planet."

I spin back around. "How do you know about the planet?"

He points at the door. "Your security man out there has a loud voice. He was yammering on about how he was going to be one of the crew chosen to explore this planet you've found. Quite talky, that one. I'd watch out for the talkers. They usually stir up trouble."

I make a mental note to put Fossick on waste detail.

"Are you prepared for what's down there? Because most of the dangers, you won't even see," he says.

"I've got a good team working on it. It's not like we're ignorant about what we'd find on a planet."

He scoffs. "Did you know, that on Earth, insects outnumber humans two hundred million to one? Imagine that. And yet we considered ourselves the superior species. Have you ever seen an insect, Jordan? In real life, I mean. Not some picture book. Did you know that the funnel spider of Australia can kill a person my size in under thirty minutes. They're only a centimeter in length. Fleas, tiny bugs the size of sand, have been responsible for millions of deaths over the centuries. They would bite rats, pick up the infection, and carry it to humans. Pus bulbs the size of your hand would break out all over the body."

I suppress an eye roll. "Is this supposed to scare me? We don't even know if the planet supports life."

"If it supports plants, it supports bugs. How do you think plants mate? They pick up root and walk over to the plant next door and say, 'Hey, baby, can I buy you a drink?' No. Insects feed on the plants, pick up the pollen, and carry it to the next plant." He sits up, moving to the edge of the bed, eager now that he has my attention. "Do you know how the Aztecs were actually conquered? A virus. Spanish sailors traded blankets with smallpox in them. Fifteen million died without any defense. Trust me when I say this, you are in way over your head and the worst part is, you don't even know it. You think you can outwit what's down there because you have a bunch of geeks crunching the odds on a bunch of scenarios? Those simulations will fail because they're not using the right variables. Your team will be dead in a matter of minutes without me."

I choke back a laugh. "You want me to bring you along? Not in a million years." The only thing worse than setting loose a bunch of armed nerds in that jungle would be to let my father loose.

"All right, but think of it this way. While you're off playing wild safari, I'll be back here making plans."

"You'd be making plans even if I brought you along. That's what you do."

"At least that way you could watch me. Who are you going to leave in charge? Loose lips out there? I'd have him contemplating mutiny before the cargo doors closed on this heap."

I'm at a serious loss. There's no way I want to bring him along, but the thought of leaving him here would gnaw at me.

"You think on it, Jordan. Out there, even if I were scheming, I'd be an asset. Here, I'm a liability."

Not for the first time I wish I had the balls to shoot him out in an escape pod and wait for the oxygen to run out.

Before I leave I say, "I told you once before if you didn't behave, you'd be back in the brig. That includes lying about who you've been speaking with. Yakovich will be in to escort you back."

The look on his face as I leave is worth it.

After visiting Sarka, this next visit should be a walk in the park, so why am I more on edge?

From the moment I met Ash, there was something that intrigued me. She wasn't what I expected. Colonel Shrives painted her to be an over-opinionated hothead. And while she is that, she's so much more. I watched her excitement that first meeting. It rolled off her in waves and washed over me, almost drowning me in their wake. Ever since then, I've been trying to keep afloat.

Not since that first regression with the doctor has she been so low. And who can blame her. It's still happening. She's still the target of someone's hate. I would have thought the events on the *Posterus* would've put an end to this, but it runs deeper. Every effort to further the investigation has brought me nowhere. I'm running out of clues. And time. The longer we wait, the likelier it is this could happen again and she could end up much worse. The only straw I have left to grasp is that Ash remembers something about the attack.

I knock on her door and wait. No one answers. I know she's in here because, like the rest of the crew, the doctor inoculated her. I could override the lock controls, but that feels too much like an invasion. After everything she's been through, I want to tread lightly.

I knock again. "Ash, open up. I need to speak with you." I hate standing out here like this on my own ship. The corridor is empty, what I can see of it anyway. It sweeps around in a circle, obscuring both ends.

I wait a few more seconds, preparing to knock again, when the door slides open. Ash is standing there in sweats. Her hair is lank and dirty, hanging in strips around her shoulder. There are still marks on her skin from the healing skin grafts and where we removed the tape. My heart drops. She looks horrible. Worse than that. She looks like she's given up.

"Captain."

"Can I come in?"

She waves me past. Her room isn't much better. The bed is unmade and there are tablets and clothes strewn everywhere. It's musty, like all her bad thoughts have sucked up the good air and left the atmosphere stale.

"You haven't been out much."

"As if you're going to let me roam the ship by myself now. Everywhere I go, there's someone waiting for me." Her hands drop to her hips as her chin comes to rest on her chest. "It would be easier if next time they were successful."

"Where is all this coming from? It's not like you to get so defeated." I soften my voice. "Talk to me."

Ash plops down on the bed and gathers a pillow to her chest, hugging it for comfort. It's in complete contrast to the first time I saw her when she knocked over a chair, so embarrassed she'd sat down without permission. "I don't do well in situations like this. If I don't have something to keep me occupied I—my thoughts take over and it isn't always sunshine and rainbows." The woman who walked aboard my ship almost two months ago is gone. Lethargy and sluggishness has replaced her energy and vibrance. The way her last few months have gone, she has every reason to be experiencing dark thoughts.

"Tell me what I can do to help. Besides finding who's behind the attacks."

She falls back on the bed and sighs. "It's not that simple, Captain." Silence stretches between us. I hear the air filter kick on. It hums for a few seconds, then shuts off.

She sits up. "Why have you been so distant lately? I understand you're busy. But besides relieving me of duty, you haven't spoken to me since the night the *Posterus* exploded." She stands up and faces me. "I could've been dead and you'd never know. I kept waiting for you to show up in the med center. Everyone else did." There's a slight spark in her eyes. An awakening as she lays down a new challenge.

What do I tell her? That I'm a coward? I have no idea how to make this right. I should have visited her, not only as a friend, but as her captain.

Honesty wins. "I did visit. But when I got there, you were already with someone, so I waited. I'm not proud of it, but I overheard what you said to Hartley. I thought it wise not to go in."

She shakes her head. "I don't remember. What did I say to him?"

"That there was nothing between us." In truth, it was the word dumb. That she wouldn't be dumb enough to sleep with me. That's what dug into me, that sleeping with me could be likened to a bad date you shouldn't have gone on. "It made me so mad, the way you dismissed it, I felt dismissed, forgettable. It made me ashamed, the way I'd acted."

"So let me get this straight? You were mad that I didn't gush like some love-struck school girl about something intimate between us? To the biggest gossip on the ship? I'm not going to talk about us to other people. What we shared was personal, not to mention against regulations. With everything else going on, I thought it best to be prudent." She pauses and gives me a sly grin. "For once."

"It's not like I was expecting you to tell Hartley, it was the way you handled it, like you were angry he'd even mention it," I say.

"I was angry. I thought Hartley would know better than to come to me with stupid gossip."

"Hartley? The king of social etiquette?"

She laughs at that. It's rich and deep, the sound more comforting than any of Ash's platitudes. It makes me hope she might actually get through this. "Good point."

I step closer. "I'm sorry I've been avoiding you." I can't even begin to explain why. It would feel like I was cracking myself open and letting her see everything inside. So I don't. Instead, I take a deep breath because the next thing I'm about to ask is more than wishful thinking, it's everything. "Can't we go back to the way things were, before?"

Her hand brushes mine, then she pulls it away. The domino effect of fluttering it causes makes me wish she hadn't. "I want to, I do. It's just that everything's changed. I know I've been rude and insubordinate, and I try not to be. But I can't help myself." Her shoulders drop as she says this last bit. "It's like I see what I'm doing, but the words are out of my mouth before I can stop them."

"Can we at least call a truce?"

"It's not like we're in this big war with each other." There's something so earnest in her eyes. "It's hard to go backward. But I can try, if that's what you want."

I almost laugh. It's definitely not what I want, but more like something I need if I'm going to keep my sanity. I nod. And now I can't put off the real reason I'm here any longer. "I know you already talked to the doctor, but I need to know if you've remembered anything from that night. Even the smallest detail will help."

Ash drops on her bed and pulls her feet under her. She looks down at her duvet, picking at the corner. "It feels like it's happening all over again. The memory gaps. I don't remember anything that night." I expect more, but that's all she says. When she finally does speak, her voice is full of gravel, like her throat has closed over a sob. "If you don't mind, Captain, I'd like to be alone."

CHAPTER TEN

The next morning, as I'm sitting down to breakfast, Hartley drops his tray next to mine. His scrambled eggs jump a foot. I jump two.

"I'm glad I caught you, Captain."

"You're not about to ask me out to dinner again, right? Because the answer is no."

He grins and picks up his fork. Instead of using it to eat, he waves it around, punctuating each thought. "No, Captain. I've postponed that area of distraction for now. No, the reason I'm here—besides breakfast," he points his fork at his eggs, "is that Yakovich came to see me. She wanted to ask about the mission and something I said when we were all meeting. Although now that I think of it, I can't remember what it was. We started talking about something else. She's really tall for a woman, isn't she?" He points his fork at me. "How tall are you, Captain? I bet you're about her height. Would you consider yourself above average?"

I'm about to make an excuse to leave when he finally gets back to his original thought. And then you couldn't budge me if you tried.

"Anyway, I remembered thinking how tall she was, she's almost as tall as me, and that's when she asked if there was another way to find out who's been in the messes after hours, besides the usual method. Said you'd be interested in the answer."

"And is there?"

"Is there what?"

Christ, it's too early for this conversation. "Is there a way to find out who's been in the messes at certain times?"

"Sure." He points his fork at the door. "Each door to the mess has a bioscanner. Everyone's scanned as they enter. It's actually pretty neat the way it works. It sucks in your breath molecules and analyzes them. Did you know, Captain, that every breath you exhale contains millions of bacteria?" His fork waves around in a circle.

I shake my head. He hasn't taken a bite of his food yet.

"Well, it's true. And the scanner can tell by that sample what sort of diseases or viruses you might be carrying. If you have something like Norwalk or Hep B—something that's really contagious and transmitted by food—then it'll sound an alarm and you'll know not to enter. It cuts down on contamination and illness on board."

He stabs a piece of egg, then jabs it toward me. Part of it wobbles and slips off onto the table. It reminds me of Ash's comment about the food when she first arrived. Most of our food is made to resemble real food but isn't. Even the eggs are a liquid substitute. The resources it would take to keep live hens on board are not worth the hassle. I've never had any trouble with our food. It's better by far than what I grew up with on the Burr station. Mostly we ate rations. Century old astronaut rations. If we had real food it was a good day. It meant the last raiding party was successful. At the time I didn't have a clue what that meant. That someone else somewhere was going without. Lives were lost so we could eat. I only thought about how hungry I was. Even the daughter of the leader isn't high on the pecking list of who gets to eat real food.

What most people don't realize about the Burrs is that they're trying to survive. Their methods are deplorable. So are the actions that forced them to raid ships to feed their children.

There was one month where powdered mashed potatoes was all we had to eat. I kept asking for freeze dried mac and cheese, which rarely trickled down our way. One packet of potatoes was enough to fill your stomach, but that's all. You can fortify them with as much nutrients and vitamins as you want. But it's still a powder that, when mixed with water, resembles lumpy mashed potatoes.

Sometimes, there'd be dried chives mixed in. I'd always pick those out because they were hard and gross.

When I moved in with Kate on the farm, it was the best I'd ever eaten. She took one look at me—a scrawny, filthy twelve-year-old—and made me a heaping plate of corn, Swiss chard and roast chicken. I don't think I'd ever eaten real meat in my life. I scarfed it down so fast I threw it all up ten minutes later.

Instead of hating bland food, I'm always thankful of what we do have. I look down at my own plate of scrambled eggs and hash browns. To me, this is a feast.

"This is all very interesting, but how does this help find who's been in the messes?" I ask.

Finally, Hartley shoves the fork in his mouth. He continues talking despite the egg. "Easy. The bioscanner records the time it takes each reading and since everyone's bacteria is unique to that individual, almost like you were a tiny planet and your bacteria were the species that lived there, then it's only a matter of checking the records and testing everyone's ecosystem."

"And there's no way to cover that?"

He leans forward and whispers, "This is about Ash isn't it? I heard she was upside down, and her—"

"Hartley, we're not discussing if this is about Ash or not. I need to know if it's possible to tamper with the bioscanner."

He puts his fork down next to his plate and leans back, folding his arms. "She's okay though?"

I've been asking myself that same question all day. Is Ash okay? I decide to level with him. "According to the doctor, she'll recover. He's more worried about her mental state and so am I. Maybe you could go see her?"

"I tried. She's not seeing anyone."

"Keep trying. She needs your support right now."

He nods, but doesn't resume eating. The mess is filling up. All the tables are occupied and it's a matter of time before someone asks to sit with us.

"Getting back to the scanners?"

"What about them? Did you know they can diagnose—"

"All I care is if they can be tampered with."

"It'd be hard, but I guess. Why not check the cameras? It would be a lot simpler. You wouldn't have to test everyone's spit." He makes a face.

"We already tried checking the video. Vasa said someone swapped the timestamp and that it would be like looking for life on another planet. Near impossible."

"That's stupid. There are a few ways you can search for a particular video, even if you don't have the timestamp." He picks his fork up and leans over his plate. "You could create an algorithm to analyze the stain patterns on the walls for instance." He gestures toward the back wall where a member of the kitchen staff is refilling a vat of eggs. "The program would look for the closest match and since that's something that's completely unique to this time period, you'd get a good result. That's if you want to get fancy. But it would be easier to check the code and look for duplicate requests."

"Wouldn't that have been masked somehow?"

"I don't see how. When you call up a video, it inputs a request, which gets tracked. And then you'd have to call up the video you're replacing it with. Rarely would you put in both requests at the same time. So the duplicate wouldn't cause any alarm because the system isn't set up to notice. But if you're looking for it, it's easy to find."

"How do we know this double request exists?"

"Because there's no other way to hack a timestamp. You need both videos pulled up at the same time."

"Huh." I have nothing more intelligent to add because my mind is working overtime. Why wouldn't Vasa tell Yakovich that? Did he suspect her of being the culprit? And then a more worrisome thought enters my head. Vasa didn't say anything because he didn't want us to know.

I stand outside the bridge and lean my head against the wall. What I'm about to do makes me sick. The metal of the wall is cool on my forehead and for a minute, I worry I'm wrong.

Further down the corridor, I hear the door to the chute hiss open. I straighten and turn. My security detail is here.

Yakovich stops in front of me. Her jaw is tight and her forehead is creased. She looks like she hasn't slept in days.

"Are we all set?" I ask.

She nods and hands me a tablet. I scan it and hand it back. There is no doubt now who's behind the attacks on Ash. I only wish we'd found him sooner.

After talking with Hartley yesterday, I assigned him and Yakovich to find the footage from the attack. With Hartley looking, it didn't take long. It showed Vasa carrying Ash over his shoulder into the mess at two twenty that morning. He was in there for fifteen minutes and then he left alone and headed in the direction of the bridge.

Hartley left as soon as the video started. I wish I had the luxury of declining to watch, but as captain I have a greater responsibility. As much as I personally want to, I can't look away just because something's difficult to watch. I promised Ash we'd find who did this and I can't let her down now.

I had Yakovich check the logs. Vasa was on hell shift, from midnight until eight. According to Hartley, Vasa left the bridge at a little after two and didn't return until almost three. He left his station logged in so it wouldn't leave a trail. But what he didn't bank on was Hartley. He searched through the code, thousands of lines, to find the exact moment Vasa left. As Hartley said, the ship logs everything, including opening doors. It goes back to the days when so many things could and did go wrong. To fix them, they needed a way to know the sequence of events on board.

Two days before the incident, Vasa entered the med center and removed a vial of ketamine, a substance that will knock a person out for several hours. The tablet Yakovich hands me is a report of the logs confirming Vasa's movements that night.

In less than a minute, Vasa's midnight shift will be over and we'll escort him to his quarters for questioning. I don't want to go onto the bridge and make a scene. Even if he doesn't deserve it, he's still a member of this crew.

Several hours later, I'm still no closer to learning why one of my trusted officers would betray me and the rest of the crew like this.

Vasa didn't deny it. He didn't make excuses. Instead, he's sat in silence since Yakovich and I entered his room. Hartley is the only other person on this ship who knows the whole story. But this isn't something we can keep from the crew. It will get out. I'd like to have the full story before that happens.

Vasa sits at his desk chair, gripping the edge. The desk is empty except for a single tablet placed in the middle. His room is as neat as the desk. The only decoration is two picture frames on the shelf above his desk. One of the photos is him with an older man and woman standing in front of a module house. I recognize the design. A stage two farm unit. Kate had one until I came to live with her, then she upgraded to a stage three. The other is of Vasa at his academy graduation. He's in his cadet uniform with his aviator insignia held out for the camera.

The sheets on the bed are crisp and tight. If I didn't know for sure this was his room, I'd think nobody lived here. The only evidence that someone lives here is the smell. It invades the room, coating every surface. It's the same sickly smell that follows him around the ship, through corridors, up chutes, on the bridge. It's a mixture of overpowering body odor and a funk that's indescribable. It's not something you want to be near, let alone breathe in for three hours.

By that third hour, I've done all the diaphragmatic breathing I can handle and I'm still fuming. It's a slow burn that creeps from stomach to sternum. It's the kind of anger that has a time limit before it erupts. I only hope we're done here before that happens.

As soon as we saw the footage, I had Yakovich search Vasa's quarters. There wasn't much there but she did find a tablet with Ash's service file and full medical history. We know how he carried out his plan, what we don't know is why.

I keep my outward appearance calm. I don't want it to show how furious I am. "You don't need to tell us how you did it, Vasa. We've already learned that for ourselves. You visited the med center the morning of the attack, complaining of a headache. You stole a vial containing fifteen cc of ketamine when Dr. Prashad turned his back. You then administered this dose to Ash at the evening meal. There is footage of you slipping it into her dinner. Later that night, you left your post on the bridge and entered Ash's cabin. You injected her with," I consult my tablet. "Protregamsyn, a substance Ash is allergic to. You then carried her to the mess and taped her up."

Still silence. He stares ahead. We've reviewed the timeline multiple times, in multiple ways. I'm hoping something will jar him enough to speak.

"If Dr. Prashad hadn't had the foresight to flush her system, Ash would've died in the mess hours before anyone found her. This is only one incident, but I'm sure if we went back and searched, we'd find that you were behind the others too." I have no idea what I can say to him to make him share his secrets. The brig is currently full. After all, we only have the one cell. Confining someone to quarters doesn't feel like any sort of punishment, unless of course, you're Ash. "Why were you trying to kill Ash? She's done nothing to you. In fact, I saw the two of you laughing together in the mess a few days before we found her."

"I wasn't behind all of them." He almost jumps out of the chair as he says this, but Yakovich waves him back down. "It wasn't all me. The first ones, the mattress, that was someone else."

"So only the sadistic, harmful ones were you," Yakovich says.

"I didn't want to hurt her." Vasa bows his head. His chest begins to heave with great sobs. "I had no choice."

"Everyone has a choice," I say.

He shakes his head. "We're supposed to be here. And she was becoming an obstacle to our mission."

"What do you mean we're supposed to be here?"

He spreads his hands. "This. Here. Can't you feel it, Captain? When we set off on this mission, didn't it feel bigger than us? Like we were embarking on something epic."

Yakovich and I exchange looks. How else would you describe a generational ship? This is getting us nowhere. I'm about to pull the plug on this interview.

"She was starting to remember. And that's not good," Vasa says.

"Ash was starting to remember? What was she not supposed to remember?" I ask.

But he shakes his head and won't tell us any more.

CHAPTER ELEVEN

I've decided we'll be ready to land on the planet Monday. Hartley recommended we call it Purple Haze because of the morning mist. All the probes we've sent down show pictures of a dark purple mist. It floats up from the marshes and valleys in the early mornings. Mani is eager to find out what makes it purple.

As much as I'm excited about this unprecedented discovery, I'm wary. Every day that passes without descending feels safe. Each step I make toward landing us on this planet screams impending doom at me. I'm not sure if it's a sign we shouldn't land or a sign I'm becoming paranoid.

In the end, I decide to trust my instincts and take a few extra precautions. To deny this opportunity would be like turning back without landing as soon as the first humans reached Mars.

A tiny part of me keeps asking, what if? What if this is it? The planet we settle on? And we found it. I'm prepared to spend the next fifty years on the *Persephone* exploring even if we never reach a destination. But what if we don't have to?

Now that we have an opportunity to see a planet it makes me want more. I've lived my whole life a few feet from the vacuum of space. This is an unprecedented opportunity. If we can find a planet in our lifetime, why shouldn't we?

I've already posted the list of who I'll be leading on the expedition. It's not a huge team, only four. Mani, whose botany expertise will be a huge asset. Foer, for any engineering issues we may encounter with our equipment. Yakovich, because anyone would feel safe with her around. If there is fauna on this planet, I don't want to announce our presence with a parade. Especially if the fauna is hostile.

I've been reading as much as I can about the early explorers of Earth, trying to glean any useful information. The early pioneers weren't much different than us. They were entering a very different world than what they knew. I skimmed over the Frontier missions to Mars and the Apollo missions to the moon, but seeing as how they were all to climates devoid of vegetation they weren't much help. The same for the early North and South Pole expeditions. This is more like the British and French invading North America and Africa. I'm determined to prepare for most if not all possibilities. I've even read a few of those *Choose Your Own Adventure* books Mani mentioned.

I have one more task before we begin landing procedures tomorrow. I knock on Ash's door. It's early evening. The ship is quiet with crew in their cabins or playing mahjong in each other's quarters. She answers her door faster this time.

"Captain."

I nod and enter at her invitation. She looks in better spirits too.

Earlier in the day, I had Dr. Prashad give her a physical to see if she's ready to resume her duties. With me off the ship and Vasa confined to quarters, I'll need someone to command in my absence. It kills me that if we hadn't discovered who was behind the attacks I would have left Vasa in charge. Or I would've held off landing until we caught the person. I'll never know for certain.

The doctor says Ash is physically ready to go back to work. She's healing well. There's only the hint of a scar on her face where Yakovich removed the tape. Mentally, Len thinks it's in Ash's best interest to work. She needs something positive to focus on.

Ash's room is in better condition too. She's made her bed. There are a few tablets on her nightstand. It looks like I've interrupted some light reading.

"I saw the list. I don't like the idea of you leading this team. What if something happens to you? What'll happen to the *Persephone*?" she asks.

"You'll take over as captain, of course."

"Me?"

"I'm reinstating you and putting you in charge while I'm gone."

She nods, but I don't get anything else out of her. I can't gauge her mood. I thought she'd be happy to be back on active duty. She balls the sleeves of her sweatshirt, hiding her hands. After a moment, she starts pacing.

"I have other news you should sit down for," I say.

"Why do people always tell you to sit down when they're about to give you bad news? Like it's going to ease the blow?"

"Have it your way." I take a seat in her computer chair and spin to face her and the room. The planet below gives off a light purple glow. It bathes her back in a faint hue. We've been orbiting for the last couple of days. It's hard to keep the crew working. Too many times I've come across a few standing at the public portholes edging each other out of the way to get a look at it. The other day, I had to give up running along the track because most of it was blocked by crew.

Most of it is a purplish blue. Hartley says there's something in the atmosphere that only makes it appear purple. When we get to the surface, it will more than likely be clear. It's only a refraction of the atmosphere.

Earth was similar when it had oceans. From space it looked like a blue sphere coated with green and yellow puzzle pieces. Now it's yellow. I spent the first decade of my life staring down at that sphere, hoping one day my dad would take me to visit. He never did. But now I have my own. And this one has water. It also has plants and trees and a whole slew of species bizarre and different from what we're used to.

It hasn't rained on Earth in over a hundred years. The only things left are hardy scrub plants. When the atmosphere burned up, most of the water evaporated with it. If you were to dig a few kilometers down, you might find some.

"What I have to say is as much good news as it is bad. We've discovered who was behind the attacks. And it was only one person."

"Who?" Ash plops down on the edge of her bed across from me. She pushes up the sleeves of her sweatshirt in preparation.

"Vasa."

"No." She shakes her head. "I don't believe it." She rubs at the goose bumps raised along her arm.

"I didn't want to either. But we have him on camera. We have logs, opportunity. Plus, he admitted it was him."

"Why? He's never given any sign that he was out to harm me."

"We don't exactly know why yet. He won't say." I don't want to share everything with Ash. I have no idea how she'll take it. I don't even know how to take it. He didn't sound like the Vasa I knew. But I didn't know him that well. How well can you know a person if they lie about who they are?

"I mean, he saved me in the filter room. Why would he do that if he was the one who trapped me there in the first place?" she asks.

I blink a few times, wondering if I heard her correctly. "What do you mean he saved you?"

"When I woke up, he was there. He had two security guards with him. He said that you'd tasked him to keep an eye on me."

Vasa mentioned something about Ash starting to remember things. I'm worried this might have something to do with it. What if her mind knot isn't what's been causing those memory gaps? When she attacked Hartley she couldn't remember a thing afterward, but this is the first time she's remembered things differently. "Why would I get Vasa to watch your tracking program? Yakovich and her team were responsible for your security. It was two of her people who found you. Vasa was off duty. That's how he was able to set it up."

She shakes her head, confused. "You interacted with him. I saw you."

"Ash, I promise you, Vasa was no where near that compartment when we found you."

She closes her eyes and tilts her head to the ceiling, at a loss for a moment. I imagine she's playing it all back in her mind. What she thinks she remembers versus reality. I'll have the doctor do a full checkup to make sure there isn't anything else in her system.

Ash runs the tips of trembling fingers over her lips. Her breathing picks up and she huffs out a long breath. "Wow. So how do I know what's real and what's not?" The way she looks at me, I know what she's asking.

"You didn't imagine that."

She nods, but it seems more of an effort to keep moving than an affirmation. If she stays still her mind will race places it shouldn't. "Okay. Okay. So now what?"

I move to take a seat next to her on the bed. "If you don't feel up to resuming your post, I don't want you to feel rushed."

"No, Captain. I want to go back to work. I need to."

"Good. Report for duty tomorrow. We'll be landing in two days." I stand and move to the door. Before I go, I say, "I want you to stay away from this investigation. Security section is taking care of it."

I get a crisp nod.

CHAPTER TWELVE

The brilliance of the sun obscures our first view as the cargo doors open. It's so blinding, my team—standing at the entrance in enviro-suits—avert their eyes. Then everything comes into sharp focus as our eyes adjust for the first time to the brightness of a sun.

What I don't expect when I step into the surrounding green, is the heat. The warmth blasts through my clear visor, bathing my face. I close my eyes and tilt my head up. I feel a cozy contentment I've never felt before.

"What a fucking hell hole." Sarka growls through the comm unit in our suits.

My contentment shatters. I debated with myself for a long time before deciding to bring him. Ash is in charge now, and I don't want her to have to deal with him while I'm gone. Plus, as much as I hate to admit it, his knowledge could be helpful. He's the only person on this ship who's ever been on a planet before. He may have his uses.

"Fucking hell." Sarka removes his foot from a giant pile of something that can only be excrement. A deep green bird the size of German Shepard parts the grass in front of him. It gives an angry honk before waddling off into the brush.

We've landed the ship on the edge of marshland. The smell is thick. It sticks to the inside of my throat. Waist high grass grows from the marsh. It looks like tiny tubes sticking out of the mud. Sure enough, when I break one off, they're hollow inside.

I've never seen so much green in one place. Even the grass fields on Delta were never this vast. Surrounding us, far off in the distance, are trees in one direction and a mountain range in another. They arc in a semicircle around the horizon.

Even though the ground feels soft, Hartley says we've landed on a rock shield that has similar properties to granite. He promises we won't sink.

Ash sidles up next to me, gripping my elbow to get my attention before letting her hand fall. "I still don't like it. You should be staying on the ship, not running off into," she waves her hand about, indicating the wilderness around us, "this."

I sigh, frustrated. We've had this argument at least three times since yesterday, and I've dug my heals in with the strength of one of Hartley's engine bots. With each round, Ash gets more and more excited. "You've made that clear. But seeing as how I'm the captain, I get to make the decisions." I turn to her so I can see that she gets it, gets how much this means to me. "I wouldn't pass up this chance to explore if I had to sacrifice several limbs for the adventure, so lay off. I'll be fine."

Even now, as I watch her scan the horizon, there's a fervor behind those green eyes. It's so intense, it scares me. I know that look well because I've seen it growing stronger in my eyes every morning. The excitement of getting here has been almost unbearable.

I hear several shouts and turn to see Sarka removing his helmet. Christ. He gasps for a few breaths then inhales so deep his nostrils flair. He grins, stretching his face almost flat. It's the first time he's appeared at all pleased since I informed him he'd be coming on the team to explore the planet.

"What the hell are you doing?"

"The air's fine. Don't get your panties in a bunch, *Captain.*" The emphasis on my rank grates me and I resist the urge to smack him. Before I can stop anyone, the rest of the crew take their helmets off. When no one convulses on the ground from lack of oxygen, I realize it's futile to protest and unlock my own.

The air is sweet, like perfume, but more subtle. There's a faint floral scent and something I can't describe, but makes me want to fill my lungs to bursting.

"The air appears to be breathable, Captain." Mani pipes up from the other side of our group. He was my first choice for this expedition. His expertise in botany and affable nature make him a perfect fit for exploring a new world. "But I can't predict what long-term effects breathing it will have on us." His chubby baby cheeks flush red, and his curls have wilted somewhat in the humidity.

Sarka slaps him hard on the back. "It'll put some much needed hair on your chest."

Mani frowns, peering down at his chest. "I'm not sure how that works." He picks at the front of his enviro-suit. "How is it going to do that?"

"It's an expression, Mani." I remember when I was a kid, anytime I didn't want to do something, Sarka would say it put hair on my chest. I wasn't sure why that was a good thing.

I turn back to the *Persephone* and take one good look at her. From this angle she looks like an old galleon, with her furled sails standing tall as masts. Both the aft and bow curve up to meet the top. She's majestic, gleaming in the sunlight.

"Take good care of her," I tell Ash.

She gives her a few soft pats. "She'll be better by the time you return. I have big plans for her."

A few crew members groan.

We set off toward the forest, south of the *Persephone*. Ash and the crew that have come to see us off wave from the edge of the cargo ramp. There's a light cheer from them as we disappear into the tall marsh grass.

As we hike through the sucking sludge, our boots already coated in a yellowish mud, we make a strange crew. Yakovich is at the front, tall and blond, with her sonic gun at the ready. Behind her is Foer, lumbering like a giant bear brushing the tall stalks aside. After him is Mani wading through the mud with high steps. Every few seconds he takes a moment to check the surroundings and make a note in his tablet. At the back of the pack is Sarka, then me. Sarka's shouldered his pack tight, all loose items secured. He marches behind Mani with measured strides, keeping his head down.

The heat is excruciating. Within minutes, I've stripped off the top of my enviro-suit. I let it hang, choosing to hike through the marsh in my tank top. Without our helmets providing a sealed environment, we're exposed to the elements. The humidity especially is wreaking havoc on my team. Mani's tank top is dark with sweat. Foer's is hanging from his utility belt.

The only one not affected is Sarka. His shirt and skin are dry and his hair hasn't moved since we left.

It's a new experience being in an environment that I can't control. I'm trying to be a good sport about it, but within the first hour the skin on my shoulders prickle and my feet hurt.

Sarka steps next to me and points to my face. "You're getting burned."

I touch my nose and find it tender. "How?" I look around, not knowing what, in this flat land, could be causing it.

He laughs and points to the sky. "The sun. Your skin is sensitive. Without some sort of protective coat, it'll get worse"

"Is it dangerous?" A wave of panic hits me. I've taken precautions, but this isn't one.

"Very."

"Are you joking?" I squint up at the sun. It's right overhead, small and bright, but the heat radiating off it leaves me to wonder if he's telling the truth.

"Not at all. Back on Earth, people used to die from skin cancer." At the word cancer, I stop dead.

"How much exposure before that happens?"

He shrugs. "It depends. But one bad burn can increase your chances."

I stop and search for anything to use for cover. We're still far from tree cover and there isn't anything else that we've brought to use. "If we'd kept our helmets on—"

"Relax. You're not going to drop dead." He smiles. It's an evil sort of smile. Then he bends down and scoops up a handful of mud from the marsh bed and begins to rub it on his nose. I can only imagine what my expression must be because he roars with laughter.

"You are joking."

He shakes his head. "Cheap and instant sunscreen."

Great. Just great. I tell everyone to stop and start applying the mud to their skin. The whole time I'm rubbing the gritty sludge over my arms, neck, and face, I'm watching Sarka do the same. I can't be sure he's not screwing with me, but I'd rather us look like idiots then risk my crew's health. I contact the ship to let them know to be careful when working outside.

Once we're coated in the fowl smelling mud, we continue through the marsh toward the tall trees ahead. A large hawkish bird calls from above. It's two, maybe three times the size of the bird we saw earlier. Its wings extend, feathers fluttering, as it soars through the sky. I've never seen anything so beautiful in all my life. I stop and stare, tracking its progress, entranced by the freedom it must feel to be part of the sky like that. It makes me long for things that will never be, things I can only read and dream about. I continue to stare at the giant bird when I realize it's getting awfully close to us.

"Uh, Captain?" Foer nudges me on the shoulder. "We should move." The bird begins diving toward us at tremendous speed.

I lunge, splashing into a pool of stagnant water as the bird stretches its claws, seeking skin. One talon rakes my back, missing its grip by inches. I push myself back up. We all bolt for the tree line, which could still be a few kilometers off or could be a few meters. It's hard to tell with the haze in the sky. For the amount of time we've been traveling, we're not getting any nearer. I throw everything I have into staying upright, which is difficult, as the marsh sucks at our feet.

Mani pants next to me, arms pumping at his sides. The only sounds are the squelch of our boots, our heavy breathing, and the rhythmic slap of our packs on our backs. The bird dives for Sarka next, but he spins out of the way.

We reach the forest. It doesn't deter the creature. Instead, it clamps on to the nearest tree with its claws. It has pincers on the tip of its wing, which help it hug the trunk. It shrieks at us in an earsplitting cry. I cover my ears to keep the noise out and the fear from swamping in. As we rush further into the trees, the bird leaps from trunk to trunk, following us deeper into the jungle. Sweat is pouring off me in liters, streaking down my face, cutting rivulets in the mud.

I sob in relief when Foer points to a fallen tree with an opening beneath the mammoth trunk. It's big enough for us to squeeze through. I push everyone under, waiting until Sarka's head disappears, then dive headfirst after him. The bird squawks above us, scraping at my legs. It's pincer scours the dirt. Behind me, Foer shouts something unintelligible at it. I wish I could close my eyes and block it out, but each sweep of its wing brings the sharp pincer closer.

There's a loud howl that quiets to a gurgle. The bird drops in front of the opening, still and silent, impaled through the head by a long-shafted weapon.

CHAPTER THIRTEEN

We trudge deeper into the jungle. We're pulled single file. Our hands are bound by a coarse rope and tethered around our waists. It's a surreal experience, finding intelligent life on this planet. Strange that in the vastness of our universe, we've encountered it here.

The rope around my wrists yanks me forward, urging me to go faster. I'm tethered to the last in line of the alien group. The cord snakes around his left wrist, while the other holds a large spear. It's a guess that he's male. For all we know their species might not have genders.

They're a strange lot, but I'd imagine if a crow were to become self-aware they'd think us strange as well. And they must think us strange. Any creature so different would. They tower over us. Their muscles bunch and flex along their lithe bodies. And their elongated beak shaped faces stare ahead, stoic. Yet instead of stamping through the forest, they glide. They're as light on their feet as if they weighed nothing.

Our four saviors, and now captors, are completely hairless. Nestled between their shoulder blades are pale gray, rough feathers. The color is only a shade lighter than their skin. The feathers flow down the length of their backs and taper at mid-thigh.

Another tug and I almost stumble over a log before catching my balance. My startled cry causes the one in back to turn. His black eyes flare, and as they do, the feathers on his back flap out stretching into wings. He ruffles them twice before folding them back. The more I study them, the more they look avian. Perhaps their bones are hollow like birds as well, allowing for their grace.

Everything feels lighter here, like we're floating. From what Hartley's explained, it's because of the mass of this planet. The gravity is lighter, we're lighter. I wonder if those wings allow them to fly. I have an almost uncontrollable urge to reach out and run my hand along the feathers. But good sense prevails.

There's a commotion ahead of us as a new group of avians joins us. Up until now, they've ignored us. Only a tug on the rope every now and then tells us they even remember we're here. But this new bunch is different. The largest catches sight of me and marches straight toward us, pushing a few of his comrades out of the way.

From his posture and confidence, this is the guy with all the power. The others defer and almost stoop in his presence. He pushes the last avian out of the way and glares down at me. He's at least two feet taller than my six foot frame but I do not stoop or concede. Instead, I keep my posture straight and stare into those beady eyes. This creature will not intimidate me in front of my crew.

There's a moment of confusion on his face when I don't submit. His eyes travel the length of my body. They stop at my breasts and rest there for several moments before coming back to meet my eyes. His perusal is clinical, detached, like he's observing an animal in the wild. He grabs my ponytail, pulling off the elastic so my hair falls to my shoulders. It's almost like he's petting me and I jerk back, disgusted.

His nostrils flare and he does that same wing flap fluttering the other did earlier. Turning, he yells at the avians behind him. It's more like a screech. I'm not sure what he's mad about until he grasps my head and forces me to the ground, and then I don't care. My ire is up. I struggle against the grip. Sharp claws dig into my temples. I'm so close to the ground I can almost taste the loamy dirt.

My hands are unbound and the rope removed from my waist before I'm yanked to my feet and hauled to the back of the line. As I pass my crew, only Sarka meets my eyes with an icy, angry stare. The rest avert their eyes out of fear or empathy, I'm not sure. When we reach the end of the line, I'm retied behind Sarka.

My own nostrils flare at the implication and I glare at the avian, throwing as much hate as I can into the effort. But my rebellion is short lived. He smacks my face and pushes it toward the ground. Screeching he marches to the front of the line.

He sent me to the back of the line because I'm female. In front of my crew, no less. My face burns in utter mortification.

"Fucking prick," I say.

Sarka turns, his face a mix between shock, pleasure, and bemusement. I stare him down, daring him to say anything. His gaze shifts to my right cheek before turning around. I touch my tongue to the corner of my mouth. I taste blood. Already I can feel the unmistakable swell of an oncoming bruise on my cheek. Any thrill at meeting a new species has soured, leaving a cold lump of dread in its place. My naïveté unnerves me. We've been thrust into a world we have no knowledge of. These creatures have their own culture and hierarchy. And we are woefully and dangerously ignorant.

I almost snort at the thought. How ignorant are we of our own species and culture? There was a time when we identified as Terrans, but does that even fit now? We're not of Earth. Few even exist who were born on Earth, and those are only due to technology. I was born in space and so am different than the humans born on a planet. My skin and eyes, as I've discovered, are too sensitive. Because of artificial gravity my bone density is different. There is no substitute for living on an actual planet. Even my abilities are different. I can't hike long distances. I can't swim or dive.

So what is it that makes us human in the first place? Is it only our DNA? A shared history, as my father claims? Or is it something more innate than even our similar molecules? Is it a universal culture that binds us? Have we changed as a species because our culture has evolved? Our habitat is different and so now our bodies are as well? Are we different from earlier humans because we share something that they don't?

I've seen things most humans before my time never had the chance to experience. I've watched Earth rotate from above. I've seen comets moving through the vacuum of space as if they were gliding underwater. I know how to move through zero gravity without puking. And I am now one of the few who has been on a planet that is not Earth.

But does this tether us to our past? Or separate us further? If we are able to resume, how will the humans on the *Posterus* change over time? Not just our biology, but our culture. As we move further from our roots in the Union, will that reflect in how we relate to each other? It makes me wonder if the avians were always like this or if this is just a stage in their cultural evolution. There was a time when humans viewed women as inferior; will the avians outgrow their prejudices too?

They tug the line forward and we continue our march through the forest. The trees stretch up above, obscuring the sky from view in a hazy green. And it's everywhere. That green. It clings to the trees in soft bundles of moss, so soft you want to reach out and pet it. Low bushes and plants cover the ground. All different shades of green, some are so bright they give off their own light. It would be intoxicating if I weren't so damn scared.

Little pink bugs with giant feathery wings flit about our heads. One lands on the back of Sarka's shoulder. I get a good look at giant green eyes and legs with pincers that resemble crab claws before he smashes it with his hand and flicks it off. The movement jerks the rope chain back and Foer stumbles and falls. There's a loud thud and a cascade of dust. Foer coughs into the dirt and staggers a few more times before Sarka yanks him up.

"Is this what Earth looked like?" I ask Sarka. I have this strange feeling of the canopy, which hangs at least a kilometer above, protecting us.

Sarka grunts. "Not even close."

"How so?"

"The trees for one. There aren't many. And they're not this tall on Earth." He gazes up at the foliage above. "I'd say they're twice as tall. And there's a lot more green. Earth is more arid."

From afar, it's yellow.

"It's the low gravity," Mani says from the front of the line. "Water can reach higher because it doesn't have to fight as much gravity. It's called the cohesion-tension theory. At a certain point the water pressure isn't strong enough to go any higher. So the trees can only grow as high as the water can reach."

"Is that why the creatures are taller as well?" I ask.

Mani shrugs. "Don't know, Captain."

"Yes and no," says Foer. He takes a moment, drawing his thoughts together. "The low gravity has an effect, but if a human were to be born on this planet we wouldn't be as tall as them. We'd be a few inches taller for sure, but not a few feet. Their height is a combination of factors."

"Is this what Earth smelled like?" I suck in a lungful, invigorated by all the scents that come with that one breath. Algae farms create most of the oxygen on the belt, interspersed with sugar cane fields and food crops, which have a low photosynthetic efficiency. These of course aren't enough to supply all the oxygen for the fleet. Each ship contains banks of what's known as silk leaves. They're a synthetic leaf with the chloroplast from a plant dispersed throughout. The result is stale and odorless.

"No." Sarka's profile and jaw muscles tighten.

"Do you miss it?"

He ignores me, which is answer enough for me. I guess it would be an admission of weakness to say he missed something. But I know he must. When I was younger, he used to share stories of his childhood with me. The way he described Earth, the independence made my head spin to hear of his adventures on the bike trails near his home. The freedom of barreling down a mountain side on two wheels. The exhilaration of conquering your fears. It all sounded exciting.

"Where do you think they're taking us? Do you think they're going to," Foer pauses for a moment, looking back at us, his eyes round with fear and uncertainty, "eat us?"

"I don't think so." I take a moment to put my impressions into words. If they were going to eat us, I don't think they would have smashed our gear. They see us as a threat and definitely have something planned for us. It may be ritualistic. That doesn't mean they won't kill us anyway. But I don't think they'll eat us. "If they were going to eat us, they wouldn't have brought the bird for food."

I don't voice the rest of my thoughts. Foer already looks like he's about to shit his pants. I don't want to add to his anxiety.

"One thing's for certain, they're sexist as hell. This should get interesting," Yakovich says.

"They're going to find out real quick what happens when they piss me off," I whisper low enough so my crew doesn't hear.

But Sarka hears. "Shush." He turns around, a warning in his eyes.

"Do not shush me."

There's a loud whooping noise ahead and I do hush as we're brought into a large clearing.

"What the fuck is that thing?" Foer stops short, causing the rest of us to collide. We're yanked forward. I falter and smack into Sarka's broad back. Unable to keep up with the forward momentum, I fall to my knees.

Sarka turns to help me. "Get up." It's a low warning growl.

But before I can regain my footing, I'm kicked to the ground by the lead avian. There's a rush of air as another swift kick finds my ribs. Instinctively, I curl into a ball. I lift my arms to protect my head. There are several more blows to my back and a club to the head. My vision goes blurry. One thought pounds through my mind: he is going to fucking regret this.

CHAPTER FOURTEEN

It's late afternoon. By the time we finally stop our trek, we're in the shadow of a monolithic pyramid. The surface, black and shiny and smooth, extends into the canopy. The top disappears in a blanket of green. It must be over a kilometer high and was constructed with precision. I lift my head, but see no other buildings surrounding it. Only wilderness reclaiming its domain. Around our feet are rough stone that might once have been a roadway, but no longer are. They're made of a lighter material than the pyramid and snake all the way around in what looks like a full circle.

And with this discovery, a new mystery. I doubt these creatures have the technology to build such structures. Their clothing and social structure appear to be pre-civilization. What little they do wear is crude and only covers what I assume are their genitalia.

If not nomadic, they haven't begun to cultivate the land in a more permanent way. Which means an earlier civilization evolved and may have gone extinct on this planet. It makes sense. On Earth, the vast majority of all species that ever lived have gone extinct. We should count ourselves lucky we didn't join that statistic.

I groan again as someone lifts the hair at the back of my neck. "He got you pretty good. If it doesn't hurt yet, it's going to."

I pull away from Sarka's rough hands, rolling onto my side again. "Leave it." I need everything to stop for a second so I can figure out our next course of action. I need to assess the situation. In one of those *Choose Your Own Adventure* books I read, you took on the identity of a spy. At one point you had a choice to sneak into a foreign castle immediately or wait until night. When I chose immediately, I was spotted and captured.

It's best to wait for nightfall before we attempt an escape. Hopefully, their guard will be down and most will be sleeping.

Sarka grips my head, turning it to the side to examine the cut. "You don't want it to get infected. Who knows what else that thing's clubbed."

"I said leave it." It comes out a little louder than I intend and we catch the attention of the leader.

Shit.

He saunters over and kneels in front of Sarka and me. His eyes roam over the two of us. Then with the speed of an automaton, his hand snatches my hair and jerks my head back, studying me. He smiles. If you can call it that. His beak-like mouth opens and a long, thin tongue darts out while his cheeks bunch. The effect is a little terrifying. He calls out to the group surrounding us. Whatever he says makes them laugh. It's more of a loud series of squawks from each, but the effect is unmistakable. He's said something about me that amuses the rest.

Sarka shoves him. The avian loses his balance and Sarka stands, towering over him. Before he can strike, I yell for him to stand down.

"Enough." I grab the material of his enviro-suit and pull him back. "I don't want anyone to provoke him." I look at Sarka, then Mani, Yakovich, and Foer to get my point across. "We keep our heads and lay low until we can get out of here."

Sarka steps back and squats next to me. Too late, I realize my mistake. This interaction has left no doubt who's in charge. Even though we don't speak the same language, both our species are clever enough to read body language.

"Quick," I tell Sarka. "Slap me. Make it believable." Before I have time to even brace for it, Sarka backhands me across the cheek. My head whips to the side. My eyes water as the sting reverberates through my whole head. If I didn't have a headache before, I sure as hell do now. "Christ. I said make it believable. I didn't say take my head off with it." He makes to slap me again and I instinctively cower. This appears to appease the Avian, who rises above us with a smug look on his face. He walks away, satisfied by my punishment.

Great. A giant leap forward for humankind and a screeching halt for women.

As the afternoon progresses, we sit in the shade and watch as they work. They're constructing something with long, stripped branches. Yellow vine is wrapped around each, holding them in place. Another group builds a fire, plucks and spits the bird. The smell of roasting meat wafts over and my stomach growls. I realize I haven't eaten anything except a ration bar since last night.

"What do you think the odds are that they're going to feed us?" Foer asks.

"I'm not eating that shit," Yakovich says, flicking stones into the bush. She's been grumpy since they confiscated her weapon and I think she's going through some sort of withdrawal.

We're still tethered at the wrists and connected at the waist. They've wrapped the rope around a giant tree on the edge of the small clearing. From here, we have a good view of what's happening.

Later, as the light changes to a deepening purple, one of the avians walks over and drops a slab of bark. Strips of bird meat flop onto dirt. Sarka immediately grabs a large chunk and rips into it.

"That's disgusting." Yakovich turns away.

"Sort of tastes like duck," Sarka mumbles around a mouthful of bird. "Nice and fatty."

I don't hesitate much before grabbing a piece myself. I'm starving and, if that weren't incentive enough, the smell of meat is intoxicating. I can't even remember the last time I had it. I wipe the layer of dirt off with the sleeve of my enviro-suit. A layer of grease comes away with the dirt.

Foer joins me a moment later. "At least it's us eating it. A few hours ago, I was kinda worried it was going to be the other way around."

I smile and shove another piece in my mouth. Juice squirts out of the fatty bits.

With the waning light, we finally discover why they've brought us to this pyramid. We're rounded up after we've eaten and brought to the base. Up close, it looks like obsidian. The stone is so smooth and shiny, it's a mirror reflecting the surrounding vegetation. In this light, as the sun finally sets, it's almost purple in color.

I've instructed everyone to cooperate with them, within reason. I don't want to antagonize them before we have the chance to escape. My biggest worry right now is the rest of the crew. We're four hours past our rendezvous time. I can only hope they didn't decide to come after us. Especially with Ash leading. Or worse. What if the avians attacked the ship? Would they be smart enough to gain access? I watch as one of the avians picks bird meat out of its claws with the sharp tip of its spear. I decide to give my crew the benefit of the doubt.

We circle the pyramid until we reach an indentation in the ground. There are large steps cut out of the earth which lead below ground. The large guy isn't in charge now. Instead, we're lead down the steps by a much smaller avian. He looks older than the rest. His skin is looser and he walks with a slight limp.

When we reach the bottom of the steps, the air is cooler and I shrug into the top of my enviro-suit. They've lit torches and placed them in holders cut into the side of the earth on either side of the steps. The flicker casts eerie shadows against the ground and walls in this little alcove. The old avian beckons for Sarka. Foer looks over at me. There's the same fear in his eyes from earlier.

I don't think they're going to kill us down here in the entrance. But when the old one pulls an ornate knife from the waistband of his coverings, I start to doubt myself.

He pulls Sarka's hand, palm up, toward him and rakes the knife across. Sarka doesn't even flinch. Sarka's bulky body obscures most of my view, but from back here it doesn't look like much is happening. The old shaman releases Sarka back to the group and eyes us for several seconds before pointing at me. I'm pushed forward. In his stooped state, his head is level with mine. He's still intimidating with a sharp beak and hard eyes that glare, unblinking, into mine.

They untie my hands. I swallow my fear as he grips my left palm, facing it up. The knife still has blood on it from Sarka. He sprinkles something on my skin, rubbing it in with long taloned fingers. I pray it's a disinfectant. With my jaws clenched tight, I brace myself for the moment when blade meets skin. When it does come, I keep steady, pursing my lips to keep from making any sound. I refuse to flinch. If Sarka can endure it, so can I.

The blood pools, dark crimson against my pale skin. The avian, still gripping tight, guides my hand to the archway of the pyramid. Nestled into a groove next to it is a small rectangular hole, large enough for my hand and little else. He motions for me to stick my hand into the opening. I hesitate for only a second. If Sarka survived, why shouldn't I? He turns my hand so the palm is facing down as I slip it into the hole. And we wait. I have no idea what we're waiting for, but the quiet surrounding us tells me it's something important. The old avian stares up at the archway, expectant, holding my elbow. Finally, he shakes his head and pulls my hand out.

They must be trying to open the doors with our blood as the key. And we don't have what they need. I try not to panic at that thought because if we're not needed any more, then there's nothing to stop them from killing us.

After trying everyone's blood, we're led back up the earth steps. I wonder why their blood won't open the doors. Or is this a test? If our blood did open the doors would that mean we would get a reprieve? Or would we be ripe for sacrifice?

The ancient Aztecs used human sacrifice to repay the debt of life to their gods. They saw it as an honor. Judging by my crew, they won't be too honored.

The sun has completely set, leaving the camp dark. There are a few torches placed at various locations to help us see. A large fire in the center throws off the most light. A group of avians sits around sharing bird meat and chatting. We're brought to the edge of the camp again, and now I see what it was they were constructing earlier. Cages. We're thrust inside, our hands tied tight to one of the branches, and left to wonder what tomorrow will bring.

I settle in, determined to wait them out, to bide my time until we can make our escape. But as my head settles against one of the skinny branches making up one side of the cage, my eyes begin to droop. I readjust, but it's no use. Soon, my eyes close and I drift into dreams about pyramids and squawking birds.

CHAPTER FIFTEEN

I become aware of the scent first. A mixture of soap and sweet florals and something else that speaks of both comfort and fervency. A finger taps my nose. My eyes snap open as a hand clamps against my mouth, muffling a shocked cry.

Ash. She kneels on the outside of the cage. There's an indescribable look on her face that, if I weren't already seated, would bring me to my knees. She doesn't say anything as she slices the rope binding my wrists and the vines knotting the cage door shut. She passes it to me, hilt first, so I can cut the ropes of those beside me.

I risk one sentence in the silence of the night. "You shouldn't have come."

She smirks and whispers, "Well, someone had to tell you, 'I told you so.'"

My only answer is a half hearted grunt. I turn to Foer and motion for him to put his hands out. Once he's free, I hand him the knife and he turns to the next person.

We slip out of camp, eager to be on our way, free of the avians and headed toward our ship. There are nine of us now. Ash brought Hartley, Chloe, and Fossick, although God knows why. Chloe was a smart choice. She's a good triage nurse. The only person with any injuries is me. I wave Chloe off the second I see her coming. They're only a couple of scratches, but she makes me take an antibiotic to be sure. And true to form, Sarka brings reality to the forefront.

"Fat lot that'll do. If she does get infected here, those antibiotics aren't going to do shit for her."

"Then what do you suggest we do?" Chloe hands me a bottle of water and I drink a third of it before I realize we should conserve. The avians destroyed our supplies, so all we have is what Ash and her team brought.

"Not get injured in the first place," Sarka says.

Fossick cocks an eyebrow. "Brilliant plan there. Spend a while on it, did you?" And now I'm not all that upset Ash brought him along.

We plod through the dark forest. I've instructed those with flashlights to refrain from using them until we're much further away. The campfire grows dimmer as we move further into the jungle. The moons—this planet has three—are now hidden by the canopy above. Soon, we're plunged into darkness and we bring out the flashlights.

Unfortunately, visibility doesn't equal stealth. Somewhere to my right, there's a loud thud followed by a softer, "fuck." I give it a few more moments to get us further from the camp before I halt the group.

"Is everyone okay?" I whisper. The crew crowds in. I see a lot of dirt, a few scrapes, but nothing too serious. The sooner we get out of here, the better. There's a smattering of nods and grunts which I take for yeses. "We'll rest up for a bit and figure out the fastest way to get back to the ship, then we'll be on our way."

I turn to Hartley. He's picked one of the leaves and is examining the underside and stem. He rubs it and a faint green glow begins to emanate.

"Do you know which way it is back to the ship?"

He nods without looking at me. "Yeah." He points behind him. "It's that way about seven or eight kilometers. Did you guys see these? They must have luciferin." He sniffs the leaf. "Or some other chemical in the veins that helps produce bioluminescence. I've seen it in certain fungi, but nothing like this." And like that he's lost in his own world, pulling the leaf apart and rubbing the substance between his fingers. He hands one to Mani and they begin breaking leaves and squeezing out the veins.

We've stopped in a small indentation surrounded by fallen logs and glowing bushes. The ground beneath us is soft, covered in a light green moss. I run my hands over the surface. It's like fur, thick and velvety.

"How's your head?" Sarka starts to lift my hair to look, but I brush him away. "You should have that nurse take a look at it."

"What happened to your head?" Ash asks.

"You should see what they did to her face," says Foer.

I stand and glare at Fossick, who's made himself comfortable on the spongy ground, pulling at the moss.

"What did they do to your face?" Ash pulls out a light, but I grab her wrist before she can raise it.

"It's fine. Let's get out of here. The longer we stand around yakking about inconsequential things, the longer we're at risk."

Fossick pushes himself off the moss. Before we move any further, a deafening squeal rips from the ground beneath us. With a loud growl, the forest floor begins to shake.

"What the fuck is that?" asks Fossick.

As the ground rises up, I lose my balance and fall flat on my ass. We all come to the same realization. It's not moss we've been standing on, but some sort of creature that's now awake and angry. Or hungry.

"Run!" I yell.

Ash grabs my wrist and yanks me to my feet. We half run, half slide down the slope of the creature. When my feet hit hard earth, earth that isn't moving, I know we've cleared its back. Ash keeps hold of my wrist as we scramble through the brush, clawing over debris and fallen trees. Her nails dig into my skin. Leaves and branches scrape at my arms and face.

"Be glad we only have to be faster than Fossick," Ash says. From the tone in her voice it sounds like she might actually be having fun with this.

"Why's that?" My pulse and breath are at odds. I for one, am not enjoying this. I can already feel mucus forming in my mouth and my legs are ready to collapse.

"He's the slowest."

"Who says it's going to stop once it picks Fossick off? Ever see a video of whale eating krill?" It's with effort I even manage to get that last sentence out. It comes out all breathy and stilted.

"Good point." Ash speeds up, her grip never easing as she pulls me through the forest.

At least it doesn't matter how much noise we're making now. The loud screeches from the creature drown us out. For the first couple of minutes, the crashes and snaps of the others are close behind. But after a while they become faint.

I try to pull free of Ash's grip. "We need to stop." I pant. "The others." I cough and sputter. "We need to stick together."

But that's the last thing either of us gets out before the ground slopes and we tumble forward. Instinctively, I tuck into a tight ball, careening down the hill. We land at the bottom in a heap of scrapes, bruises, and heavy breathing.

"Christ, that hurt." My ribs are screaming at me. I don't even want to see how that last spill added to the bruises already mottling my torso. I lie there for a good while, in what seems to be a tiny valley, staring at the expanse of stars overhead.

"Huh." Ash, too, is lying flat on her back watching the sky.

"You okay?"

Her face glows in the light of the moons. She has a smile so wide I'm worried she might have whacked her head a little too hard. "That was something different. I've never run from a live animal before." It's the first time in ages she's sounded like the woman I met at the start of this mission, full of excitement and wonder.

I can't take my eyes off her. While she stares up at the canopy, lips parted, eyes scanning the leaves, I memorize her face. A breeze parts the branches high above us and a soft blue glow filters down. It highlights her hair, making the auburn appear silver in the light and copper in the shadows. Her skin is so pale it almost shines and her lashes stand stark, framing dark eyes.

"What about you?"

I know what she's actually asking. Am I having fun? I'm not. This is not fun. I can't bring myself to validate her feelings so I take the question at face value. "Sure. I grew up on a farm, remember?

I'd much rather Janice, our dairy cow, chasing after us than that thing."

Some time later, she asks, "How's it been with Sarka?"

I'm surprised at first. I thought she'd fallen asleep. I still don't know what he did to her and my imagination has been eating away at me. It's such a contrast to think of the two sides of him. The one, I see as my father and the other, the leader of the Burrs.

"He's been protective, which is strange."

"And that bothers you?" When I nod, she asks why.

"Because he doesn't have the right to care. We're related, but he's not my father." Even as I say the words, I know they're not true. There was a time when he was. It may have been a very long time ago, but there was a time when I never doubted his love for me. Was that the naïveté of a child?

Ash shrugs. "When it comes to family, it's complicated. I've always kind of resented my dad because of who he is." She snorts. "I even use my mother's maiden name so no one knows we're related. But I can't deny that I still want his approval. It's stupid, but I still care what he thinks."

"Well, I don't care what Sarka thinks about my decisions or choices." Is that true? "If circumstances were different, he'd be in prison, not frolicking through the jungle with my crew."

Ash laughs loudly and it guts me. How can she so easily push everything that's happened aside and find humor in our situation? "Sorry. I had a mental picture of Sarka skipping through the forest. It's…" Her face falls and she stops laughing. "It's a better way of thinking about him."

"Do you want to talk about it?"

"No."

"It may help."

"It won't help. It'll make me relive it over again. And I never want to do that. If you're worried that he—. You don't need to. He never touched me like that." She sits up and hugs her knees, turning her head away from me. "The way I see it, it was a test I had to pass. And I did. Now I never have to wonder if I have the guts to hold onto my convictions." Her voice is soft and faint.

The humidity hasn't lessened. If anything, it's gotten worse since the sun set. It feels like I'm sitting in a giant vat of my own sweat. I pull the top of my enviro-suit down. I have no idea what time it is, but as soon as it gets light, I want to head back to the ship. From there we can arrange search parties.

Ash stands. She drags a large fallen branch over to us and begins to hack off the leaves. "As soon as it gets light we should start looking for the others," she says.

"No. We need to get back to the ship as soon as possible. Sarka will have one plan, and that's it. He won't give a shit about anyone else. And if he makes it back first, he'll leave us all behind."

"Do you know which way it is?"

As she says it, my heart sinks. I have no idea where we are in relation to the *Persephone*. And then another bigger question pops into my mind. "How did you find us?"

She turns, giving me a hard long stare. "Let's just say the doctor helped out with that."

The trackers. I'd like to say I'm sorry, but I'm not. They proved more than worth the moral dilemma. "Do the others know?"

"No, and I'm not going to tell them." Ash drops a pile of leaves next to me. "What were you thinking?"

"I've already gotten a lecture from the doctor, I don't need one from you as well. And seeing as how I'm the captain—even if people keep forgetting—I get the last say."

"What does that mean? 'People keep forgetting?'"

I scrape the leaves into a pile and lay down, resting my head on the crunchy pile. "Never mind." The ground isn't too bad; the tall grass adds an extra cushioned layer. I take a deep breath and ease my bruised ribs down. "Let's get some sleep."

I close my eyes, listening to the cacophony of evening animals. How did this expedition go so wrong, so fast?

Chapter Sixteen

With the morning, comes a concert of birdsong. There must be thousands of them, the din is so loud. Nature's alarm clock. There are low baritones and high sopranos. Even a few warblers with calls so intricate they could pass for human vocals.

I sit up too fast and my ribs ache in protest. I'm debating whether I want to see what my abdomen looks like or if it's better to stay ignorant. Ash, who's sitting a few feet in front of me watching the sun rise through a hole in the canopy, turns around. Her mouth drops.

I rub my face. Patches of dirt flake off in my hands. The remnants of yesterday's provisional sunscreen still coat my face and arms. The first thing I'm going to do when we get back to the ship is take a long, hot shower and wash all this grime away. I must look like a swamp monster.

"Your face." She slides over and kneels in front of me, taking my chin. She turns my head to the side. The bruise must be larger and darker than I realized. Her fingers graze my cheekbone, tracing the length. I pull away, distancing myself. I'm all too aware of my body's reaction.

"It's nothing. We should go." But as soon as I try to stand up, I suck in a sharp breath and sink back to the ground. Christ, that hurt.

"What's wrong?"

Before I can deflect, Ash unzips my enviro-suit, reaches in, and pulls up my shirt. We both gasp at the deep scratch running along my torso from when I fell. In one spot, I can see the faint outline of the avian's footwear.

"Lay back. I'm going to check if you broke anything."

"I've broken a rib before. They're only bruised." I take a few breaths to steel myself and then in one quick move, push myself off the ground.

Standing is better. It hurts less. I zip my suit. The morning air is already thick with humidity, but my suit feels like a shield of sorts. I feel like I'd be revealing more than skin if I removed my enviro-suit. Exposed somehow. I'm embarrassed I let it happen, and every bruise and scratch is proof.

But I only make it twenty minutes before the insulating nature of the suit begins to boil my skin. We're headed back into the deep forest, both not sure of the correct direction, but it's important we keep moving. If we can find some of the others, even better.

Another thirty minutes and I unzip the collar. My drenched shirt clings to my breasts and torso. Rivulets of sweat stream down my chest and back, pooling at the waistband of my shorts.

Ash has shed her enviro-suit, choosing to trudge through the forest in boots, a shirt and skin tight shorts. She carries the suit over one shoulder.

I wish we could contact the ship and check in, but unfortunately, that's not an option. The comms unit is in the helmet, and we left all of them back at the ship. They're for space walks, not nature hikes, which is why they're so stifling. I pull at the open front, trying to flap some air into the suit.

Ash turns back in disgust. "You're making it hotter just looking at you in that." She stops, running her eyes down the length of me. "What's the point of making it back to the ship if you're going to drop from heat exhaustion before we get there?" She smirks. "Honestly, Jordan. You don't strike me as the modest type. But if it'll make you feel better, I promise not to look."

I roll my eyes. But I do unzip my suit and peel it off. Ash helps me with my boots so I can tug the pant legs off. The air, when it hits my skin, feels fresh. I sigh in relief as the fire begins to cool. Ash stares at me, eyes growing narrower as they rake over all my cuts and bruises. Her eyes stop on my forearm, lingering at the finger marks.

"What the hell happened to you? Why does no one else look like they staggered into trees lined with broken glass?" She stands, pulling my attention to her. "And don't tell me, it's nothing."

My skin prickles. The sun has risen above the tree line. Even under the canopy, the humidity is like warm bath water. Every inch of me is sweating. Both the situation and conversation make me uncomfortable. And I have no doubt she'll dog me until she gets an answer.

"I offended their leader." It's simple, yet truthful.

"How?"

I shrug and start walking in the direction I hope Hartley pointed to yesterday. Why couldn't I have gotten separated with him? At least he would've ignored me in favor of the local flora. And I could be certain we were heading in the right direction.

"That's it? That's all you're going to tell me."

"There's nothing more to tell. I don't speak their language so I can't be a hundred percent certain. I'm pretty sure it had something to do with being female."

"You're joking."

"I wish."

We walk in silence for the next kilometer or so. My thoughts turn through my next plan. Moving forward is the only way to deal with it, to stay ahead of the turmoil. If we don't meet up with anyone or come to the edge of the forest soon, we're going to have to reevaluate. Our best bet is to find high ground or see if there's a tree we can climb. If we can get above the canopy, maybe we'll spot the ship or the mountains in the distance.

I stop and look at the height of the trees in front of me. They start big and taper to a point at the top. It could be they get very thin, or it could be that they're so high they only look tiny on top. From the cavernous feel of the jungle, I'm going to guess the latter. There's no way we can climb high enough.

Ash steps next to me and hands me a ration bar from her pouch. "So, are we going to talk about why you felt it necessary to implant trackers in the entire crew and not tell anyone? Dr. Prashad wouldn't even tell me why you did it."

I take a bite of my bar. It's hard as wood and doesn't taste much better, but it's food and my stomach isn't picky right now.

"Don't think we're not going to talk about it because I let it drop last night."

"I don't have to justify my decisions to you."

"You're right. You don't. But when I signed on, you said that the only way this crew was going to work well together is if we did it as a team. And not only that, we had to think of ourselves as family. Going behind everyone's back and implanting trackers is not thinking like a family or a team. It's a serious ethics violation. I'm surprised you'd do it. Even more surprised Dr. Prashad went along with it. What's next? Mind knots?"

I crumple up my wrapper and shove it in my enviro-suit pocket. "What I did isn't even close to that. I had a good reason. It saved lives." I continue walking. It doesn't even matter which direction, we're so lost. For all I know we could be heading back toward the pyramid and the avians.

"You don't think the people who invented those mind knots in the first place said the same thing? It's for their own safety. Just think, if we can monitor them while they're in battle, we can send reinforcements. We can evacuate them faster."

I grit my teeth and keep walking. I'm mortified that she would think this is anywhere near the same thing. The trackers are harmless and temporary. They wash out of your system after a few weeks. And we can't control anyone with them. They were there to make sure she stayed safe.

When I saw her in the mess, trussed up, something inside me broke. And I can lie to Prashad, but I can't lie to myself. I couldn't bare to see Ash hurt anymore. It was the only way I could keep her safe. I would do it again if it got the same result. But that answer goes against who I am and everything I stand for. To act so unprofessional and yes, selfish, to benefit one person is so out of character for me.

"I don't have an answer for you. Not if you want me to be truthful."

She stops dead. "That's crap and you know it." Even the forest has stopped to hear my response, all birds and bugs have ceased in that moment. She purses her lips. The deep green of her eyes shimmers in the muted light. She's got that fierce look she gets when her mind is set on one goal. There will be no winning this argument. So I do the next best thing, I give up.

"It's done. And I stick by it." Even if it wasn't needed in the end. I needed it. It was a safety net, knowing she was safe gave me peace of mind.

"I know why you thought you needed to do it. But I could've handled it myself."

Christ, I want to smack her sometimes. It's this attitude that she's invincible that drives me mad.

"This is why." She takes my hand. "There are always consequences."

I nod. It's too damn hard to distance myself. And I knew that going in. In fact, I went in eyes wide open, knowing it would hurt like hell coming out the other side. But I was too weak. At the time, I didn't care about consequences. And now I'm left with the burn of it.

I pull my hand free and continue forward.

By midday, I know we're heading in the wrong direction. It's all new. We've entered an area of the forest where everything is pink. The trees and undergrowth are coated in some strange fungus. I halt Ash, scanning the trees for any sort of leverage to get higher up.

Ash follows my gaze. "What are you thinking?"

"We need to get an overview of the area, figure out which direction to take."

Ash bends to inspect some of the pink fungus. Before she can reach out and touch some, I grab her wrist and pull her back. "For all we know, it could cause necrosis."

"Good point. No touching the pretty pink fuzz. It sort of reminds me of a book my mom used to read to me. All the trees had these cool pink wispy tops before they chopped them all down."

We head back in the direction we've come, searching for trees that will allow us to see more of the forest. But most of them are tall without any lower limbs to climb. After another kilometer or so we hear a loud thud. It's followed by a string of obscenities that would make even Sarka blush. Ash takes off before I can stop her, not that I could in my condition. I follow at a slower pace, but when I come over the ridge, I forget my injuries and scramble through the underbrush.

Hartley and Yakovich are struggling up an incline. Even from the back I can tell Yakovich broke her leg. It's bent at a strange angle and hangs limp, toeing the ground.

Chapter Seventeen

"They set traps, Captain." Yakovich grits her teeth. "They're hunting us down." Sweat pools at her brow, dirt and blood streak her face, but beneath I can see the ashen pallor. We need to find a way to get her back to the ship as soon as possible before she goes into shock.

We've laid her down on a patch of bright green moss—after checking it was, in fact, moss—at the top of an incline. I don't know how she's managed to make it this far, or how she's even conscious at this point. Her leg is bad. I'm no medic, but I know enough to recognize a compound fracture. Part of the bone is sticking out near her ankle. And there's a shirt—Hartley's since he's not wearing one—tied around the wound. I could smack him, but it's obvious he has no medical training whatsoever.

I untie the shirt and pass it back to him. I examine the damage like I know what I'm doing when all I want to do is puke at the sight of bone piercing skin.

Everyone's hovering over me, watching, like any second I'm going to become magic and fix her leg. Even though I know it's only in my head, their breathing becomes claustrophobic. I need to get them out of the way.

"Hartley, I need you to go find me two long thin branches, and some vine, if you can, to lash the sticks to her leg. How much water do you guys have?" Hartley shakes his head. "Do you still have your water canister from your pack?" Hartley unclips a one liter bottle from his belt and passes it to me. "That's it?" They both nod. "Okay,

Ash, I want you to help me set her leg, then I want you to go see if you can find some water." Everyone's standing there, motionless. "Hartley, I'm going to need those branches sooner rather than later."

"On it, Captain. I'll go find you the straightest sticks you've ever seen." He dashes into the underbrush, streaks of sunlight dancing off his pale, scrawny back.

"Where do you need me?" Ash looks up at me from across Yakovich, even if her concern isn't in her voice, it's all over her face.

I point to Yakovich's thigh. "I need you to hold the top of her leg while I apply traction. We need to get it aligned before we splint it."

Ash repositions herself next to Yakovich. "Hey," she says as she crouches next to her. "Quinn, this is going to hurt like a bitch, but I promise you'll feel much better when we're done, okay?" Ash wipes some dirt from her cheek before turning back to me.

"Quinn, I want you to count to ten, okay? It'll all be over in ten." I wait until she nods. When she's not looking, I hold up three fingers for Ash to see. She nods and we both grab Yakovich's leg. Her ankle is tacky with blood and it takes me a moment to find a firm grip.

"Everybody ready?" I ask. They nod, both with eyes so fearful I wonder if my expression mirrors theirs. I can only hope I've managed to tamp my fear down and project a confidence I don't feel.

When Yakovich gets to three, I pull out and down as hard as I can. I hear bone popping back into place and hope it was just my imagination. Yakovich's scream is so loud, nearby birds take off in flight.

Ash turns back to Yakovich. "It's done. We're done. We're going to splint your leg and you'll feel much better."

Yakovich preempts my next question. "Hartley doesn't have his first aid kit with him. He dropped his pack back at the clearing."

Ash perks up. "Wait a second." She reaches for her enviro-suit and pulls out a clear plastic bag the size of her palm. "It didn't fit in my pack, so I stashed it there." She turns it over in her hand. "It's got aspirin and some antiseptic pads with some gauze." She shrugs, "It's not a lot, but…"

I take the kit and open it. I want to laugh at how ineffectual the two inch antiseptic pads will be. There's a gaping hole in Yakovich's leg. The aspirin will help. I smile anyway and thank Ash. At least it's something.

Ash leaves to find water and I'm left alone with Yakovich in the middle of a strange and noisy jungle. With natives hunting us. Let's not forget the natives.

"I'm sorry, Captain. I didn't see the trap until it was too late."

I reposition myself so I can hear Yakovich, whose voice has become hoarse and far too soft. "It's not your fault. This is all a new experience for us. We're trying to get through it as best we can."

"I'm going to slow you down now." A tear escapes from the corner of her eye and slides down her temple. "Captain." She takes a deep breath and wipes the tear away. When she collects herself, her voice is strong and decisive. "You should leave me behind. I'll be fine for a little while if you hide me in the bushes." She rubs the tears that are now flowing down her face. "I'll still be here when you can come back with more crew and weapons."

"Stop being so goddamned noble. No one's leaving you behind. Even if you were missing both your legs, I wouldn't leave you."

I ball my enviro-suit and lift her head onto it. I pick a large leaf and fan her face. It probably doesn't help cool her down much, but it keeps the bugs from landing.

"I don't want you to worry about me. I'm not going to die out here, Captain." She shakes her head from side to side. "There's something so final about dying in a place like this. On ships you get jettisoned into space, so you get to keep moving, you know? I've never spent much time in places that didn't move. Not even on the Belt. I grew up on ships. We were always moving. The idea of being stuck in one place after I'm dead is the scariest thing I can think of."

"No one's going to die. It's only a broken leg. We've already done the hard part and now we're going to splint it and we'll carry you out of here. With three of us, it won't be any trouble." I keep the leaf moving. It seems to have a calming effect. Her eyes start to droop. "That's right. Save your energy. You're going to need it."

When the others return, we devise a sort of stretcher out of vine and the thin bark. It's sturdy enough to lift Yakovich. She fades in and out of consciousness, while the three of us distribute our strength. We lift her using two of the less straight branches Hartley found.

As we raise her, I pay close attention to Yakovich. She doesn't flinch, and that worries me more. Her skin is almost gray. I'm sure she's going into shock. I gave her two aspirin and half a liter of water, leaving the other half liter for the three of us to ration. We're going to have to find a water source before we reach the ship. Hartley assures me it's only four kilometers from our current position.

Progress is slow. Ash and Hartley carry the poles in front of the stretcher while I've got the rear. This deep in the forest, there isn't a lot of give when it comes to the underbrush. It's covered in tangles and dead bushes, fallen vines and rotten trees. My hand is killing me. The cut along my palm has reopened and the mixture of blood and sweat is making it difficult to hold the pole.

My boot squelches into something soft and I cringe to think what it might be. I try to keep my mind occupied on other things. After all, it's like compost. Only with animals and vegetation. It's what allows more vegetation and animals to thrive. It still doesn't stop me from getting creeped out every time the forest floor sucks at my boot.

By late afternoon, we're all covered in sweat and dirt. Dehydration is my biggest concerns. We're leaking so much fluid I'm afraid we're going to shrivel up like raisins in a dehydrator. Every crack and squawk, every rustle has me tensing. If they're hunting us, we're doing an excellent job of announcing our location.

"What do you think they want with us?" Ash asks. Every few minutes she rubs her palms on her shirt and switches hands.

"I'm more worried about what's in that pyramid they want opened." Both Ash and Hartley turn with stunned expressions. "You didn't see the giant pyramid?"

They shake their heads in unison, dumbfounded. Hartley's face lights up like he's discovered how to create wormholes from juice mix. "There was an earlier civilization that lived here."

"Yeah, that's what I thought too."

"How do you know these guys didn't build it?" Ash asks.

"Pyramids require a lot of resources. They usually denote a civilization with agriculture and a higher form of labor division. These creatures are definitely in a pre-civilization state." Sometimes I wonder if Hartley spent his childhood devouring textbooks.

"Also, they wouldn't be trying to open it with our blood if they had. They might think we're the builders and want us to open it for them. They've probably created myths around these structures and how they got there." It's also probably why they're hunting us. But I don't mention that part. If they see us as a hostile invasion on their territory, they will kill us.

"They used your blood?" Both Hartley and Ash ask this at once, each with very different intonations. Hartley is so intrigued, he might wet himself a little.

"Why? What do you think it means?" I've been wondering why they would think our blood would open up a locked door.

"It could mean a lot of things. But they've deciphered some meaning at the entrance of the pyramid that calls for a life substance of some kind. Did anyone's blood open it?"

"No."

"And they've obviously tried their own." He walks on in deep thought, his mind working over the problem. He's so excited he's seemingly forgotten we're carrying an injured crew mate through the jungle. Finally, he turns back and asks, "Did you see any symbols on the door?"

It was dark, but I do remember seeing etchings along the top of the door. "Yeah, there were two circles joined together, not quite like an infinity but more like a Celtic knot. There were a few others but I couldn't make them out."

And then chaos.

I don't even see the avians until they're upon us. I feel the tip of his spear pricking my shoulder. The musk stench of his body is so close it's overpowering. I turn and stare up at the leader. His eyes are black pools of hate.

CHAPTER EIGHTEEN

We break through the forest and stop. Ahead of us is the strangest, most confusing thing I've ever seen. We've reached their village. Instead of finding caves or huts like I'm expecting, their homes are hundreds of feet above us.

Ash and Hartley are as mesmerized as I am. Hartley's mouth drops at the spectacle of hundreds of avians soaring overhead. The light filters through the canopy and catches their wings. When spread wide, they allow them to glide between the trees.

The avians have hollowed out the trunks. At that height, the circumference is still considerable. Each tree has a small platform to provide a spot for landing. Next to each dock, they've strung rope and small logs for bridges.

I'm curious. If they can fly, why do they need bridges between the trees? Then I see why. Some of them don't have wings.

Ash nudges me. As we move close enough to see details, I discover they aren't underdeveloped wings or even stunted. They're bound in natural rope, cutting the circulation until they fall off. As we're pushed through the throng of avians, we realize those who've had their wings removed are female.

It's easy to distinguish the females once you know what to look for. They're shorter and darker than the males. Also, the females are in constant motion. They rush around carrying baskets of food or prepared hides. Most appear to spend their time on the ground and I don't blame them. If I couldn't fly, I wouldn't want to be anywhere in the sky. Why do they stay?

Ash leans over and whispers, "Why do they let them do that?" Her face is contorted in bafflement. They look like slaves, cowed and broken. And I know Ash can't understand being dominated, because no one could ever break her. There isn't a force in the universe that would make her submit.

But I know. I saw it on the ships growing up. There were people so broken they had no option but to live each day as if the next would never be any better. They gave up. I've seen what it's like to live without hope. They don't care if they live or die. That's why they're forced to have kids. It's why my mom had me. It anchors them to their oppressors. But my mom wasn't cowed, she was biding her time until she could escape with me.

That's where the revolution should begin. If you have no fear of death, and you have nothing to live for, rise up and scream.

We're shoved onto a platform and hoisted into the canopy. It's slow and with each pull more of the lower village comes into focus. By the time we get to the top, I can see the network of trees strung together. They reach far off into the distance like a city in the clouds. As the sun sets, light streams through the branches like tentacles reaching out to snare us in a trap. A sense of dread forms, small and tight in my stomach, as we're led along the rope bridges to a dark hollowed out trunk.

We're not alone. As my eyes adjust to the darkness, two other bodies come into focus, Fossick and Foer. Dread unfurls and creeps through my body.

"Where's everyone else? We haven't seen Chloe or Mani," I say.

Foer shakes his head, but doesn't answer. He has a large gash on his chin and he's cradling his arm. Fossick looks filthy. Dirt coats his arms and undershirt. His knees are scuffed and coated with dried blood. For several minutes no one says anything.

Then Fossick asks, "Where's Yakovich?" and I look away as tears fill my eyes. I want to tell them we had no choice. But that's the coward's answer. The truth is, I couldn't think of any way to save her.

"We had to leave her behind." I scrunch my eyes shut. I can still see the fear in her eyes as we left. She's going to die out there, and we all know it, including her.

"We didn't do anything. That was all you, Captain," Ash says.

I don't know if there's anger behind that comment, but there's judgment. If Ash had her way, we would have all died fighting to bring her along. When she punched that avian in the face, she didn't think it all the way through. She never does. That's why I had to make the decision for her. She may never forgive me for holding her back. But I don't have the luxury of being noble. When faced with losing one crew member to save three, the odds were against Yakovich. I can't gamble with lives like that. But Ash doesn't care about these things. She only sees the black and white of it. As Captain, I have to view the world in gray.

"We're not going to leave her behind. I'm going to get us out of here. Even if I have to search the entire goddamned planet, we're bringing her body back with us. I'm not going to leave her on this planet." I stand, unable to still the anxiousness deep inside me. "I promised her I wouldn't." I turn toward the inner wall, unable to look Ash in the eye. I pick away at the bark, pulling at the fibrous strands that line our hollowed out prison cell.

"I'm sure that's a comfort, Captain." Ash's voice is hard and mean.

I turn to confront her. "Would you rather we all died? You think they would have hesitated to smash us in the back of the head and leave us there? We're not alive because they need us. We're alive because they haven't figured us out yet. I've seen their kind before. I grew up surrounded by that mentality. The second we become a nuisance, they'll kill us. We'd all be dead right now if I hadn't stepped in."

Hartley reaches up and places a hand on Ash's forearm. "Why don't we turn our energy to getting the hell out of here? I, for one, don't want the giant homicidal birds to kill us."

Foer raises his hand. "I'm on board with that."

Ash rips her arm free of Hartley's grasp and sits in a far corner.

I go back to picking at the inner bark, going over our options. "Was Sarka with you guys?"

"No. We haven't seen him since the giant moss monster."

"You think he'll come for us?" Foer, always the optimist. I hate to crush his hope.

"Davis Sarka has always been a man for himself. Always will be." By now, he's made it back to my ship, taken charge and left us here to rot. "We're on our own for getting out of here." I take a seat facing the others. "So let's figure this out. Any suggestions?"

Over the next hour, we go over every scenario we can think of. I've gotten everyone to dump out what they've still managed to hold on to. This leaves us with a couple Band-Aids, an empty water canister, a compass, and a protein ration pack. All the tools we need for liberation.

The door crashes open and another body stumbles into the room. For a brief second, I hope it's Sarka, but the form is too short and stocky.

It's Mani. He looks like he went swimming in mud. He's still wearing his environmental suit, it's ripped and covered in dirt and green streaks.

"Owen! I thought the moss monster ate you," Foer says.

He shakes his head and slides down the wall. His mop of hair tries valiantly to follow the motions of his swiveling head, but it's lank from the humidity.

"I'm glad you're safe."

"If safe is locked inside a tree, fifty meters up, waiting for angry birds to eat us, then I agree with that assessment," Fossick says.

"Keep your sarcasm to yourself, please. It's not helping," I say.

He raises his hands in surrender and slumps back against the bark wall.

"Are you injured anywhere?" I ask Mani.

He shakes his head and hugs his knees to his chest. "What are those things?"

"Doesn't matter what they are." Fossick begins to pace. "When we come back with the *Posterus*, those things won't stand a chance." He kicks the door. "We'll wipe them off the planet."

I'm struck dumb by the comment. Even if it was from Fossick. I can't believe one of my crew could even think like that. Worse, say it out loud. "The *Posterus* is not coming back here. In fact, we keep this planet to ourselves. If anyone ever mentions a word about it, I'll make sure you spend the rest of your life locked up in the brig," I say.

"Why? We've found exactly what we've been looking for—a habitable world. Why would we turn our backs on that? Because there's another species here?" Foer asks.

Fossick snorts. "An inferior species."

Foer leans forward. I can tell how much he wants this to be the end of it, the end of our searching. "We can find a quiet continent and make our home there."

"Yeah, Captain. We don't have to harm them. It's a big planet. We could find another section to inhabit, they wouldn't even have to know we were here," Mani says.

"And what happens when we outgrow that little section of land and we want more? You don't think we'll find enough justification to take it away from them? Fossick's already given us the best excuse. They're inferior. Right, Fossick? So what does it matter if we push them out of their homes? Besides, it wouldn't be like we were kicking them out. We would give them something in return. We could show them how to shoot their enemies instead of clubbing them over the head."

"You're going to side with them? Even after what they did to you? What they did to Yakovich?" Fossick asks. If it had only been Foer, I know I could have crushed these ideas right here and now. But Fossick never lets anything go. He'll hold on to this long after everyone's forgotten. But I still need to try. The other crew members will at least consider what I'm saying.

"We're the intruders. We don't belong here. No matter how many platitudes we tell ourselves, it would still end the same. We'd force them out, and we have no right to do that."

I hear a loud commotion outside and motion for everyone to be silent. The door opens again. The soft sunlight filters in, silhouetting the shape of a large avian. I hope again to see Sarka's smug face, but instead I hear a shrill squeal. Two muscular avians shove Chloe through the door. She tears at their arms, screaming, kicking, lashing out at anything she can dig her nails into. They drop her on the ground with a loud thud and slam the door shut.

She takes a moment to breathe. Then she's up again, pounding on the door. She screams every expletive she knows, and a few creative ones I've never heard before in Spanish.

No one moves, too afraid they'll be collateral damage. After a few minutes, when I realize she isn't going to relent any time soon, I lay a hand on her shoulder. She whips it off and goes back to hammering at the door.

I grab both her arms and pin them down at her sides. "Chloe, calm down. If you use all your energy banging on solid doors, you'll have nothing left to help us escape."

This last word has an effect. "Escape?" Her voice is hoarse and small. She looks up at me with fear, pain, and anger, then collapses at my feet. "Good. I hate jungles." She rubs her hands together, trying and failing, to clear them of the dirt they've accumulated. "I hate heights and I especially hate dirt." She looks at each of her crew mates until she finds Ash, who's lounging against the back wall, watching the show with a hint of amusement in her eyes. "Why did you have to bring me? I didn't want to come. I told you I didn't and you still insisted. You said it would be like a walk in one of the parks on Alpha. This is nothing like Alpha." She lifts her arms. They're covered in grass stains and scrapes and there's a large gash along her left elbow. "Alpha doesn't have animals walking around trying to kill you." Her crisp blond hair hangs stringy and greasy. "Why couldn't you have brought Len?"

"I couldn't leave the ship without a doctor. You were the next best thing. It was unlikely that we'd need major surgery out here." She bites her lip to stop from laughing. "Besides, you're handling it like a champ."

"Fuck you, Ash."

"Okay." I hold up my hands. This is going tits up real quick if I can't get them working together. We need to focus on getting out of here instead of tearing each other apart. "Chloe, did you manage to hang on to any part of your kit?"

She shrugs and rummages around in her utility belt. She pulls out a few ration bars, a med kit and a flashlight. Hartley pounces on the flashlight.

"Now this I can work with."

CHAPTER NINETEEN

The mood is somber after my little speech and Chloe's arrival. Fossick is off in the corner talking with Mani. I know I didn't get through to Fossick. He'll be dreaming of cities and wealth long after we leave this planet. I hope he doesn't manage to infect anyone else with his ideas. Mani is pretty affable and tends to go along with the crowd. I'll have to keep a close eye on Fossick, see who else he talks to. It makes me wonder if he's what the conquerors of Earth were like. It's one of the only constants from our history.

Humans are takers. We see something we like and we take it, by force if necessary. I don't want our legacy in this solar system to mirror that. Part of the reason I signed onto the *Posterus* mission was to start fresh. And not only my own life, it was human nature I wanted to erase and begin again.

"God, Mani, you're making me hot looking at you. Aren't you boiling in that thing?" Ash tugs at the arm of Mani's enviro-suit, who looks down at it as if he'd forgotten he was wearing it and shrugs.

Cooped up in this tree hollow, it's like forty degrees, it must be over fifty in that suit. He unzips the front, like it's a favor to Ash and he couldn't care less if he boils to death.

"Hey, Mani, what supplies do you have left?" Hartley asks as he disassembles Chloe's flashlight.

Mani begins to empty out his cargo pockets. There isn't much. Another protein ration and a spare canister of compressed air.

Hartley snatches up the air canister. Most of us ditched our spare when we removed our main tanks before heading out. His face is pure glee. "Now if only we had kindling for a fire, I could rig a blow torch of sorts and cut through the hinges on the door."

"Use some of the tree bark the Captain's been shredding. If you can find some hard sap that'll help. Pitch is a great fire starter," says Mani.

"Will that work?" I ask as I lean over to inspect the hinges on the door. They are made of a tough looking braided twine.

"If we're lucky and I can actually get a fire started and the canister has enough air in it to weaken the hinges, then maybe."

"There's a guard outside, maybe even two. We need to think worse-case scenario. Without a weapon I don't know if the six of us could overpower two of them at the same time. That's three on each guard." The way Ash's mind works impresses me. I can almost see the calculations in her head as she weighs the odds of each scenario. "But if we can get the door open and then lure them in one at a time, then it's six on one and those are much better odds. What do we have that we can use as a weapon?"

Fossick picks up the flashlight. "We can hit 'em over the head with this." He whacks it a couple times against the floor to demonstrate.

Hartley yanks it out of his hands. "Give me that, you idiot. How do you think we're going to start the fire? If you've damaged the filament in the bulb I'm going to shove this thing up your—"

"Okay," I cut him off. "Let's start collecting hard sap and any scraps of bark we have. Mani, take your enviro-suit off, we're going to rip it into strips to use as garrotes."

We spend the rest of the afternoon preparing and waiting for dark to fall. If we're going to escape then our best bet is to wait until everyone's asleep. We manage to collect a good selection of pitch along with a pile of shredded bark.

Before we lose all light for the night, Hartley removes the bulb from the flashlight. He carefully chips away at the glass before screwing it back into place. We surround Hartley, fascinated, as if he's the fire and we're mesmerized by his flames. He packs the space around the filament first with pitch, then with the shredded bark and sets it aside.

Now we wait.

"Was Sarka with you, Mani?"

He shakes his head. "Sorry, Captain. I haven't seen him since we all separated."

Figures. Unlike the rest of us, Sarka was trained to survive in this type of environment. As I look around the room, I realize most of our survival instincts are primal. We weren't raised in the wild. We've only ever been in controlled atmospheres. Synthetic air pumped through pipes to mimic Earth's lower atmosphere. LED lights designed to simulate artificial sunlight. Even on Delta, we pretend we're living on a planet and not trapped in biospheres on giant rocks orbiting the sun. But it's all fake. The real thing is much scarier than I imagined. I'm more impressed our ancestors made it out of the ice age.

Now, we huddle in fear on our four main colonies. A species ostracized. I can't imagine the possibility of billions. Our two thousand kilometers of land mass is laughable compared to the five hundred million we once had. It's no way to live. But neither is kicking an indigenous species out of its habitat so we have somewhere to fuck up again.

As the last of the light seeps out of the room, we crouch in anticipation. Everyone has their task. We're all just waiting for the right moment before we implement them. I wind the strip of Mani's environmental suit around each of my fists. It cuts into my wound, causing a sharp pain, but I don't care. I have one goal: wrap this strip of fabric around the neck of the first avian who enters.

We wait another hour before deciding the time is right. We want to take the guards out as quietly as possible. Hartley picks up the flashlight. He's arranged himself by the door with the canister of compressed air. He flicks the flashlight button on. There's a quick burst of light, our anxious faces imprint on my mind, then nothing.

"That's it?" Fossick whispers. "I thought you said it would start a fire."

After the flash of light I can't see anything. I can only hear rustling over by the door.

"I'll try again, it's not an exact science, you know? There's a lot of luck in starting a fire this way." More rustling, then the click of the flashlight again. The room is briefly illuminated before going dark again. And then, so slowly I might be imagining things, a tiny glow begins to emerge from the top of the flashlight. Hartley adds more shredded bark to the small fire until there are tiny flames curling up pieces of bark. He lifts the canister of air and positions it near the fire. The first spurt creates a tiny fireball that wafts into the air before extinguishing. He adjusts something on the canister and sprays again, this time lifting the fire into the flow of air. It creates a harsh stream of fire, which Hartley adjusts to narrow it. He hands the torch to Mani, whose job it is to keep the fire going in case Hartley needs it again.

Now that he has a steady stream of fire, Hartley gets to work on the hinges. Ash is beside him, ready to cut through the hinges as soon as they begin to weaken. She's using the only sharpish edge we have, the lid of an empty water canister. She tried cutting with it earlier, but there's a hard layer on the twine and she couldn't get through it.

"Crap." Hartley leans closer into the hinge. "It's taking longer to cut through the rope than I planned. I was kind of hoping it would catch and burn away, but this braided twine doesn't seem very flammable." He wipes the sweat from his forehead and stands to cut the second hinge. "Try to pull the braiding apart, Ash. I've gotten the top layer, that might make it easier to unravel."

Hartley starts on the top hinge while Ash works away at the first one. The rest of us sit useless in the background, watching them work, waiting for our turn at action.

After a few more minutes the canister of air sputters and dies. Hartley lets out a soft expletive. "Sorry, that's the best I can do."

"Give me some more light. I'm almost through." Ash grabs Mani's hand and positions it closer. I can't see around her, but when she gives a tiny cry of triumph, I know she's made it through. "One more to go."

Mani and Ash stand to work on the top hinge while the rest of us sit and wait. The waiting is the worst part. The back of my neck prickles from the heat, my palms are sweating and I have an unrelenting urge to start pacing. Even though I want to, almost need to, I can't. It will make everyone else anxious, more so than they already are. Instead I ask how it's coming, in return, Ash grunts. I'm not sure if that's a good sign or not, so I leave her to it.

Finally, after what feels like hours, Ash lets out a soft, "Ha." She looks at me, her smile elated. Even through all the dirt and the small bruise now forming on her cheek, she's beautiful. I smile back. The moment stretches.

Hartley coughs beside me, breaking the moment. "What now, boss?"

I shake my head a little to refocus on our task. "Now we lure the first guard in."

Foer and Fossick lift the door from the frame. Without the hinges it comes away easily. Standing in front of the door, his back to us, is one of the avians. He holds a large spear in one hand and what looks like dinner in the other. At the noise, he turns, his face scrunched into a scowl.

This is the moment our plan can all go wrong. His next action determines our fate. If he calls out to the others, we're done, but if he comes into the room, we have a chance.

Foer and Fossick back into the room. They're still clutching the door, leading the avian inside. Chloe pokes her head out the door, acting as lookout. As soon as the avian's across the threshold, Ash kneels on the floor behind him. I use her back as a springboard to toss the homemade garrote over his head. I jump off and pull down with everything I've got. His wings flap out, knocking Ash and Hartley to the floor. He thrashes about, catching Mani in the head with his spear and Fossick in the stomach with the tip of his wing. I pull tighter on the garrote. My ribs howl in protest and the sweat on my palms makes it slip.

I want to scream with the effort, but quiet is essential if we want to escape unnoticed. His sputtering changes to a guttural coughing and he falls to his knees. Foer grabs the arm with the spear. Ash pulls the spear, trying to wrench it free, but his grip remains firm. I tug harder, but it does nothing to ease his grip.

Then, Foer bites the avian's wrist and he drops the spear. His wings flail out in furious motions. My crew dodges the attacks until everything goes completely still with one loud thwack. Ash holds the spear above her head, ready to strike again if he moves. But he crumples to the floor.

Breaking the sudden silence is our chorus of heavy breathing. Everything's stopped. I let loose the garrote around his neck and slide to the ground, exhausted.

Ash does the same. Between breaths she says, "Thank fuck there weren't two of them."

Hartley and Foer laugh, but it's weak given the circumstances.

"I say we use the rest of the environmental suit and tie his arms and legs," Ash says.

"Good idea. Then we'll replace the door and make our way back to the lowering platform."

We make quick work of our tasks, not willing to hang around any longer than necessary. As we creep along the rope bridges, I'm reminded of a similar night over twenty years ago. Only this time, I'm in charge of the escape. Is this how my mom felt leading people into the unknown? Terrified she'd fuck up somehow and lead them all to their deaths?

CHAPTER TWENTY

The moment my feet touch the hard, solid ground again, I almost faint with relief. I resist the urge to bend down and run my hand through the loose soil to confirm I'm back where I belong. Although I guess that's not accurate either. I've spent my life in space. The gravity on asteroids isn't the same, not even with the help of simulated gravity. Now that we're on a planet, it's not exactly what I was expecting.

Living in space is easy. We don't have most of the things that can kill you on a planet. Is this what life on Earth was like? Before we'd mastered our environment with cities and civilization? At one point, we weren't the top of the food chain. We were one of the links, making our way through the world much like the rest of the animal kingdom. But at some point we adapted and moved our way up the food chain. Now, confined to space, we've learned to adapt yet again.

Far from the village, Ash lets out a whoop of celebration and does a fist pump before high-fiving Hartley. I wish I could celebrate with them, but the cost was too high. We're a strange bunch, stomping through the jungle, flanked by soft neon leaves. We're all down to our undershirts and those thin shorts that always ride up your backside. The ones they give you for space walks. Each of us sports more than a few scrapes and bruises. We haven't showered in days and judging by the wide berth the avians gave us, we stink.

But at this moment, they're happy, and they deserve to be. We're free and clear of danger, until we encounter the next moss monster or native. Hartley will lead us back to the ship. At least someone thought to keep their compass. And with any luck, the ship will still be there.

Ash turns to look back at me, her smile fading. She slows her pace to fall in step next to me.

"What's wrong?"

"Nothing." I shake my head. I don't what to bring her mood down.

"You're thinking about Yakovich."

I shrug but look away. "I don't want to talk about Yakovich."

"I'm sorry I snapped at you. I know you were only doing what was best for the crew." She kicks a fallen branch out of the way. "It was the right decision, even if it didn't feel like it at the time."

"Ash, you don't have to placate me. I'm used to having people not agree with my decisions. But the great thing about my job is that I get my own way no matter if they do or not."

We follow the others in silence for a few moments. We're on some sort of trail, which isn't the best idea. As soon as the avians discover we're gone, this will be the first place they look for us. But I'm reluctant to veer off the path in case we discover another type of native out to kill us.

"For somebody who's in the business of taking orders, you don't do so well at it," I say.

She stares up at the canopy before responding. "I was five the first time I disagreed with my dad. He wanted me to make my bed every morning before coming down to breakfast. I thought it was silly because it was going to get messed up again when I took my nap in the afternoon and again when I went to bed." Her face darkens as she continues, and I know she's not recounting a good memory. "And I'll never forget the look on his face when I said that, like it was the most stupid thing he'd ever heard. He took hold of the table with both hands." She demonstrates the grip. "And upended it. Cutlery and dishes flew everywhere. And he screamed. It was the first time I'd heard him yell like that. If there was no point to making a bed in the morning than there was no point to setting the table for breakfast. No point in even getting up and going to work. He said, that if we let the little things run to chaos, our world would follow. It all sounded so stupid to me at the time. And I realized then, my life would be this long string of orders I didn't want to follow. So I made up my mind that I would find a way to make those orders my choice."

"And then you joined Union fleet."

She laughs, but it's more sad than happy. "I discovered that I don't actually like being in charge, too much stress and responsibility. But I don't like being one of the many either." She shrugs. "It's weird. You're the first commander I've ever disobeyed, but also the only one that I would follow anywhere."

I'm floored. I have no response to her statement, but there's a warmth radiating from the pit of my stomach.

We keep walking, following the others along the path. Every so often there's a sharp incline followed by a steep downslope.

After our third Ash says, "My mom would've loved to see this place. She used to dream about Earth even more than I did."

"You said she was a twin?" It must be strange to have a sibling, someone to share in the mischief. Ash nods. I want to ask how her mom died. She's never talked about it, but I don't want to pry either. I hate when people do it to me.

"We were on Epsilon." At my confused look, she clarifies. "When it happened. When my mom died." We reach another sharp incline and I grab Ash's arm when she slips on some loose dirt. I hold on a little longer when we reach the top.

"It was a Burr raid."

"You don't have to tell me if you don't want to."

She squeezes my hand and lets go. "No, I want to. I've been thinking about her a lot since we've been here. She loved stories of Earth. More so than my dad. He loved living on the Belt." We're much further back from the rest now. I wonder if that's intentional so she doesn't have to speak so quietly. "We were there visiting one of the mining homes with my cousin. They came on the third day. A small group of them. I don't even know what they were there for, food I guess, who knows. I was only ten at the time. The whole thing was like a video game. My cousin and I had been playing around in one of the complexes when we heard this loud boom. When we entered the main promenade, there were fires everywhere. People were on the ground, covered in blood and debris." Ash stops to pick a twig out of her boot and let the others move even further ahead. She chucks it aside before continuing.

"There was this one woman, she'd lost both her legs, but she was still trying to crawl away with her arms. I remember feeling sorry for her because she wouldn't give up and you could see how much pain it was causing her. Then she looked up, looked right at me, and I realized it was my mom. She'd been crawling toward my cousin and me, trying to make sure we were safe." Our pace has slowed so much, we've almost stopped. I want to wrap my arm around Ash, but I don't want to make her feel uncomfortable. She stops completely, right in the middle of the trail and turns to me before she continues the story. "I couldn't move. I stood there and watched as one of the Burrs came over and hit her in the head. He turned to us, ready to do the same thing he'd done to dozens of other people that afternoon, but I still couldn't move. To my right was this old man. He'd tripped over someone, a young woman. I started to run over and help him, but my cousin grabbed my arm and pulled me away. The last thing I saw of that old man was his head bouncing off the ground. I kept hoping that he was dead before he hit." She pauses, cracks a few knuckles and looks back up at me. "My cousin said he died so we could both live. But I've always wondered if we'd stepped in, could we have saved him? I always said I'd never let it happen again."

I motion for us to keep moving. I don't want to get too far behind the others. "You can't save everyone." It's something I learned early on. Even before we escaped the station. Raids would go out with dozens of men and only a few would come back. My dad always said it was the cost of doing business. He treated his men as resources, no more valuable than the items they brought back with them. It's a cynical way to look at the world. For a brief moment, I see the world as he would've experienced it. From the time he was in his late teens, Sarka was an object. A resource. Something to consume and discard once it no longer had use. If that was my life, would I be like him now? God, I hope not.

"Only a dozen or so people survived out of hundreds, my aunt and my cousin included. My dad went ballistic."

I'm about to reach for Ash's hand when we halt. The others have stopped on top of a small hill overlooking the clearing we camped at the other day. Beyond stands the pyramid, dark against the night sky.

"Holy shit. It's massive. When you said pyramid, I pictured something smaller. The shape, yes, but not the size," Hartley says.

Ash is in as much awe. In the moonlight it looks even more impressive. The black stone reflects the moon and surrounding phosphorescent leaves.

"Come on." Hartley waves us forward. "Let's see if we can get inside."

"Whoa, Hartley, hold up." I grab his arm, holding him back. "We need to head back to the ship. We don't have time to get sidetracked."

"But, Captain, don't you want to explore? This is the whole point of our mission, to discover other cultures. This," he holds his arms out, indicating the massive pyramid before us, "is the greatest thing humans have ever discovered. This is ancient technology created by an alien species. And isn't it amazing how much it resembles our own?" He has a point. And I'd be lying if I said I wasn't curious to see what's in it. But is it irresponsible when it puts us in a compromised position?

"We may never have this opportunity again," Hartley says.

"Okay, but if we can't get in within an hour, we leave the mystery to the pyramid and head back to the ship."

As soon as I say, "okay," Hartley skips down the hill toward the pyramid.

When we get to the familiar doorway at the base of the stairs, Hartley feels around the ground near the base of the door. Finally he stands, brandishing a sharp rock. "What's everyone's blood type?"

Mostly everyone shrugs except Ash who calls out, "O negative."

"Ash, get over here and give me your hand."

She glances at me first before walking over to Hartley and giving up her hand. Hartley drags the edge of the stone across her palm, opening a long nasty gash. Before she even has a chance to scream, he's shoved her hand in the recess next to the door.

"You couldn't have used your own blood?" She wipes her hand on her shorts.

Chloe clucks at Hartley. "Do you have any idea how easily that can get infected?" She grabs Ash's hand before she can wipe it on her shorts again. No one seems more surprised than Ash that she even cares. Chloe pulls out her med kit and begins drenching Ash's palm in disinfectant.

"Ow." Ash pulls her hand back.

"Do you want to die out here because you're a big baby?" Chloe holds out her hand. Reluctantly, Ash places her hand back in Chloe's.

"They already tried that, Hartley. Blood doesn't open it," I say.

"I think I figured out what the two circles mean, Captain. The avians discovered that you need blood to open the door, but that's only part of the key. When you mentioned that they tried Sarka's and it didn't work, I started to wonder if the two circles were a sign that it was only a certain type of blood that would open it." As soon as he says this, we hear a loud crunch and a deep rumble as the door in front of us begins to open. "O negative can be used as a universal donor, but only in emergency situations. There may still be antibodies that can cause problems during transfusions but I figure the pyramid wouldn't know the difference in this situation." He grins and takes a deep breath. "And it worked. Ash's blood opened the doors." Not for the first time in my life, I'm reminded I have the wrong type of blood inside me.

CHAPTER TWENTY-ONE

I've stepped in something." Foer groans, halfway down the stairs. "You think there are animals in here?"

"Nothing's been in here for centuries." Fossick calls forward from the back of the line. "It's only your imagination."

"It didn't sound like my imagination."

There's not much light to see by. Hartley rigged up branches of the phosphorescent leaves to use as torches. They throw eerie shadows against the walls as we descend into what looks like a vast, dark pit.

"That's not actually true, Fossick. Animals can squeeze into surprising things," Hartley says.

Mani laughs. "They're resourceful little fuckers."

"I once found a rat carcass in the hydrogen chamber of one of my prototypes. The opening was only twenty-five millimeters wide."

"Gee, thanks, Hartley," says Fossick.

"You're welcome."

It must have taken several decades to build this. The outside is massive, but so is the inside. We've been walking for over twenty minutes without reaching the bottom. The smell is getting mustier too. I'm having second and third thoughts about agreeing to this. We should've left well enough alone. How do we know we're not walking into an ancient booby trap?

But why would they make a door if they didn't want people to enter? Or, maybe it's the right kind of people. How many avians had to give their blood before they figured out theirs didn't work? It makes me more worried that ours does work.

Ash halts in front of me and raises her fist for us to stop. She looks at me. In the glow of the green phosphorescence, her eyes flare like emeralds.

"There's something up ahead. And the air's changed. Can you feel it?"

I nod. It's thinner somehow, and it feels more claustrophobic. I turn to Hartley. "You guys stay here. We're going to investigate."

We creep closer and find another door like the one at the top of the stairs. We call to the others. As they join us, Ash and I inspect the door. It also has a recess next to it.

"How's your hand?" I ask Ash. She lifts it to the light and we both inspect the gash. It's already clotting.

"It's fine. I can reopen it. Doesn't hurt much," Ash says.

"Let someone else do it. You don't need to reopen yours. It'll get infected."

"We don't know how many doors we're going to find in here. And who knows if there's anyone else who can open a door. It's easier if I do it."

I hold my makeshift torch up to the recess. Above it is a series of dots. "Hey, Hartley, what do you think these mean?"

He peers over my shoulder, mumbling as he reads. "Wow, this is amazing. They've set up a sort of access code to get through the door. It's not about the blood, you have to figure out what the next sequence is." He points to a panel below with oblong stones sticking out and extra holes underneath. "We need to place the stones in the right spots to get the door to open."

"Can you figure out the right sequence?"

"Of course I can. Give me a few seconds to think it through." Before he's even finished speaking, he's rearranging the stones in the holes. As he sets the last peg, the door creaks, then opens.

"What was the sequence?" I ask.

"It was simple. I don't think they were trying to be difficult."

Simple. Right. Ash and I exchange a look.

"Hartley, your definition of simple is our definition of difficult," Ash says.

Hartley points to the series of dots, which to me looks like a jumble of nonsense. I'm amazed that Hartley's brain can create a pattern out of it. "We have a list of numbers represented by the dots, one, one, two, three, five and so on. Then they ask for the next number in the series, which you get by adding the last two numbers in the sequence together. It's known as the Fibonacci sequence. It can either start with a one or a zero. Although it would be hard to represent zero on this grid. I bet these avians haven't discovered zero yet."

"And that's unusual?" Ash asks.

I check to make sure everyone is still with us. Foer, who's holding one of the makeshift torches, stands near the back. His jaw and cheekbones protrude in the light.

We've now stepped into another corridor, leading us down on a slight incline. If I were a religious person, it might feel like we were walking deep into hell. A very dark and musty hell.

"Zero is not an easy concept to accept. You think nothing of it because you learned to use it in early math class. Imagine never having seen zero before and then someone says, here is something that represents nothing. It would stump you. Humans didn't even come up with zero as a placeholder until the Babylonians and even then that was a rudimentary precursor to our current zero."

Again, I wonder if Hartley spent most of his life reading textbooks.

As we descend, the corridor gets narrower, forcing us to move in closer together. Ash pushes in front so she has the lead. I'm about to argue with her, but the look she gives me tells me there's no point. She's put herself in the line of fire. I wish some of the crew could have at least a tenth of her bravery. Fossick's staked out the back of the line, ready to turn tail the minute we encounter problems.

"I don't get it though. What's so big about zero? If it doesn't represent anything?" Mani asks.

"But it does represent something. Often, it represents the absence of something. Without it, we wouldn't have algebra, calculus, advanced arithmetic, or even computers. Imagine our world without computers."

"And what makes you think that the ones who built this pyramid have discovered zero?"

"They were far more advanced than this pyramid suggests."

When we get to the end of the hall, there's another series of dots to the left of the door with a panel of blank holes. Ash and I hold up our branches of phosphorescent leaves so Hartley can see the numbers.

I'm glad we have Hartley with us because math isn't my strong suit. As one of my calculus instructors used to say, I'm not bad at math, just lazy. I can't help it, numbers hold no fascination for me, not the way they do for Hartley.

He reads out the list of ten numbers—a few times—before reaching for the pre-cut stones. Ash stops him.

"Wait, I want to see if I can get it," she says, still holding on to his arm. I lean in closer, astonished they can find a pattern in these random numbers. I read them to myself, two, nine, three, one, eight, four, three, six, five, seven, but they're still nonsense.

Hartley grins. "Did you get it?"

"Two," she says. He smiles, displaying teeth that glow green in the light.

"Yep." He puts two stones in the two spot and the door opens.

"How the hell did you come up with that number?"

"There's two sequences. Two, three, four, five, and nine, eighteen, thirty-six, seventy-two. The seventy-two was missing a two. The second sequence doubled the number each time. You see?"

"Ugh, that hurts my brain thinking about it." I follow Ash and Hartley through the doorway.

This room is different. The realization is immediate. We've reached the main chamber. There's a blue glow coming from the center. It casts odd shadows around the cavernous room. I step forward and stop everyone from walking any further. The light is moving.

"There's someone here," I whisper. They all freeze, listening for any sounds. All is quiet. All is still except for the flickering coming from the mass of objects in the center of the room.

I motion for everyone to stay. Then, I creep to the side and edge along the wall. My heart is pounding in my chest, thumping against my ribs so hard I can't breathe. I look back at the group. They're all crowded around the doorway. Fossick looks ready to bolt the second trouble comes, Ash is ready to run forward the second I give the word. Chloe, looks fearful, Foer and Mani are watchful. Hartley is kneeling on the floor, examining something at his feet.

As I come around to the source of the light, I realize it's coming from a bank of monitors. They're displaying scenes from the jungle and the avian village. I take a step closer. It's not the village we were at. There are at least five different villages displayed on the monitors.

I stop when I see a figure seated in front of the monitors. It's slumped forward with its head resting on the table. Its arms hang limp at its side. I step closer, treading as lightly as I can in my boots. There's still no movement by the time I make it to the set of monitors. I nudge the figure's shoulder. Nothing. I pull back its shoulder. It weighs almost nothing. The second I touch it, I know it's dead. There's no warmth left in this body and hasn't been for a long time.

As I pull it upright, the head falls back. The face has a frozen grimace and dead eyes. The face is similar to those of the avians, only the beak is much less pronounced. It's more like a hard shell where our noses are. Goose bumps pop up on my skin and I stumble back. I take a quick look around, but the room is empty except for the monitors and dead guardian.

"It's okay, we're clear."

My crew steps around the workstation.

"Oh, wow. How long do you think he's been dead?" Hartley asks.

"A hell of a long time." Foer picks up one of the arms and lets it drop. Dust from his skin floats up into the stale air.

Everyone coughs and covers their mouth.

"Not necessarily. They constructed the pyramids in Egypt in such a way that aided in mummification. It's possible this pyramid is similar," Hartley says.

"The technology is incongruous though. Do you think whoever built this pyramid are the same species as this guy?" Foer asks.

"This pyramid is ancient. There's little chance the monitors have anything to do with the original builders."

"Why are they spying on the avians?"

A million more questions flit through my mind. How did this guy die? How long has he been here? Is anyone coming back for him? But even if we were to examine this chamber for days, we wouldn't find the answers we're looking for. There's no way of knowing any of this. Even though the avians have tried to access it, they can't. Perhaps the watcher was a scientist, observing a more primitive species.

It's obvious that he's not the same species as the avians. He doesn't have a full beak and doesn't look as tall, which means he could have evolved somewhere else. It's hard to see what he would've looked like before he became a gray shrunken figure.

As my crew chatter around me, I realize the more profound implication of this find. There is not only intelligent life on this planet, but intelligent life in this solar system. And they're capable of space travel. If they didn't evolve here, they must have arrived by ship. Is the ship still here? Is it hidden somewhere? It's unlikely he came alone. Where is the rest of his crew?

But none of this matters right now. We need to get out of here and back to the ship before the avians discover we're gone.

"Captain, come take a look at this," Foer calls me over. He and Mani are in one of the far corners, examining the wall with a leaf torch.

I step around the dead scientist to see what they're looking at. They point to a series of carvings in the stone wall. There's a whole mural of drawings. We step back to get the bigger picture of what it could represent. It's covered in symbols. There are hundreds, thousands of tiny pictures. They're grouped in four different quadrants. Most of it is gibberish. Without knowing what the symbols mean, there's no way we can figure it out. Still, it's pretty impressive. It gives insight into why this chamber was built. Not some lair to spy in secrecy.

"All right. It's time to go. We need to get back to the ship." As I say it, I realize it's already too late. A warm glow spreads into the chamber, casting our shadows against the wall. I look over and see four avians standing in the doorway.

CHAPTER TWENTY-TWO

Ash pushes me out of the way before I have a chance to react to the avians storming into the chamber. Their eyes are wide in what I'm guessing is astonishment. This must be a big moment for them, entering the inner sanctum of the pyramid. With only imagination to fuel the avians' speculation, I can't help but wonder what they thought they'd find. As their astonishment turns to anger, it's clear that this is not what they were hoping for.

Were they expecting riches, weapons, or secrets of some kind? Instead they get a dead scientist and a wall of cryptic messages.

It was reckless to give in to our curiosity. It wasn't our discovery and we should've left it alone. And instead of finding answers, I only have more questions. Will they understand what's going on? I doubt it. And I don't want to be here when this becomes even more confusing for them. I don't want them to destroy it before they have a chance to understand what it means to them. Right now they're not advanced enough to fully appreciate what this place is.

"We need to get them out of here. They'll destroy it before they understand it," I say.

Ash and the others nod, but even as we decide this, there's no way the seven of us can take four of them. The numbers aren't on our side.

The leader smashes his club into one of the walls, and a piece of history is forever gone. Before she could have even thought of the consequences, Ash wedges herself between the wall and his club. She spreads her arms wide, blocking any further destruction.

"No!" I yell. He swats at her, but she ducks out of the way. Before Ash has a chance to counter his next move, he hits her in the jaw with his other fist. When she's doubled over, he rams the club into her stomach and she falls to her knees.

He sneers something at her. Ash pulls herself up, slow, as if she's afraid she might crumble. As he's about to swing the club again, a loud, piercing sound echoes through the chamber. The avians cover the small flaps on the sides of their heads. The leader takes another swing at Ash, but before he can follow through, he crumples to the ground.

Behind him, Sarka stands in the doorway, a gun in one hand and a knife in the other. There are four other crew members with him, all aiming weapons at the three avians still standing.

I kneel next to the leader, there's a large burn mark from the blast on his back. His breathing comes in short bursts like he's trying to catch his breath after a long run. I reach for his neck, looking for a pulse, but even if I could find one, I have no idea what it's supposed to feel like.

It doesn't take long. Within seconds, his breathing stops and his eyes become glassy and vacant.

"You didn't have to kill him," I say to Sarka.

"You're welcome, Captain." He offers me an impudent salute.

There's no use talking to him when he's like this. All gloating and full of himself. I guess I should be grateful he came back for us. It's obvious he's been back to the ship for reinforcements and weapons. The four crew with him are decked out in appropriate clothing for this weather and terrain. They have weapons, rations, and water. I look down at my own clothing, or lack thereof. I'm wearing dirt-encrusted boots, a skimpy tank top, and shorts that expose my bloody knees and mud covered legs and arms. Blood, dirt, and bruises cover more than half my body. I look as if I've been giving us a tour of all the mud pits in the region instead of trying to get us back to our ship.

"What should we do with these guys, Captain?" Hapta, one of my armed security asks. He steadies the gun, aimed at one of the smaller avians. There's a quick fluttering of wings, but the avians remain silent and still. They've now learned what guns do. It shames me to think my people were the ones to teach them.

"Bring them outside. You two." I point to Fossick and Foer. "Carry this one up and place him on the ground next to the others. Hartley, you and Ash figure out how to seal this pyramid back up. I don't want them coming back in here until they can figure it out on their own."

The night air is moist by the time we reach the surface. A coming dawn tinges the sky pink and there's a sweetness to the wind I can't place.

We leave the avians tied near the base of the pyramid and begin our journey back to the ship. With Sarka in front and me bringing up the rear, we make a ragged bunch.

I have to say, Sarka as a savior doesn't sit right with me. He always has an agenda and I can't figure out what it could be in this instance. There would be no reason for him to come back for us if he'd already made it to the ship. Unless he had a harder time taking it over than he thought. Perhaps this is him playing nice, showing the crew he can be a good guy. It's a ploy, but one they may not be expecting. Either way, I'm happy he did. I don't think I have any more fight in me.

This entire adventure has been more than enough to serve me for two lifetimes. All I want now is a hot shower and clean uniform. If I never encounter another living creature that wants to eat me, kill me, or steal my blood, I'll be happy.

Ash falls back to walk beside me. "It's kind of sad isn't it?"

"What's sad?"

"That it's over. Even with all the danger, it was exciting discovering a new species. I mean, this is proof that we aren't alone in the universe. There is other intelligent life and we were the first humans to discover that." Her face, though streaked with dirt and micro scratches, is lit from within. And when she says it like that, it does sound exciting.

It makes me wish I'd been on the same adventure as her. Instead I'm wracked with guilt over Yakovich and that avian Sarka killed. It wasn't his fault we invaded his planet and broke into an ancient shrine. It still feels wrong that we used our technology against him in such a disastrous way. The implications of his death could be huge. For all we know, we could have started a chain reaction that will destroy his species. Jesus. I hope I'm not as arrogant as I sound.

One thing is for sure. We have not left his planet better than when we found it. Why must this be the enduring human trait? We are more than takers. We are destroyers. We're like three-year-olds who've never learned to share. If we can't have it, then we don't want anyone else to either.

Ash interrupts my thoughts again. "I don't know about you, but the first thing I'm doing when I get on board is taking a shower."

And like that, an image of Ash, water sluicing over her naked body, invades my mind. I look at her and my stomach coils in a tight knot. Her eyes darken. It may be my imagination, or wishful thinking, but I could swear there's invitation in those eyes. I turn away and take a long swig of water before my thoughts get too out of control.

"We could all use a shower," I say.

"Not exactly what I had in mind."

My stomach does a loop-the-loop like one of those old-fashioned airplanes.

The sun is up and we haven't even reached the ship yet. Everyone's panting, dirty, and sweaty. The only person in his element is Sarka who pulls back, stepping aside to let the others pass.

"Are you okay?" he asks.

I nod. "Nothing getting the hell off this planet won't solve."

He stops and puts a hand on my arm to hold me back. Ash walks a few paces then turns back and slows, waiting for us at a respectful distance.

He pulls a canister of water from his belt and takes a long gulping drink. "The most important thing to remember is to hydrate. You'll die of thirst before anything else. Not to mention, it brings on heat stroke faster which can cause fevers and delirium." He motions the canister to me, but I shake my head.

"I'm glad you're safe, Jordan. I'm surprised I made it back to the ship before you did."

"Why didn't you come back sooner? You took off into the jungle and left us. For all you know, a giant moss monster could've eaten us."

"You're a big girl. And you had Ash with you. So I figured if there was anyone to worry about, it would be the jungle." He takes another drink.

"Thanks. For coming back for us. I know it went against every instinct you have. But thanks."

"I'm not always the monster everyone else makes me out to be."

I don't answer. Instead I examine the dirt at my boots and feet. I know he is a monster. That's what makes this so hard. I know he's done every bad thing people have said about him, and worse. He doesn't do anything unless it helps him. I know rescuing us fits into his agenda somehow. I just haven't figured out how yet.

"We better get back before people start to wonder where we are."

He touches my arm again, looks over at Ash, and says, "I know you don't want me talking about your mom—"

"Then don't."

He holds his hands up in surrender. "I'll say this. She would've been proud of you. You may not think I knew her. But I know she loved you more than anything in the world. She'd be proud of what you've become. Not a lot of people can survive in conditions like this. Believe me, I know. I've seen guys harder and tougher looking than you two who grew up in this stuff and still couldn't hack it."

When he offers me his canister this time, I take it. After a tentative sip, I take a few more, realizing how thirsty I am. It's almost empty when I hand it back.

I motion for him to lead the way. He salutes, this time like less of an ass, and heads out to catch up with the others.

"What was that about?" Ash asks.

"I don't know. He's planting the seed for something. I'm not sure what yet. He used the whole 'your mom would've been proud of you' line."

"Is it possible—and you know I'm the last one to defend him—but could his intentions be in the right place for once?"

"No. Let's hurry up." I don't like how far behind we are. I can't even see Foer, who was in the rear. Even Sarka is a good ten meters ahead of us. And the sooner I get out of this humid jungle air, the happier I'll be. I never thought I'd miss the fake air of the ship, but I do. "Can I have some of your water?" I don't know why I'm so thirsty.

"Sure." Ash unclips her canister and hands it to me. She grabs my arm when my hand misses the canister. "Are you all right? You're very flushed."

The disorientation has worsened, along with my thirst. My knees buckle and I drop to the ground.

"Jordan." Ash's voice sounds far away and I struggle to keep her in focus. She's kneeling next to me, pouring water on a piece of cloth and wiping my face and arms. It hurts, I try to push her away. I'm so tired right now. All I want to do is curl up and fall asleep.

"Jordan." It's a deep male voice this time. Sarka. He's so loud his voice echoes through the jungle. He says my name again and it sounds deep and scratchy. That's the last thing I remember.

CHAPTER TWENTY-THREE

My heart pounds. So do my legs. The grunting behind us is only getting closer. I don't even risk a quick look to see how much it's gained on us. The image of this ugly snarling beast is already imprinted on my mind. I have no idea what the hell it is, but I know I don't want it anywhere near me. It looks like a mix between a rhino and an alligator, all claws, teeth, and horns.

Up ahead, Ash stumbles and falls to a skidding halt a few feet from the edge of a ravine. With my momentum, I don't have time to stop, and I trip over her. We tumble, head first, down the steep slope into the ravine. It takes several seconds to reach the bottom. When we do, I'm sure of two things. One, we've escaped death by impalement, and two, Ash does not make a good landing zone.

I turn my head toward the panting on my right. Ash closes her eyes and rests her hands on her heaving stomach. She's alive. We're alive. That's something at least.

It's been twelve hours since Sarka stranded us on this goddamned planet. I've never been so scared in my life. Not even during the explosion on the *Posterus* before I knew whether Ash was alive or dead. No, this is a different feeling. For the first time in my life, I'm not sure whether we're going to be alive this time tomorrow.

It's been twelve hours since I woke tied to a tree. Ash was a few feet away, ready to spit fire and murder.

Sarka drugged me. He played me. Again. When Ash bent to help me, Sarka smacked her over the head and tied us both to a tree. He must have told the crew that we're dead. That's the only reason I can see the crew leaving us here.

And they did leave us. When we finally got free of our binds and made it to the ship, it was gone. The giant indent of her hull was the only thing to prove the *Persephone* was ever there. And now it's the two of us, stranded on this fucking planet.

We decided we should head in the opposite direction of the avian encampment. It meant we had to begin our travels on marshland, which turned to scrub, then desert. We may have saved our skin from burning by covering it with mud, but it didn't keep the heat out. By the time we reached the jungle an hour ago, we had heat stroke.

Ash and I didn't make it very far into the jungle before we encountered our welcoming committee. We've been running ever since.

"You okay?" Ash asks.

"I think so." The shade offered by the canopy feels wonderful. "Do you think this is how early humans lived? Always running for their lives?"

"They were better equipped than us. We've spent a total of forty-eight hours on a planet. We'll get the hang of it."

"Sooner rather than later, I hope." We're in a small grove of trees. They tower above us, the tops lost far above. The ground is mossy and soft, with only a few smooth stones acting as islands among the sea of green. In the background, I can hear buzzing, soft bird calls and a light wind shaking the leaves. And, almost too faint to catch at first, the trickle of water.

I sit up. "Ash, do you hear that?"

"My confidence breaking? Sure, I've been hearing it all morning."

I snort. Make that two of us. "No, I hear water."

Ash sits up too.

"It's coming from that direction." I point to a stand of bushes where the trees become thicker. I help Ash to her feet and we begin the search.

It only takes about five minutes before we're standing next to a stream. It's not very wide, or deep, but it doesn't need to be. I'm on my hands and knees ready to scoop the first liquid I've had in twelve hours into my mouth when I notice Ash. She's also on her knees. Instead of drinking, she's stuck her hand into the water and is wiggling her fingers in the current.

"What? You don't think it's safe to drink?" I ask.

"So much water. Can you imagine what it would be like to take this for granted? For this feeling to be so mundane that you wouldn't even appreciate it?"

Without responding, I search through our pack for water pills. After years of living on asteroids, drinking water from all over the galaxy, you come prepared. I pull out the canister and dump four pills into my palm, passing two to Ash. There's no point in hydrating if we spend the entire night vomiting it back up. These pills, a staple of any Belter, will prepare you to ingest anything.

"Ash, you should drink while we have the chance. Who knows what else is out there waiting to make dinner of us."

She enjoys the feel of the water for a few more seconds then bends forward and scoops water into her canister. While she indulges, I look around. Smooth rocks pepper the bottom of the stream. Neon yellow fish with tiny spikes undulate between long, flowing reeds. Further down, there's a fallen tree impeding water flow. A family of long necked birds sit along the edge dipping their heads into the water. They scoop up the neon fish and throw their heads back, sliding them down their throats.

"Our best bet is to follow the stream." I wipe as much dirt off my face as I can. "It'll give us a fresh source of water and hopefully lead us somewhere good to camp tonight." We spent last night out on the flat desert. But the sunset we watched made the searing heat of the day and the bitter cold of the night worth it. I've never seen anything so breathtaking. It was like the heavens landed at the edge of the desert and put on a light show. It was better than any nebula or galaxy spiral I've ever seen. The combination of reds, oranges, and pinks warmed me from inside until I thought I'd explode.

Thanks to the pack Ash was wearing when Sarka left us, we have the ability to make fire. Unfortunately, there was nothing in the surrounding desert to make fire with. Instead we took turns at watch, trying to share what little body heat we had. Tonight, I'm determined we'll have some sort of shelter and a fire.

"The closer we stick to water, the more likely we'll encounter unfriendlies." Ash wipes the excess water from her mouth with the back of her hand. It slashes the encrusted mud on her face across her cheek.

We're both so filthy, I'm tempted to suggest we wade into the stream and clean off, but decide it's too dangerous. Ash is right. We shouldn't stick so close to the water for long. I pull the pack around and fish out another canister. "Let's fill up as many canisters as we have and move within hearing distance of the stream. We'll head upstream and find the source."

After about two hours, the jungle hasn't changed much since we began. Every now and again we'll see tiny rodent like creatures dart out from the underbrush. Large green feathers, almost like leaves, stick out of their spines. Their ears bounce as they move and flop forward when they stop. If I knew how, I'd catch one. I'm sure they taste better than any rations we have in our pack.

Rations are hard packed squares. They resemble cardboard and taste like roasted almonds coated in wood pulp. The whole thing is unsettling. They're designed to last for decades in storage, so any resemblance to actual food is discouraged. But they keep our stomachs full and that's the important thing.

"So, are we going to talk about it?" Ash picks a small leaf from a bush and begins to tear off strips, dropping them as we walk.

There are several things we need to talk about and I'm not sure I want to talk about any of them. Not yet. "Which it are you referring to?"

"The fact that your dad stole your ship and left us stranded on a planet to die."

Part of me is as numb as that sentence. Another, smaller part, is so confused, I want to keep it buried until I have time to dig it back up and examine it. "I'd rather not."

"It might help." She tears off another leaf.

"Help how?"

"If you keep it bottled up, it'll just fester. There's no way you're not pissed about this."

"If you want to know whether I'm surprised, I'm not. It doesn't hurt as much when you expect betrayal."

"You mentioned you couldn't understand how people seek approval from their families. I didn't understand how you could feel that way until now. If it was my dad I'd be pissed. Aren't you pissed?" She stops talking, afraid maybe she's gone too far.

I sigh. As always, she's determined to push. "Can we drop it? I don't feel up to talking about it right now."

She grabs my wrist, stopping me. "Don't do that. You always do that. Why can't you let down your guard for once?"

I pull my arm away and continue walking. "Not everyone is capable of sharing everything about themselves."

She catches up to me and stops me again, this time, by stepping in front of me. "Won't share."

I groan. "Can we please have this conversation later?"

"And by later, you mean postpone forever?"

All around us the jungle vibrates. Birds flutter and squawk above us. The leaves bristle. Insects buzz below. And the humidity strangles us in a vice. My pulse picks up, beating to the rhythm of our surroundings. It's got me on edge and I have no idea how much longer I'll stay calm with Ash pushing me like this.

"I need time to figure this out. Can you respect that?"

Her eyes drop to the ground, then raise back to me. She's hurt, but she nods. "I can respect that. I know I don't have any right to ask you these things. I just wish you'd trust me more."

"It's not about that. I do trust you. I need a little time to get perspective. That's all." I take her hand in mine. "I've had a lot of time to think about my past. I've had twenty years to put my feelings about my dad to rest. And having them resurface like this…it's hard to know how to deal with them. Even though I know him, know what he does, I didn't ever see him like that. Now everything's different. I can't dismiss what he did with some childhood filter."

Ash nods. I'm not sure if she gets it or not, but at least I've silenced her questions for now. I keep walking. I want to find shelter before we die of heat exhaustion.

At the sound of the water, Ash picks up her pace. "Do you think it's another river?"

As we get closer, the trees begin to thin out. I want to warn Ash to slow down, to wait for me. We have no idea what's out here, but before I get a chance, she's disappeared. I break into a run, going as fast as I can without injuring myself. When I finally catch up, I almost crash into her. She's standing at the edge of a clearing, staring out at the most beautiful sight I've ever seen.

CHAPTER TWENTY-FOUR

I'm surrounded by rainbows. They dance in and out of sight, caught between water vapor and sunlight streaming through the canopy. Spread before us is a waterfall so tall, clouds obscure the top. It empties into several lagoons. These spill into lower lagoons until all have emptied into a small bay with water so blue, it's more like turquoise. Lush green vines hang from each terrace, suspended in mid-air. It looks more like something out of dream than a real place.

I look over to get Ash's reaction, but she's no longer standing beside me. There's only her shirt, which lays discarded next to me. She tugs at her left boot as she hops toward the edge of the water, throwing each cast off piece of clothing behind her in her haste.

"Ash!" I yell. "We don't even know if it's safe yet."

Instead of listening, she pulls her bra over her head and I'm distracted by the sight. The sun glints off her long, slender back. Next, she takes off her briefs and I look away, embarrassed to be watching her undress.

I hear a splash and look again. Ash is treading water a few meters from the edge. Her smile is so big, it takes over her whole face. It's breathtaking.

"Come on." She waves for me to follow her.

I approach with caution. What if there are creatures living underwater waiting for some idiot to jump in?

"Don't be a wuss. It's fine." She flips onto her back and swims a couple strokes. Her breasts bob with the motion, and I blush. I actually blush. I feel like I've been caught peeping into the girl's locker room.

"For once in your life, do something impulsive." She dives in and swims toward me.

I recall the last impulsive thing I did. Another image of Ash's nude body invades my mind. It plays back in full color with surround sound. She pops out of the water and splashes me.

"Nothing's going to happen. I promise." She laughs and dives down again. Her legs kick in the air. Water splashes in her wake. It's hard not to get caught up in her enthusiasm.

"Is it deep? Can I stand on the bottom?" I ask when she surfaces.

"No, it's pretty deep. Jump in, we'll swim over to the waterfall."

I hesitate. There's nothing I'd like better than to shed these grimy clothes and cool off, and Ash makes it look so inviting.

She rolls her eyes. "Keep your clothes on if you want."

I sigh. "I can't swim."

It's Ash's turn to look embarrassed. Her cheeks pink up and her gaze drops to her arms treading water.

Swimming is a privilege on the Belt. We recycle all water through sophisticated filtration systems, even our urine. But a large part of the supply comes from mining carbon-rich asteroids. It's dangerous, and expensive, making water one of our most precious resources. Only those living on Alpha would have the money or the arrogance to fill a pool with it.

"I'll keep you from drowning." She cups her hand and sends a wave of water toward me, soaking my shirt.

I laugh. It's such a foreign sound. I don't remember the last time I was in a good mood. But I am. It amazes me the way Ash can forget we're stranded on a planet, vulnerable to any number of deadly creatures. Before I overthink it any more than I already have, I pull my wet shirt over my head and toss it next to Ash's on the rocks.

When I'm naked, I turn and see Ash treading water a few feet from the edge, watching me. There's no mistaking the lust in her eyes. Heat spreads from my chest like a tidal wave. My skin prickles. We stare at each other. Ash floats in the water and I stand naked on a rock a few feet from the edge. For an instant, I'm happy we're on this planet. Instead of dread, I'm actually experiencing anticipation.

It's me who breaks contact first. As I make my way to the edge, excitement coats every part of me as if I've already submerged myself in the lagoon. Before I'm able to lower myself into the water, my foot slips and I plunge into the depths of the cool lake. There's a moment of panic when I realize I can't breathe and I kick, hoping to propel myself toward fresh air.

Strong, warm arms envelop me, drawing me to the surface. Ash is centimeters from me. I cough and sputter. Any hope of intimacy shatters.

"Kick your legs for me." She props me against her body and pulls a large piece of bark toward us. "Here, grab on to this, I'll pull us toward the waterfall."

I hoist myself onto the makeshift raft and begin kicking while Ash pulls from the front.

The spray hits us long before we reach the waterfall, coating us in tiny droplets. Each one gleams in the sunlight, making it appear as if we're decorated with tiny diamonds.

The main waterfall is too powerful to stand under. There are several smaller streams that act as showers. I position myself under one, holding the rock face.

The water is clean and cool as it washes over me. For some reason it smells like flowers. If I close my eyes, I can still feel the sun through my lids like a red glow. Is this what it was like? To live under a sun? To wake up to it casting light over the horizon and to drift off to bed in the waning hours? I peer over at Ash, her eyes are also closed, but there's a small crease on her forehead. Is she thinking the same thing I am?

Without opening her eyes she says, "Do you think he's coming back for us?"

It takes me a moment to come back to reality and figure out who she means. When I do, my heart sinks. I shake my head. "No. He's not coming back for us." This is it. But for the first time, I can see the possibilities. We just need to figure out how to avoid the avians and embrace our long lost hunter-gatherer. After all, I could have it worse; I could be alone. A small part of me feels guilty. After all if it wasn't for me, Ash wouldn't be stuck on this planet. But another larger part is happy that she isn't stuck up there with him.

"I'm sorry, Jordan. I wish things were different." She swims over to me, treading water, her breasts a few feet from me.

I'm finding it hard to focus. The sun has added some color to her shoulders and face. The creamy white of her collarbone blends with the freckles. They map the contours of her nose and cheeks. I want to reach out and kiss every one of those freckles.

I'm about to pull her close, when she says, "But we have to come up with a plan. Surviving in this place is going to come with a steep learning curve," and brings me back to reality with a crash. She's always thinking ten moves ahead.

I swallow and push my libido down deep. "Our first step should be finding shelter for the night. After that, we can worry about food. Tomorrow, we can start exploring. If we're going to set up a permanent place, I want it to be as far away from avian settlements as possible."

We indulge ourselves a little longer before climbing out and resuming our journey.

The sound of the waterfalls blends into the background when we spot a small band of avians. There are four or five of them, all male, carrying hefty spears and what looks like one of those giant birds. It's plucked and spitted. I pull Ash to the ground and look about for a place to hide or run. We have one gun between us, but I'd rather not have to use it. The less interaction we have with the locals, the better. Ash points to a large slope to our left, which would lead us away from them, but at what cost? It looks pretty steep and thanks to the forest, we can't see the bottom. Who knows what's waiting for us down there.

"Unless you want to try to crawl under a bush, it's our best option," she says.

I crawl over to the edge and peer down. There are trees scattered here and there, but there are several large rock formations. A loud cacophony breaks through the jungle. I wonder if it's their laughter. And why not laugh? They're heading home with a kill, large enough to feed their families. My stomach rumbles to remind me how empty it is.

I start down the incline. Ash stumbles for a moment, then regains her footing. Tiny rocks, pebbles, and some rather large boulders trace our path down the side of the hill. Only a few more feet and we'll reach the bottom. Only a few more feet, yet I still manage to catch my boot on one of the larger rocks and crash into a pile of boulders at the bottom. I lie there for a second, catching my breath. My back is screaming. Pain radiates all along my left elbow.

"Watch out for the landing. It's a bit bumpy." Ash smirks and pulls me up.

"Says the graceful swan who sailed down without any problems," I say.

When I finally get a chance to look around, we're surrounded by trees.

"Do you think they saw us?" Ash asks.

I look back up the steep hill. The rock slide has covered our tracks. "I doubt it. But it's still a good idea to find cover for the night. We should start looking for a place to make camp."

"How does this look?" Ash points to a small cave in the side of the hill.

CHAPTER TWENTY-FIVE

And now we're camping.

When I was ten, I found a pile of books in a crate from one of my father's raids, long forgotten. It didn't contain anything of worth in their minds. But for me, it was a goldmine. I read every one of those books. Most of them were science fiction, with dreams of time travel and utopias. All with futures that would never happen. There was one about a group of girls who journey into the Canadian wilderness. To camp. For fun. This concept was so foreign to me. Why would you leave your dry, safe, and clean home to venture out into a dangerous, dirty, wet, and cold forest? And yet, this was a thing humans used to do. I can understand in the army you're forced into it, but volunteering? No, thanks. How do people stay clean with all this dirt around? Even now, minutes after a swim, my skin is sticky. The humidity keeps my skin coated in a constant sweat, which is like glue.

"Isn't this great?" Ash stomps through the cave entrance with a pile of wood in her hands. "I've always wanted to go camping." Why am I not surprised? Of course she would love this. For her, it's an adventure. As long as life isn't boring, she's happy.

She dumps the wood in a pile near the entrance and stacks them along the side for later. "In grade nine, our class took a trip to Gamma where they grew the evergreens. They wouldn't let us have a fire so we couldn't roast marshmallows or make s'mores. But it was so beautiful sleeping under the stars. Ever since, I've wanted to go camping for real."

When I was in grade nine they took us on a tour of the industrial farms. If you didn't already live on a farm, they required you work on one during weekends, to prepare for the day you graduated. I was lucky Kate had a small herd of pigs and a field of corn. But it also meant I grew up knowing way too much about pig shit and how to use it as fertilizer.

I don't relay my story because I don't want to intrude on Ash's happy mood. It's not her fault she was born on Alpha. Most of the time I don't think she realizes how lucky she had it.

"God, I wish we had marshmallows." She sits back on her haunches and looks at me with an expression of intense horror.

I stand up from my poor attempt at making us bed mats, worried. "What? What is it?"

"I just realized I'll never have chocolate pudding ever again. Even if this planet did have something like cocoa beans, I'd have no idea how to make them into chocolate. I don't even know how pudding's made."

I laugh. Of course that's what Ash would miss most. Forget real beds or hot showers, which is what I'll miss most.

We spend the rest of the light hours gathering what we'll need for the night. While Ash tends to our cave, I head out in search of food. Our pack only has a few ration bars and I don't want to use them up in the beginning. It's better to save them until we're so hungry we'll eat anything. Anything tastes good if you're hungry.

I don't have much luck finding food. I spend a lot of time watching what the birds and tiny rodents are eating. I don't know much about surviving in the wild except if there are others eating it, then it's safe for us.

I return with a small bundle, enough to tide us over, but soon we're going to have to learn to hunt. I'm confident we'll find a way.

When I return, Ash grabs my arm. I dump our dinner as she leads me to the back of the cave. The only light is a small backup flashlight we found at the bottom of the pack. The cave isn't very big, or high. By the time we reach the back we're stooped. The smell of the jungle recedes. Deeper in the cave, it's musty and smells like an old box.

"Look," she sweeps the light across the back wall. Painted in dark hues of red, yellow, and brown are bipedal figures in warrior poses. They carry large spears aimed at herds of animals which look much like Earth's cows. The animals are spotted with large brown noses but with tufts of hair traveling down their backs. But the bipedal figures aren't the avians we've seen. They don't have wings. Instead they look more like tall, skinny humans.

"What are the chances an earlier species painted these? But eons ago when they were still evolving?" I ask. Excitement bubbles up. This is an incredible find, almost more so than the pyramid, or the avians. Evidence two different species developed cognitive intelligence on this planet is beyond thrilling.

"That's great and all, but not what I wanted to show you." Ash lowers the light. There, in a small pile on the ground, is a disintegrated pack with the letters ASA surrounded by a blue circle.

Ash kneels down and picks it up. "It's an old NASA pack." Debris falls from the opening, including a few bones. At one point it made a nice home for some small animal. Before that, it was a survival pack for a NASA astronaut—an organization that hasn't existed for over two hundred years.

She turns it over. On the other side is an unmistakable logo. This pack was from the doomed Frontier IV Mars mission. Which makes the pack exactly two hundred and twenty-five years old. It is, in fact, from the last ever NASA mission.

The space program was canceled after that. Too many missions had failed or turned up too little scientific worth. Humans had hoped to terraform Mars, to colonize it as a secondary Earth, but it became evident that the resources required would be too great. Humans had other worries. If that mission had been a success, things might have been different.

By that time, resources on Earth were becoming more scarce. Our planet could no longer sustain billions of people. When the resource wars started, Earth was already doomed. By the last years of the war, it couldn't even sustain millions. Thousands fled to the north and south, hoping to escape the extreme weather. But by then, it was too late. The stratospheric ozone layer no longer existed.

For the first time ever, the world came together to help rebuild the protective layer, but there was a miscalculation and, instead of saving Earth, it resulted in most of the remaining water being evaporated into space. This last blow was the single defining factor in Earth becoming uninhabitable.

Without water, crops failed. Famines became global, taking children and the elderly. Several years without food decimated the human population. Billions died. In essence, we'd created our own mass extinction. After a century of rebuilding, a little over a million exist.

We only survived because we took extreme measures. The asteroid belt encircling our galaxy was our only option. With over two million asteroids in the belt, most of those over a kilometer wide offered resources. They have land, minerals, and water. The smaller outer ring gives some protection from stray asteroids. And the larger dwarf planets are stable enough for settlements. But it's a makeshift solution. The Belt isn't sustainable indefinitely. It isn't our home.

This pack represents the last of Earth's optimism. The last of our hope for a bright future.

"But how?" I run my hands along the stippled surface.

Ash opens the bag, but anything that was in there is long gone, dragged out by animals.

"The same way we got here, I'd imagine," she says.

Whatever brought us here must be a natural phenomenon. Hartley thinks it's a wormhole. "I wish Hartley was here." Not something I ever thought I'd say. "He might be able to explain it better."

"The ship must be close by. Do you think they survived? Or was it brought by animals who used this cave for shelter at some point?"

Two hundred and twenty-five years. Who knows what shape the ship would be in now. If it's even recognizable. But there's a chance. If it is still around, it would be better shelter than this cave.

"We should look for it," I say.

Ash's face responds for her. She lights up. "Hell yeah, we should. Imagine finding it? One last mystery of Earth solved."

We make a plan to start out tomorrow morning.

We settle into bitter berries and something hard and nutty. It's almost inedible. If we're going to survive here, we'll need to find better food.

Ash shivers. "I will never complain about mess food ever again. What I wouldn't give for some tofu loaf right about now." Her shoulders slump and I know she's thinking about chocolate pudding.

"Tomorrow we'll find something more edible. Perhaps we'll even be able to trap an animal and have some meat."

With our bellies full and a decent fire going, talk soon turns to what our long-term plans are.

It's depressing to think we'll spend most of our time avoiding the avians and scavenging for food. Our skill set is not going to help us. A few days ago, I'd never breathed a natural atmosphere let alone worried about what local fauna could eat me. Humans haven't had to deal with these problems for thousands of years. Once we established civilizations, we never looked back. Who would want to spend over six hours a day looking for food? There are better things to fill our time with. Each generation saw the creation of jobs that hadn't existed when they were born. New technologies took over, even if it wasn't better. It's hard to topple the notion of progress.

Ash, of course, is excited by all this. The challenge of her against nature is too thrilling to let go. If there's one thing I know, it's that Ash always comes out on top.

"We'll need somewhere permanent. We can't wander around for the rest of our lives." I poke a fallen log back into the fire. It sends sparks into the air. We don't need a fire. It's still humid out, but it's more to let animals know we're here, and they shouldn't mess with us. "Although, we're not exactly sure what their seasons are like, or if they even have them. Maybe we'll have a summer home and a winter home." I look over at Ash who isn't even listening. She's mesmerized by the fire, off in her own world.

"How bad could it be though?" she says.

I have a sudden uneasy feeling. She's got that crazed look she gets when she has an idea she knows I won't like. Her green eyes are so light, they're almost hazel. In the firelight they look luminescent. "The seasons? We won't know until we experience them."

She waves her hand erratically. "No, the ship. The Mars ship." That uneasy feeling blooms to a full panic. "How bad could it be? They built those things to withstand anything. It's possible it could have survived two hundred years."

"In a humid jungle? Not a chance. Besides, even if it is habitable, we'll have a lot of work to do on it."

"I don't want us to live in it." And this is when the panic threatens to become an anxiety attack. "No, I want us to fly it."

CHAPTER TWENTY-SIX

I wade through the shallow pond toward Ash. She's lying naked, stretched out on a flat rock, soaking up the late afternoon rays. The surrounding trees cut the sun into shapes, painting her body in light.

We've been searching for two days and still haven't found the ship. It's either long disintegrated or buried so deep in the jungle, no one will ever find it. Despite Ash's optimism, I'm still skeptical. It's not likely it survived in the jungle after two hundred years. No matter what engineering feats it possesses.

"Even if we do manage to find it, how are we going to get it to take off?" I asked after our first day.

It was almost dusk. The sun was about to dip below the horizon. We'd spent the better part of our day looking for things: food, water, an ancient Earth spacecraft. We were sitting against the hard rock face outside our cave with our boots off.

"First of all, they designed those ships to take off from Mars after five years with little energy input. We can combine solar energy and hydrogen to power take off and the basic systems. And second, this planet has a much lower escape velocity than Mars, so it'll take a lot less energy to reach orbit." She's always so sure of herself. Does she have any doubts at all, or does she honestly believe that we'll be able to launch an antique into orbit? This is all so unrealistic, I can't afford to get caught up in her optimism.

"That's if it doesn't have a giant hole in the side from crashing on this planet," I said.

She wasn't deterred. "How do we know they crashed? What if they landed it? Let's worry about finding it before we worry if we can fly it."

"As practical as that sounds, I don't want you to get your hopes up. There's a very real possibility that we'll never find it, and if we do, that it won't even power up after so long."

While searching for food that first day Ash found this small pond not far from the cave with fresh water. It's like our own private pool where we can go at the end of the day and nothing disturbs us.

When I reach the rock, I hoist myself up and lay beside her. It's smooth, and hot from the sun. Warmth seeps into my back, but it's nothing compared to the heat of Ash's arm next to mine. It's like a tiny fire spreading through my whole body. She turns and now the length of her body presses against mine.

"Staying here might have its benefits." Her voice is low in her throat. The sound vibrates down the side of my arm.

I don't have much self control left. Since that night in the showers, my imagination has been playing it back in full holo surround. Each time only amplifies the sound and feeling. Sometimes, I change the ending. I don't run out on her. We go back to my cabin and do all the things I've dreamed since she walked into my life.

Her fingers dance along my stomach. She leans down and whispers in my ear, "If there were no rules, what would you do to me right now?"

The sounds of evening surround us. Animals settle into their nests and burrows for the night. The sun hangs low, hovering at the horizon. It casts a fiery light over everything, charging it with energy.

I sit up.

"Ash—"

"Shut up."

Something unfurls inside me. A deep need I've been holding at bay since that night in the showers. Now it's awake and demanding attention. My mind races through every dirty thought I've ever had about Ash. My reason pools somewhere low. Her lips crush into mine. They're soft and warm, and I part for her.

I put everything into the kiss. All my wants, needs. Every moment of longing flows between us.

When we break, we're both breathing hard. I coax Ash back on the rock, kissing her neck, her shoulders, following the line of freckles. "Turn over."

She flips onto her stomach.

I move her damp hair to the side. It looks darker when it's wet, almost a crimson next to the pale white of her neck. Her muscles jump in rhythm as I kiss my way down her back. I stop for a moment to tease and admire. She turns her head to the side and closes her eyes. Her lips part. The edge of her breasts are visible, pale and supple. I trail my fingertips up her inner thigh, starting at her knee and stopping before I reach the sweet spot. Her hips start to pump, seeking relief, but I place my other hand at the small of her back and push her down.

Her tongue darts out and licks her lips.

I run my fingers through her folds, achingly slow. She's so wet, I slip inside. She groans from somewhere deep in her throat and I almost speed up just to hear the sound again. Every part of me fills with the need to go fast and, simultaneously, to draw it out as long as possible. She bites her lip and buries her head in her folded arms.

She pushes against my hand, bucking up. I take my fingers out and circle her opening. She gasps. So do I. The sun reaches the horizon and in one last spasm, bursts into a spectacular explosion of warm light. It spreads through the glade, bathing everything in red and orange.

I grip Ash's hip and sink deep inside again. Her muscles contract, gripping my fingers. She's on the brink of exploding. She arches up. I pull out and circle her clit. I'm rewarded with that throaty groan, which almost becomes a growl as I thrust back inside.

At that sound, with her grip on my fingers, something deep inside me snaps. I clench and almost join her as she comes. A thin sheen of sweat coats her back. Light plays along her muscles as I draw the moment out.

I lie next to her, panting along with her. The sun dips below the tree line and the pond is slowly cast in a deep purple.

"What is it about water?" I ask.

She sighs.

Above us, the first stars peek through the break in the trees. There's no comparison to seeing them through ten feet of metallic glass. Even on the *Persephone* they're dull compared to this. From this vantage point, they sparkle, almost like they're dancing with each other in the night sky. It's breathtaking.

"They say sailors used to navigate by the stars. They'd memorize the constellations and follow their path. It would be scary to navigate with nothing more than your memory to guide you," I say.

"If I lived during that time, I always pictured myself a pirate." And she would've been too. I can see Ash as a pirate captain on the high seas living only for her next adventure. I picture her standing on the quarter deck, her auburn hair whipping in the sea breeze. "What about you?" she asks.

I sigh, knowing too well what it would've been like for someone like me growing up in that era. "Married to a man I can't stand, pushing out babies."

"Nah. You're not the conventional type. You'd have found a way to be in charge. I can see you as a captain for the British Navy, pretending to be a man so you could live free." She squeezes my hand. "Who do you think would win between us? The Navy captain? Or the debonair pirate?"

I turn to look at her. She's silhouetted against the night sky, but I can make out the smile on her lips. "You would win. You always come out on top."

She turns toward me with an eyebrow cocked. "Always, huh?"

The only way to describe the look she's giving me is lascivious. It's all want, need, and seduction. My stomach curls in on itself at that look. I'm tempted to give in, but one look at the darkening sky and I think twice about it. I begin to sit up, but she pulls me back down.

"A few more minutes," she says.

It's been so long since I've seen her this content, I'd give in to almost any request. Under her breath, she's humming a tune. It's so soft I can't make it out.

"Did your mom ever sing to you when you were a kid?"

I shake my head, then realize she can't see me in the growing darkness. "Not that I can remember." I don't think she had much to sing about. "Although my dad used to, when I was very young. I'm not even sure what song it was, I can only remember the melody." I hum a few bars, but Ash isn't sure what it is. It's a strange hidden memory. I'm surprised when it pops into my head. I'd had a nightmare, and my dad was consoling me. He sits on the edge of my bed. The window frames the moon. I know by morning the space station will rotate and the Earth will be visible in that window. Because of the light behind, he's silhouetted. I don't remember his face when I was younger. Or maybe it hasn't changed in all these years, only that stretched scowl, which never appears in my memories.

"My mom used to sing to me. My favorite was 'Twinkle, Twinkle, Little Star.' I never understood, until now, what it meant to twinkle." She takes a deep breath. "It's so much better than I imagined."

"We should head back. It's getting dark."

Ash points to the rock holding our clothes. "It's okay. I brought a flashlight."

But I've made up my mind even if my body has other opinions. I don't want to risk getting caught in the middle of the jungle in the dark. We know nothing about this planet. Every time we let our guard down, it surprises us in unpleasant ways.

"The last thing I want to do is wade through this pond in the dark." What if there are creatures that only come out at night? I shiver at the thought.

With the waning light I can see Ash trying to work out a way to convince me to stay. It wouldn't take much at this moment, so I take the initiative and slide off the rock. The water's much cooler now that the sun's gone down.

Reluctantly, she follows and we make it back to the cave without incident. But when we arrive, we're introduced to the joys of outdoor living and given a lesson in how much we still have to learn.

The cave is in shambles. The leaves for our makeshift bed mats have been strewn across the cave. They litter the floor with green and brown debris. The food I'd collected earlier is scattered, most of it eaten or taken.

"Well, shit," says Ash from behind me.

I sigh. On the outside, I keep calm, but inside I'm reeling. The weight of it, being here, crashes down on me. It's never going to be easy living in this place. Ash is kicking some of the wood back into the fire pit. She's so despondent. I can't have that.

"Why don't you get the fire started while I try to salvage our beds. We may have to dip into rations."

We work separately until the flames from the fire jump and spark. The light dances up the walls, partnering with the shadows and sashaying across the ceiling. There's something hypnotizing about fire and it pulls at me. Sitting next to Ash, with her shoulder pressed against mine, there isn't anywhere I'd rather be. There's something about her energy. Even sitting still like this, it calms the fire and anger inside me. It's almost like a counter balance. I can't explain exactly what it is about her, but I like this version of myself when I'm with her.

"Thank you, by the way."

It's hard, but I drag my eyes away from the fire. "For what?"

"I never said it before, but I want to say thanks for choosing me. I would never have gotten to experience this." She waves her hand in the direction of the jungle and the back of the cave. "I've experienced so many firsts on this adventure. Things I never thought I'd ever see, and it's because of you."

"But—"

She waves off my protest. "Even if we don't find the ship, and even if we die on this planet, I'm still thankful. Especially since I got to experience it all with you." She hesitates, but only for a second, gauging my reaction. She leans in, her eyes on my mouth, and seals her heartfelt declaration with a kiss. It's slow at first, like she's discovering my lips for the first time, but soon becomes something more urgent.

She tugs my shirt off, but before I can reach for hers, she pushes me to the ground.

"My turn." She begins to kiss down my neck, along my collarbone. She runs her fingers across my chest, skimming the tops of my breasts. The sensation travels down, spreading along my skin, sparking a fire all the way to my toes. "I love your skin." She bends to kiss the top of each breast.

I reach up and entwine my fingers in her hair. It's so silky. She kisses between my breasts, running her thumb along the sensitive skin underneath. My back arches at the contact. I've never been so in the moment as I am right now. Every kiss, caress, every spot Ash touches, I feel deeply. She places her hand flat on my stomach as she takes my nipple into her mouth. My hips buck at the sensation. She eases her hand downward, running it along the inside of my waistband. I don't think I can take much more teasing as she peppers my stomach with soft kisses.

She inches my shorts down, skimming her fingers along the outside of my thighs as she does. Every part of my body shivers as she stares into my eyes. Her eyes are dark and full of lustful intentions. By the time she leans down and glides her tongue along my folds, I'm already a goner. It's like nothing I've ever experienced before. It's as if my skin is contracting and expanding at the same time, undulating along my body. I am cool and hot all at once. At any moment, I'm going to explode.

Ash takes her time exploring, teasing and it's almost my undoing. My moans echo through the cave and into the night. Finally, she presses her tongue hard into my clit. My vision contracts and I can't tell if my eyes are open or shut.

"Oh, God, Ash," I say, when I'm finally able to speak. "There are no words."

Ash crawls up my body and sinks into me. "I know what you mean." As we fall asleep, entangled next to the fire, she whispers, "I love you."

I turn to tell her the same, but she's already drifted off to sleep.

Chapter Twenty-seven

O n the fifth day, we find the cliff. We admire the view and would've moved on, except Ash spots something that doesn't belong in a jungle. At the bottom. The very deep, hard to reach bottom. This will take some definite thinking.

We've spent most of the last five days in the cave. Or at the pond. It's been hard pulling ourselves away from each other. But we can't live in that cave forever.

The cliff runs a few kilometers along what was probably once the coast. Far off on the horizon, the ocean glistens. It juxtaposes the sea of green, which stretches out below us as we stand at the edge.

"How far down do you think?" Ash peers over the edge. She kicks a rock and we listen as it disappears into the tops of the trees below.

"Far. Every tree we've seen so far is gigantic. If these are the tops, then the bottom must be a kilometer below."

Behind us stretches flat rock, half a kilometer to the tree line, which leaves us exposed. It took a lot of convincing to even get me to come out to the edge. One gun between us is useless if we're outnumbered. We haven't seen any avians out this way, but it doesn't mean they aren't around. I'm still not used to fauna. It makes me feel as though we're constantly being watched.

"We should jump," Ash says.

The comment comes out of nowhere. I stare. Is she joking? "Be serious."

"I'm one hundred percent serious."

"We'd die."

"No way. The canopy would break our fall. Those leaves are bigger than we are. They'd catch us."

"I'm not jumping, so forget it."

I gaze out at the expanse. A bird soars high off in the distance, circling something below. It spreads its wings, gliding in a hypnotic circle. I'm mesmerized, until the wings collapse upward, and it spins feet first into the foliage. There's a loud squawk and the sound of greenery ripping. That makes my mind up. I will not be jumping.

There must be another way down. The cliff veers in a semicircle, meandering into the trees off to the right, the same to the left. Our best bet is to follow the edge and hope for a more gradual descent. The sun is at its zenith, which tells me we have about five hours of sunlight left. Not enough time to explore much more. I'm wondering if it's even worth it. All we can see is a flash of something whenever the wind moves the leaves. It could be anything. Then again, it could be something.

"Let's make camp. Tomorrow we can try to find a better way down."

Ash is on her stomach, peering over the edge. "What if we climbed down the rock face into the trees?"

"Without proper repelling equipment? Not on your life."

"There are footholds here. It's doable."

I shake my head and begin walking toward the trees. There aren't any caves around here that I've seen so we'll have to take shifts keeping watch. We've been collecting food as we go, so there's plenty to eat today. I still haven't gotten the courage to try for one of the small creatures yet. We need something more substantial than the berries and legumes we've been finding along our way. But I have a feeling looming starvation will help that endeavor along.

I hear the danger long before I see it. The noise, a series of birdcalls, sharp and loud, comes from our left. Ash stops and crouches low to the ground. I join her, but my gut tells me we've been tracked for some time. The trees are still too far, and we're out in the open. It's why I didn't want to come this way.

"There." Ash points to the trees closest to us. A group of four avians, all with large spears, are coming toward us. They tuck their wings in tight, crouch low, and hold their spears at the ready.

I look to the right. The trees appear even further than before. We'll never make it. I'm guessing they're pretty accurate with those spears. I've seen them take down much larger animals than us.

Behind us, the semicircle of cliff edge looms. I hand Ash the gun and pick up the only thing I can find that might be of any use, a large rock. I heft it in my palm, ready to throw it.

"There isn't much charge left." The whine of the gun powering up accompanies that statement. "There's enough to take down two, maybe three."

I grip my rock tighter. "It'll even the odds a little."

The group is only fifteen meters away now, coming up fast. The leader cocks his head to the sky and crows. They all stop about ten meters back.

The sharp edges of the rock dig into my palm from gripping it too tight.

Several loud caws rip through the air. But the sound doesn't come from the group in front. I look around. Five more avians are approaching from the right.

Ash grasps my hand and crushes it tight. I look over at her and think: this is it. But instead of the fear or resignation I'm expecting, there's a gleam in her eyes.

"Do you trust me?" she asks.

Do I? She's reckless, yes, but her actions put her in harm's way, not others. So I nod.

"Good." She squeezes my hand again before letting go.

Before I can even reassess our situation, Ash takes off, sprinting toward the cliff.

"Ash! You crazy ass," I call after her. I turn in time to see her sail off the edge.

"For fuck's sake! Ash!" I look down at the rock in my hand and contemplate my options. There are very few. Best case scenario, the avians capture me. More likely they'll kill me and roast me for dinner. I look behind me and my heart constricts because I know I'm going to do it.

I chuck the rock to the side and sprint for the cliff. The edge comes up much faster than I'm expecting. Behind me, I can hear the thumping of their feet as they begin pursuit. Several loud caws follow. I don't waste time looking back. Looking back is a death wish.

And then I'm at the edge and there's no choice. No more time to change my mind or second guess myself.

Fuck, fuck, fuck.

The last thing I think before my feet leave the safety of solid ground is, if I survive this, I'm going to kill Ash. It's possibly the last thing I'll ever think.

And then I'm airborne.

My stomach launches slower than me, lodging somewhere in my throat as I drop. The screaming I hear may be me, but I'm not sure. All my thoughts are on the mass of green coming closer.

When I hit the top level of foliage everything goes dark as I'm enveloped by layers of leaves. They tear at my arms and legs, slicing into the tender skin of my neck and face. And then there's the noise. Falling through canopy is loud. I'm surrounded by a thunderous roar as I reach out, hoping for some sort of purchase. Tiny vines begin to curl around me, slowing my descent. Eventually, I'm able to grab a bunch of them and stop my fall.

I take a deep breath. Holy shit. I'm surrounded by green. Above me, I can make out the hole I made as I crashed through the canopy. There's the faintest circle of blue sky. The ground below is nothing but hope.

"Jordan." Ash is a few meters above me, sliding down one of the vines toward me.

When she reaches me, she brushes a lock of hair from my face, tucking it behind my ear. Despite the myriad emotions swirling around my head, it sends a shiver through my body.

"You jumped." She couldn't be happier about that. "I knew you'd jump."

"This is the dumbest idea you've ever had."

Ash's grin takes over her whole face. "It's only dumb if it didn't work."

"If it hadn't worked we'd be dead."

Ash waves me off. "Semantics." She's actually having fun. Damn her.

"So how do we get down?"

She scoffs. "I'm the ideas girl. You're the problem solver."

After a few minutes of trial and error, we figure out that the tiny vines are strong enough to hold our weight. It's slow going, but we manage to drop a few meters at a time by sliding down the vines.

"I wish I could've seen their faces when we jumped." Ash tugs a vine snaking around a branch before grabbing on to it.

I don't say anything. I'm still kind of mad we're in this situation. It's true that we're stuck on this planet because of me. It was my father who stranded us here. But this? This situation is definitely on her.

"Why are you moping? It could be worse. They could've followed us," she says.

And almost as if on cue, we hear a loud crash above, followed by several whooping sounds.

We're still half a kilometer above the forest floor. There's no way we can reach it before they catch up to us.

"They can glide, right?"

I don't say anything, just nod and slide down faster. My ability to think ceases, I'm in panic mode now. Grab and slide, grab and slide. The vines are rough and unforgiving and my palms start to burn.

The ripping and whooping above us gets louder. And closer. I risk looking up, I shouldn't, but I do. Three avians glide toward us using the vines and tree branches spiraling out from the trunk. Their descent is graceful, like a dance. Unlike ours, which resembles a toddler trying to walk for the first time.

My hands ache. They've started to bleed and still we're not going fast enough. The rush of leaves above is deafening. And then all momentum stops. Something grabs me from behind and I'm pulled up. I call out to Ash, but she's too far below. I turn, expecting to see the long beak of one of the avians. The pack I'm wearing has caught on one of the branches.

I only debate for a second before shrugging out of it. There's little time to regret the loss of all our food, water, and tools. As soon as I'm free, I fall several meters before catching myself on a branch. It knocks the wind out of me and I lose precious seconds recovering.

"Behind you," Ash calls from below.

I don't turn in time, but it doesn't matter. The excruciating pain on my right shoulder tells me what's happened. One of the avians has caught up and grabbed me. A sharp claw digs into my clavicle. The claw is almost pure black, like the pyramids, only not as shiny. A stream of blood spills down the front of my shirt the second he pulls it out. For a moment, I do nothing, just stare at the gaping wound in my shoulder.

The avian straddles me on the branch, a foot on each side of my body. His clawed toes wrap around the branch, sinking into the soft wood. He picks me up like I weigh nothing, and hoists me over his shoulder. The blood from my injury smears down his back, the contrast of dark red against pale gray is stark.

He shouts something at the rest of his group. I don't need to speak their language to understand. They have me.

"Hold on." Ash's voice sounds much closer than it should be.

"Ash, get out of here."

She doesn't listen. Of course.

The avian's wings flap against his back a few times before opening full width. Up close, the feathers are dirty, covered in mud and dead insects. And they stink like rotten earth, as if he's dragged them through a compost heap.

"Don't move." Ash's voice is now only a few feet away, and I'm not sure if she's talking to me or the avian.

I twist in time to see her draw the gun and fire at his leg. He shrieks and falls backward, squeezing me to his chest as he reaches for the branch above.

"I said don't move." Ash fires again, this time, at his head. The blast decimates his face, and still he doesn't drop me. I have a sickening view of the labyrinth of branches and vines below us. As he falls backward, that view changes to the two avians above.

I scramble to free myself from his grasp before he drags me down with his dead weight. It's no use. My equilibrium is off and I can't figure out which way is up and which is down. Before gravity takes me, Ash latches on to my wrist. Gravity and momentum almost rip my arm from its socket, but I'm no longer falling.

The earlier excitement is gone from Ash's face. Her eyes are still bright either from the excitement or the strain of holding on to me.

"Can you climb down on your own?" she asks.

My shoulder kills, but if I don't try, I don't even want to imagine the alternative. "I think so."

We stick close to the trunk where the branches are thicker, but it leaves us with less of the vines to grab onto. Ash needs to help me on almost every branch. Every time I lift my arm, the bleeding gets worse.

We hit the ground, almost in unison, just missing the maze of giant roots heaped around the bottom of the tree. I don't even have time to dwell on my injuries because Ash grabs my arm and pulls me up.

"Come on. We need to move."

Judging by the angry shrieks behind us, I agree.

As we sprint away along the jungle floor, I take stock of our situation. We're now without weapons, food, water or even water containers of any kind. All our rations, medical kit, and fire starting equipment dangles a kilometer up in a tree. There are at least two avians chasing us through dense underbrush. And if they don't kill us, a million other things will.

I burst through a rather grabby bramble and find Ash sitting on the ground. She snatches my arm, holding me back.

"Don't. There's something there. A barrier of some kind."

There's nothing in front of us except a clearing with dijon-colored grass and some stunted trees. I search the ground for something to throw and find a jagged rock. It's heavy and solid.

We've been on this planet for a week. If there's one thing I've learned, it houses a lot of secrets. Nothing should surprise me anymore. And yet I'm floored when the rock bounces back and rolls to a stop at my boot tip. There's some sort of shield guarding this section of the jungle. A moment later, two avians barge through the same bramble and stop a few meters from us.

CHAPTER TWENTY-EIGHT

Ash hauls herself to her feet, ready to square off against the two avians standing a few meters away. They're weaponless, which doesn't necessarily mean we can take them. They're stronger and faster than us. And even though it's only been a few days, they look taller than I remember. And much angrier.

"Seeing as how you're the ideas gal, what do you suggest?" I ask. We're in limbo, stuck between two menacing bird men with carnage in their stance and a shield we can't see.

Ash lifts the gun and fires our last shot at the avian on the right. He stumbles forward and sinks onto one knee, clutching his chest. The blast is deafening in the relative quiet of the jungle. It sets off an explosion of birds in the nearby trees. Without saying anything, she takes my hand and runs. This is more suicidal than being target practice for the avians.

"We'll get our asses fried on that shield."

Ash points at the ground. "No, we won't. Look at the grass."

And that's when I see a distinct divide. The grass inside the shield is yellow while the grass on our side is lush and green. The line meanders in a gentle curve around the clearing until we reach a thick copse and a rushing river. The river curves back around in the direction we've come. That's where our escape route ends. It's several meters wide, and thick and angry with debris from last night's storm.

Ash drops a rock into the rushing water. We lose sight as soon as it hits the water with a quick splash.

"Looks pretty deep," she says.

I take a step back. When she turns, I can see the question on her lips, but I shake my head. A calm pond is one thing. There is no way I'd risk getting swept away in that. With our luck, we'd get brained by a passing log and drown before we made it around the next bend.

I look back through the shield. From this angle, everything on the other side is hazy. We've run half the circumference of the shield. I can see the avians crouched together through the clearing on the other side. Their bodies are vague forms moving through a fog. I can make out one avian laying the other down on the ground. He pulls something from his friend's garments and stands, searching the forest until he sees me. A jolt of surprise stiffens his body as he spots me. That same jolt shoots through mine as he begins running in our direction.

"Ash? Whatever we're going to do, let's do it soon. There's one more, and he's heading for us."

Ash is squeezing herself through several large bushes. She's managed to jam half her body in, but we'll never make it through before he gets here.

I begin searching the ground for anything to pry apart the branches. That's when I spot a smooth metal sheet near the ground at Ash's feet. I crouch and run my hand along the surface. It's cool and almost silky beneath my fingers. At the bottom right is a triangle with a spiral etched into it. I circle the grooves with my finger. Nothing happens.

I look up. The avian is halfway around the shield.

I push my thumb into the spiral. It fits, sinking into the metal. A faint hum follows. My thumb is punctured. I yank my thumb back and examine it. Blood beads in a spiral formation.

I glance in the direction of the avian. He's so close I can hear his grunts as he sprints toward us. His gaze isn't on us, instead it's focused on the ground. He must have figured out how to see the shield boundary.

The hum gets louder. In fact, it's now more of a whine.

"Jordan." Ash jerks herself free from the bushes and points at the base of the shield. There's a distinct orange glow emanating from the circumference of the shield. It radiates up from the ground.

He's less than a minute away.

The field is now shimmering. And expanding. Before I react, it moves and envelops me. It's like stepping through a membrane. I hear the background noise in the jungle, the bird calls, wind in the trees, animal chatter, and the rush of the stream. And then I can't. On this side of the shield, it's deathly quiet. Everything is still. There's no wind, no animal sounds. Nothing.

My skin tingles. I run my hand down my arm, but other than the strange sensation, nothing's out of place. I turn, expecting to see Ash standing next to me, but she's still on the other side of the divide.

I scream at Ash to move.

There's a spark as Ash reaches out to touch the shield. She yanks her hand back, and screams something, but I can't hear her. I point to the control unit on the ground and hold up my thumb, hoping she understands. I search the clearing on my side for a similar box to lift the shield. But there's none, only dull, flat grass.

And then it's too late.

The avian tackles her. My world stops. I'm paralyzed by the scene in front of me. Ash twists and pulls the gun from her side holster. I hope for one last shot, but its charge is dead. She doesn't waste much time finding another use for it; she bashes the hard metal into his jaw. It's enough to give her leverage to kick herself free. She scrambles to her feet, half crawling, half running and slams her foot into his face. He shakes his head, dazed.

We stare at each other through the invisible divide for only a second before she takes off toward the river. I've never seen her so terrified. She jumps into the river. And then she's gone. Like the rock, she disappears with a quick splash into the snarling mass of brown rushing past.

I scream her name even though she can't hear me. The avian stands. He takes one look at the river, decides it's not worth it, and turns his attention to me. His eyes crawl from my scuffed boots, up my bruised and battered body, stopping at my dirt encrusted face. He looks puzzled and curious. He extends one of his clawed hands, but is quick to pull it back when the shield flares on contact.

It must work like the pyramid's entrance, with blood. Although, for whatever reason, my blood can open this. Who would go to all this trouble to guard their secrets?

The avian paces in front of me. I'm not sure which of us is in the cage.

After several minutes, I sit with my legs crossed, and spend the next fifteen minutes planning. Priority number one is finding Ash. As soon as the avian leaves, I'll search out another shield control. There must be one on this side, or how would people get out?

He spends those several minutes throwing various objects at the shield. Everything bounces off. Finally, after what feels like an hour, he cocks his head, listening to something in the distance. The avian takes one last glowering look at me, then turns and takes off the way he came.

I wait several more minutes to make sure he's gone for good. I pick myself up and head off in search of a way out of this silent trap. I find a way out a good fifty meters in the direction we came. I'm worried I've wandered too far in case Ash manages to find her way back.

She's a good swimmer. I'm concerned her luck has run out, but I have to believe she survived the river.

I trace my way back and follow the river downstream. The rushing water doesn't abate. If anything, it gets rougher the further along I go. Twenty minutes later, I come to a stop. Ahead is a large rock face, the same cliff we came from. It is a solid mass, stretching up into the sky. The water smashes into it, splashing in an arc before continuing its destructive journey around the bend.

I hear my name, it's faint and coming from the direction of the river. I run toward her voice. About ten meters from the cliff, Ash clings to a giant rock halfway between shores. The river careens past, collecting everything it passes.

I stop at the bank and sink to my knees. We lock eyes for several seconds. There's no way she can swim to shore with the water rushing past this fast. She's too close to the cliff. She'd smash against it. The rock is too far to reach out to from either side of the river. I watch, helpless, as branches and giant pieces of bark sweep past her. It gives me a chill, being this close to such dangerous water and not able to do anything about it. Even if I could swim, there's nothing I could do for her from here.

A small tree sails down the river. Its roots are still fresh, twisting out from the trunk in all directions. The branches collect smaller debris as it races through the rapids. One of the claw-like limbs snags her arm. She loses her grip on the rock and spirals back into the current. My heart constricts. She flails and thrashes, disappearing under the water for five heart-stopping seconds. She reappears several meters closer to the cliff face. She smashes into a smaller rock and clings to it.

Whatever I'm going to do, I need to do it fast.

I search the undergrowth for a branch that's long enough to reach her. There's nothing that long or straight laying about. I stomp into the forest, kicking at fallen leaves and decomposing soil. It shoots a musty smell into the air. I grab on to one of the vines to keep myself from slipping and that's when I have an idea.

I yank at the vine until it comes loose. There's a lot of it. I drag it out toward the river. The tiny barbs coating the outside dig into my hands. I double-check that Ash is still in one piece, then begin wrapping one end of the vine around the base of a tree on the riverbank. The other end I tie in a loose slipknot noose.

I drag the whole thing closer and call out to Ash, "I'm going to throw you this end. Grab on to it and I'll pull you in."

She doesn't say anything, only nods. Her skin is deathly pale, accentuating her freckles which stand out like constellations.

I coil up a good section of the vine and whip it as hard as I can. It lands a few feet to the right of her. It's in reach, but she doesn't try for it. I pull the vine back in and try again. This time, she lifts her hand to grab for it, but immediately clutches the rock again.

She shakes her head. "I can't let go. The current's too strong. It'll sweep me away."

I examine the lasso, wondering if I can throw it to land around her body. But if I aim wrong or throw it too hard, I could dislodge her.

And then I get another idea. It's crazy. I watch as another tree shoots past. Sometimes we need a little crazy.

I untie the end with the noose and wrap it around my waist. I secure it with several hard knots, but the entire time I'm shaking my head wondering how it came to this. What is it about Ash that makes insane plans seem possible? I once thought working three shifts was crazy. And yet, in the past week, I've done more questionable things than I've done in my whole life combined. Hell, in the past hour, I've jumped off a cliff and am now about to jump into a ferocious river of death with nothing more than a vine tied around my waist.

I yell, "Ash, I'm going to jump and grab you and then haul us back."

"No. You can't even swim, what if the vine comes loose?" She shakes her head. "Stay on shore. We'll figure something else out."

I take a deep breath, back up to get a good run, then jump. The snarling blackness looms up and captures me, stealing my breath. Goddamn, it's cold. I miscalculate and shoot past Ash at blinding speed. The vine snaps taut. I choke as the pressure squeezes all the breath out of me. I swallow a mouthful of water and sputter. Fear like I've never known seizes me. The enormity of my situation hits home. This is the dumbest thing I've ever done. I pull myself back to shore and climb up the slippery bank. It takes several minutes before I catch my breath.

When I look back at Ash, hanging on with everything she's got, I know I'll try again. It's worth the risk. She's worth it.

This time I begin further upstream, compensating for the quick current. When I jump into the cold river, it's not such a shock this time. As I whip past, I manage to seize Ash's waist. I can only hope the vine holds when it snaps tight. She clings to my back as I haul us in.

We're both panting by the time we make it back to shore. Ash stretches out on her back and stares up at the sky above. Her chest heaves with each giant breath she takes.

"Promise me you'll never do that again." She turns toward me. Her eyes are the deepest green I've ever seen. Darker than the moss coating the rocks along this valley.

"What? Save your life?"

She turns on her side with her back to me and I can't gauge her mood.

We spend the next half an hour getting our breath back and drying out before heading back toward the shield. This time I insist Ash goes first. But we both have no problem crossing.

Ash still hasn't said anything since the river. It makes the creepy stillness inside the shield all the more unsettling. I can't tell if she's still stunned or she's angry at me for saving her. I know now's not the time to broach the subject.

Ash stops short and I almost crash into her.

"Holy shit," Ash says.

Up ahead is a squat white ship with the word *Roebuck* stenciled along the side.

Chapter Twenty-nine

"Holy shit." Ash circles the spacecraft. It's white and cone shaped with red streaks running the length, like racing stripes. Each side has a different insignia, representing the three nations that funded the expedition. NASA, ISRO, and CSA. Nations that haven't existed for over a hundred years. It looks in pristine condition, except for one long scorch mark down the side.

I look up. Even though it's invisible, you can almost see a shimmer as the sun tries to penetrate the field. It barely filters through, giving the surrounding vegetation a death mask.

The ship sits in a small clearing. The trees surrounding it are all misshapen, growing at odd angles. There isn't much green here. If the sun doesn't filter through, then I suspect the rain can't either. The eerie quiet makes it all the more desolate.

We appear to be alone, but someone has to be maintaining the shield. I have so many questions, I don't even know where to begin.

I find Ash, her hand pressed against the side below the CSA insignia, peering up in wonder. As soon as she spots me, her face falls.

"What is it?"

She drops her hand. "Nothing."

I can't resist either, the impulse to touch is too great. I run my fingers along the surface. It's not smooth like I would have expected. Minuscule stippling covers everything. "From Earth." It's such an obvious statement, but I can't help the awe that creeps into my voice. The last time this ship was touching ground was somewhere on Earth. And now it's here.

Before I can come up with a plan of action, I hear a pop and a swish from the other side of the ship.

"I figured out how to open it. Dead simple. You'd think they'd have some sort of locking mechanism in place."

I follow Ash's voice, circling the spacecraft, until I reach the other side. Ash has already climbed two of the five steps and is peering into the darkness.

"Be careful. We don't know how it got here. Anything could be inside."

She's takes one more step up, then pauses. It's the only time I've ever seen her uncertain. She turns back to me and descends the steps.

"You're right." She stands to the side, looking expectant, like she's waiting for me to give an order. "We should be more cautious."

I'm stunned. I'm not sure where this newfound restraint is coming from, but it's weirding me out. "Are you okay?" I'm worried she hit her head on a rock when she jumped into the river. From here, she looks fine. There's only minor bruising, which could have come from any number of things, but no open cuts or wounds.

"Do you want to wait a bit? See if anything comes out?" She motions toward the door.

Screw that. I want to see what's inside. But I'm not going in blind and unarmed. I search the ground around our feet and the landing gear of the ship. It's sunk into the soft earth. And judging by the amount of vegetation around the base, I'd say it's been here for a long time.

The ground is strewn with rocks and grass, but no weapons. I venture toward the trees and find a fallen branch. I use the ground as leverage to ram my foot through the center. A nice sharp piece splinters off. I stomp on it again and break off another piece, which I hand to Ash.

"Let's stay alert. If there are people in there, they've been watching us for a while now." I grip the jagged branch. "I don't want anything to take us by surprise."

Ash grabs the handrail to mount the stairs, then stops and turns to me. "Can I go first?"

"What the hell is wrong with you?"

Ash doesn't answer. She gazes off into the distance, her mind somewhere else. I give her whatever time she needs. It's obvious something's bothering her.

Finally, she says, "I used to have pretty good instincts. Or I thought I did." She shrugs. "Now I'm not so sure." She looks like her world has been upended.

"That doesn't make a whole lot of sense." I cup her cheek. Her eyes, when they look up into mine, are sullen.

"I'm not doing us much good here, am I? All I've done is get us into one mess after the other. My stupidity has almost gotten you killed, not once, but twice now." She sighs. The sound is so loud it almost echoes. "And then I started thinking." She hesitates, like she doesn't want to admit the next part. A few seconds go by. She looks away before she says, "It's always like that. I'm always like that. I thought it was initiative." She pulls my hand away from her face. "All those things my father said. Every time he lectured me, I shrugged it off because I knew best. But what if I don't?" This last bit, spoken into her chest, is so quiet. "What if I've been remembering everything wrong? Not for the past couple of months. Not because of the mind knot, but because of me?"

"None of us knows what to do all the time, including your father. Is this about the last communique he sent you?"

She frowns, not sure what I'm talking about. And then realization hits. "No. I didn't watch it. I didn't want to hear another lecture."

"I'm not always right either. In fact, most of the time, I don't know what to do." I shrug. "But you suck it up because it's part of the job."

"But you always seem to know what to do."

"That's probably why I'm in charge. I'm good at guessing." I motion toward the ship. "So let's go find out what's inside."

I don't mention the memory gaps. I don't want to show how worried I am. What if she's right and there's some lasting condition because of what Sarka did on Europa? It's hard for me to say because I never knew her before then. So we'll have to wait. I'll have Dr. Prashad examine her when we get back to the ship. If we get back.

As soon as we enter, the lights switch on. Much of the ship is motion activated. I decide to start us from the bottom of the ship and work our way up. The first few decks are cargo holds, still packed with everything they'd need for the flight. It isn't until we make it to the fifth deck that we encounter anything of interest. And it's possibly the most interesting thing I've ever seen.

"Are they alive?" Ash asks.

We're standing in what must be their common space. But it's tiny as all get out. Portholes the size of our heads puncture the walls. Dust motes dance in the light streaming in.

In the middle of the round, open space are two coffin-like pods. They are hooked up to several machines. Inside the pods are two humanoids, one male and one female. Most likely they are part of the crew of the ship. They're naked with several tubes attached at key locations in their necks, chests, and thighs.

I check the readout. There are no vital signs. "Long dead." The only thing the pods are doing is keeping the bodies from decomposing. In fact, half the energy of the craft is being used to keep these pods active. If we're going to launch this ship, we'll have to redirect that energy to the engines and guidance systems.

There's only two of them, but the Mars mission ship had a crew compliment of five. Are the others on other decks?

"The big question is why are they here at all?"

Ash leans over one of the pods and peers inside. "It's kind of eerie. They look like they're taking a nap."

"They're well preserved for two hundred years. Centuries ago humans used to mummify their dead. Like that political leader they had on display for centuries. Before they bombed his mausoleum to pieces."

"It's so strange, creating a place to go visit your dead."

"They used to bury their dead in giant parks. There were markers to tell who was where. I imagine people used to get comfort, thinking their loved ones were still hanging around, enjoying all the trees and flowers."

Ash, always the pragmatist, makes a face. "What a waste of space."

"Let's finish checking the rest of the ship. We might find some answers to all these questions," I say.

But we don't find any answers. Twenty minutes later, we reach the bridge and find it empty like the rest of the decks. It's very—I don't want to say primitive—but it's the first word that pops into mind. A second later, I amend it to sparse.

Because the ship tapers, the bridge, which is at the tip, only has space for three seats. They're bunched together near a large screen below an impressive console. Each chair has an elaborate seat belt harness akin to an old-fashioned parachute. It gives you an idea of how fast the ship has to go to reach orbit.

I take a seat in the pilot position. There are about a million buttons and switches lining the console in front of me. They're color coordinated. A third are blue, another third red, and the rest are black. Only one is green. Unfortunately, we can't use the ship to communicate with the *Persephone* because the technologies are incompatible.

"Are we going to be able to fly this thing?" Ash lowers herself into the copilot seat.

"There isn't much to it. Seal the ship and hit launch." It sounds a lot more simple than it is, but the later Mars missions were almost all automated. There's no doubt the astronauts of that era could calculate liftoff. But it was much safer having the computer do all the complicated calculations. We don't have that same knowledge, but luckily we don't need it. This ship was built long before access codes, but well after space suits.

"It's a bit like time traveling." Ash's got that big grin on her face. Part of me is happy to see her sense of adventure is back, but another part—the part that knows better—is a little terrified.

"It definitely makes you appreciate what you have." You could fit eight of these on *Persephone*'s bridge. It would've become cramped real fast during the three month trip to Mars.

"It would've been fun. I mean, you'd definitely have to be more choosy about who your flight mates are." Ash starts opening compartments and rummaging around. A minute later, she pulls a large plastic booklet from underneath her seat. "Well, the good news is, I found a flight manual."

"What's the bad news?"

"We're going to have to learn how to fly this thing." She flips through several of the thick pages. "Shouldn't take more than a day or two."

Instead of excitement, I'm homesick for my own bridge. A bridge that's currently commanded by a thief. And it's time we took it back.

In the end, it only takes us a day and a half. Ash is a quick study. The short prep time works in our favor for several reasons. We lost all our food and rations during our escape from the avians. Any food on this ship has rotted ten times over. But I'm most worried that whoever put the crew in pods will come back and catch us here.

While Ash studies the manual, I figure out how to dismantle the shield. We don't want to take any chances of it interfering with liftoff. It takes half a day, but I manage to figure out how to shut it off. It uses the flow of the river as a power source. All I have to do is divert the water. I take a broken piece of the inner hull of the ship and jam it into the stream like a dam, stopping the water from reaching the mechanism. In less than an hour, the shield goes down. When it does, the real countdown begins. With our protection gone, anything can wander in. It's not only the avians we have to worry about.

I spend an entire afternoon checking the structural integrity of the exterior of the ship. In two hundred years, not much has degraded. Plastic is hard to breakdown. The shield helped as well, keeping the elements from degrading the metal. To say I'm surprised is an understatement. I'm astonished we even found the ship, that it's also still functional, doubly so.

"This might seem like a silly question." Ash asks from her spot in the copilot seat as we prepare for takeoff. "But if we don't have any food, how are we going to survive once we're up there?" Ash points in the vague direction of the sky. And she's right. Once we leave here, we're leaving behind stability. There are many dangers on this planet, but they're survivable. Our deaths aren't as inevitable as they are if we launch ourselves, without resources, into the unknown. But I don't plan on us being in the unknown for long.

"I have a backup plan. Something I set up with Hartley a while ago."

While there's no way I could've guessed Sarka would strand us on this planet, I knew he would try to take over the ship. I had Hartley create backdoor access codes so he could stall the ship from leaving the planet. All we have to do is get this ship into orbit, attach ourselves to the *Persephone* when it passes us, and use those same backdoor access codes to gain access through a hatch.

Her face after hearing my plan is a mixture of incredulity and awe. "I don't know whether to be proud that my crazy ideas are rubbing off on you or worried. That is the most bat-shit crazy thing I have ever heard."

"It'll work." I turn my back to her, hiding my face, hiding my worry. "Are we ready to go?"

"Good to go."

"Then prepare us for takeoff." As I say this, my stomach climbs into my throat and hangs on with a death grip, preparing for the worst.

In all honesty, I'm not too sure of the plan either. But I don't want Ash to know that. I've discovered over the years that pretending confidence sometimes helps. I've given this whole plan a fifty-fifty chance of working. That's pretty shitty odds. But Ash tends to come with a thirty percent win rate, so that ups our odds to eighty. Not too shabby.

We debated what to do with the two pods. We only ever found those two and no evidence of there being more. I'm not sure what happened to the three other crew members. Maybe they died on arrival, or before the ship even landed. In the end, we decided to bring them with us. There was no way for the two of us to move the pods off the ship. And the idea of a burial was not even an option. I didn't want to leave them behind on this alien planet. I can decide what to do once we reach orbit. So, in essence, there will be four humans leaving this planet. I couldn't help but think about Yakovich. There wasn't a safe way to go retrieve her body before launching the *Roebuck*. But we'll come back for her. I made a promise.

As we buckle ourselves in the snap from our belts is loud. It echoes in the stillness of the cabin. I look down at my station. There's a sticker on the edge of my arm rest. It's a gray alien giving me the finger. I wrap my hand around it as Ash presses the green button. The engines start, drowning out all other sounds with the weight of four engines igniting.

It's go time.

Chapter Thirty

We break through the clouds fast. Our ascent is so quick it's easy to miss the details. The flash of the sun, the blur of the pinkish clouds as we blast toward the dark blue stratosphere.

I grip the arm rests of my chair. Ash grabs her knees. She presses them together as if the tighter she keeps herself the less likely our speed will rip her apart.

The rattle of the ship tells me not only is this possible, but pretty damn likely.

A red warning light flashes. Then, in comedic slow motion, the entire board flips red, like a surge of old-fashioned dominos. One goes, so the others have no choice but to follow.

I find myself thinking of choices. How one action leads to another. One simple decision creates a cascade effect, like those dominos. I'm trying to decide what the catalyst was that led me here. Was it choosing to stay in that cave? If we hadn't, we would never have found the NASA satchel and gone looking for the ship. But it goes further than that. It goes back to landing on this planet in the first place. If I'd played it cautious and reported back to the *Posterus* instead of landing, we wouldn't be here now. But not landing on this planet is a little like asking a flower not to bloom, a supernova not to explode, and your lungs not to breathe. We wouldn't be explorers if we hadn't landed.

But the real reason we're here right now isn't because we landed in the first place. We're here because of Sarka. If we hadn't brought him along, if I'd stood up to the captain on the *Posterus* and left him behind, we wouldn't be in this mess. In the end, I proved myself right. I can't trust my father. There was a glimmer of hope that he'd changed. But he's like that scorpion in the parable. He can't help himself. It's in his nature.

One moment of weakness, one capitulation has led me to this ship and this crazy idea. That one choice is the reason I'm hurtling through a planet's atmosphere at 30,000 kilometers per hour toward probable death.

The way life amplifies your regrets is savage.

A pure white smoke fills the cockpit now. It hovers against the console like a wall of cloud. With no wind, no gravity, it has no where to go. If there is artificial gravity on these things, we haven't figured out how to turn it on. It's just as well. I don't plan on us being here for long.

"Fuck, yeah," Ash screams as we reach escape velocity, break free, and push through the exosphere.

I grip the armrest tighter. "Fuck."

And then, as quick as it began, it's over.

As instructed, Ash brings us into a high orbit. From above, the planet looks so lush and green. With the atmosphere softening the edges, it gives it a dreamy appearance. It's much more serene than the reality of the place.

The best thing about these Mars ships is they're built to survive. They're sturdy stock, like the Neanderthals of the Homo genus, it takes a hell of a lot to break them. Unfortunately, like that ancient species, they don't have the brain capacity of the newer models. We have basic navigation, but not much else. Once we reach orbit, we'll be without power. We'll be at the mercy of the planet's gravitational pull. If all works out as planned, the ship will settle into a natural orbit. We can see where we're going and where we've been. We have proximity sensors—so the ship will warn us if we're about to crash into something and vice versa.

"What's that noise?" Ash asks. A blaring fills the cabin, warning us of something.

I wave some of the smoke out of the way. It floats to the edges of the cockpit.

"It's a proximity warning. From what I can tell, the *Persephone* is coming up behind us." I flip through several more screens until I find the exact distance. "It's about thirty kilometers away. Can you slow us down and match speed?"

"I can try. If I vent atmosphere from our forward compartment, that will push us back. Should slow us down enough to exit the ship. The rest is up to chance."

Ten minutes later, Ash and I are waiting in the aft compartment. We're ready to deploy the *Roebuck*'s emergency chute. All early shuttles and spacecrafts had them. The early shuttles had drag chutes to help slow them down and reduce the stress on breaks and tires. They changed the design of the ships for the Mars missions because they needed to land on surfaces that were uneven, so they used chutes to both turn and slow down the spacecraft.

Today, we're going to use it for something it was never meant for. A grappling hook. If we time it right, we'll hook one of the aft sails of the *Persephone* and hitch a ride. Once we're confident our tether won't snap and send us whirling into space, we'll go for a little walk.

A piercing alarm sounds next to my head. Ash slams her fist onto the panel, shutting it off. The silence buzzes. We have two minutes to deploy the chute before the *Persephone* passes us by and we miss our opportunity. Miss this window and we'll be stuck out here forever. Which on the plus side—with our lack of resources—won't be very long.

I adjust the gloves of my space suit. These earlier models are much bulkier than I'm used to. Not that I have much call to go for space walks. I look over at Ash, she has this shit-eating grin on her face. Like this is something she's always wanted to try and now's her chance. It looks like the suit is consuming her. It's several sizes too big for her. There were only two on board and she insisted I have the smaller of the two. The stiff material creates an awkward shell around her, unlike her regular suit which molds to her body.

I check our countdown. One minute left. In the distance, a small speck breaks from the mass of stars dotting the horizon. As she moves closer, I begin to see the details of the *Persephone*.

She's a beautiful ship. Sleek, if not modern. The matter sails bulge, obscuring the back of the ship from view. But they don't deter from the trim shape.

We've slowed as much as we can. Now it's up to the strength of the chute cables. I'm confident they'll hold. Thirty seconds to go.

Ash nudges my arm. "I want you to know, if we don't make it—"

"We'll make it."

"Yeah, but just in case." Her eyes are wide and earnest. "I wanted to tell you how much…" She turns away for a second to gaze at the view spread before us. "I enjoyed serving under you." There's so much more left unsaid. But we don't have time. I nod as the last alarm blasts through the small exit bay.

The *Persephone* looms large and intimidating. It's so close it looks like it's going to crash into us.

Ash punches the release button on her left and the chute deploys. At this range the chute won't have time to open. Instead it'll get tangled with the matter sail on the *Persephone*'s aft compartment. We hope.

There's twenty seconds of silence as we hold our breath and watch the silver canister arc through space. It pings the hull and bounces off. My heart plummets. And then, as if the impact was too much for the canister, it explodes and a long navy chute deploys. It catches a corner of the sail, entangling itself.

Before we have time to celebrate, the *Roebuck* lurches and spins to port as the *Persephone*'s momentum takes over and drags us forward. I fall to my knees with a hard thud and slide toward the aft portal, which is wide open. I try to grab on to one of the rails, but the bulky suit is clumsy to maneuver. I start to panic as the edge gets closer. These suits don't have built in propulsion. If I fall out of the ship, I'll be flung into space and left to drift until I run out of oxygen.

I must look like a mad woman as I scramble for something—anything—to grab hold of. I'm breathing too fast for my carbon monoxide filter and the glass on my helmet fogs up.

"Calm down." In one fluid movement, Ash grabs my arm and snaps us on to the cable chute with a large carabiner. It's all very slick. I'm still recovering when she clips my waist lead on to the cable. At the same time as all that, she manages to disengage the *Roebuck* from it's tether.

"How did you do that?" I ask.

"I set a timer for disconnect."

"What if we hadn't left the ship yet?"

"We had a tiny window to leave. God, you're lucky, because that really was bat-shit crazy." Her grin is so large her lips have almost disappeared. And coming from Ash, it's a compliment. But as I stare up at the *Persephone*, which is now only several hundred meters above us, I question my sanity. Would it have been so bad to live out the rest of our lives on that planet? We had food, water, shelter, not safety, but there's no such thing as perfect.

Or maybe there is. Seeing the *Persephone* again, I realize this is the only place that has ever felt like home to me. I've spent my whole life running to somewhere. I was always escaping. The station, the farm, lower ranks, bad assignments, none of them gave me comfort. Everything I've ever done has led me here. It's no wonder I couldn't leave it behind. There is no force that would allow me to let someone take that feeling of contentment and safety from me. There is no substitute for it. Not even Ash. As much as I love her, in the end, it would've only been a makeshift home if we'd stayed on the planet. I belong in space.

This is unreal. I've never felt so small in my life. Next to the planet, we're dwarfed. It's like we've fallen into a glass of black liquid with tiny, far off flecks of light.

We make our way, hand over hand up the cable. It's long and arduous, and I'm sweating by the time we're even halfway. A sensor on Ash's air tank flashes. I tap her on the back and she stops.

"What is it?" she asks.

I pull myself closer. Her oxygen tank is a little less than half full. They were full when we left, but these aren't the same as the tanks we're used to. These use gas oxygen, while ours use liquid oxygen. It's lighter and can hold eight hundred times more than the gas. We're going to run out of oxygen before we reach the ship.

"We're using too much oxygen. We need to slow down."

Ash frowns. Her brow furrow is almost hidden behind the thick glass of her helmet.

"I know it doesn't make sense, but the more we exert ourselves, the more oxygen we use. If we keep our pace nice and slow, then we may make it."

Ash looks behind her at the *Persephone*. We still have a couple hundred meters to go. Even from this distance, the ship appears giant. The sightline down the length of the cable makes it seem far.

"I've got a better idea." She wraps the cable around her wrist twice and grabs my arm. "Hold on." Almost as an afterthought, she turns back to me and says, "Don't worry, this won't damage the ship."

Shit. What the hell is she up to?

Ash oscillates the cable up and down in long, fluid movements. The strong, inch-thick line, begins to move. It goes slow at first, then picks up momentum, until it's swinging in front of us. I hold Ash tight and watch as the true brilliance of her mind unfolds in front of me.

The matter sails are intricate and complicated, therefore expensive. Because of this there are many safety features built in to protect them. One of which is that, at the slightest provocation, the sails will retract.

It only takes a few good swishes for the sails to feel the movement and close in on themselves. As an added bonus, the cable begins to wind its way around the sail frame, pulling us toward the ship.

"You're brilliant."

And she knows it too. Her face is calm and smug, almost like she'd planned this from the start.

Within minutes we're an arm's length from the ship and only a meter from the nearest hatch. I use my backdoor access codes and the hatch opens.

As we stand in the decompression bay, the silence of the vacuum still around us, I can't help but feel we've entered the belly of the beast.

CHAPTER THIRTY-ONE

After we reestablish pressure, I remove my helmet and suck in air. It tastes beautiful.

"We don't have much time. I'm sure Sarka's had Hartley set up all sorts of alerts for anything unusual." Ash dumps her helmet on the floor and rips off her gloves, tossing them aside. "So what's the game plan now?" Her hair is sweaty and wild.

"We get to engineering. When I had Hartley set up those backdoor access codes, I had him set it up so that if my command codes were ever replaced, I could input a secondary set and they would nullify the replacement set. The trouble is, I can only input those secondary codes from a secure location."

"So the bridge—"

"Which would be crazy," I say.

"Or engineering—"

"Which is bat-shit crazy. There's a good chance Sarka has posted people there to make sure Hartley doesn't make trouble."

"Do you think we'll have a problem?" she asks.

As much as I'd like to believe my crew is loyal only to me, I know there will be a few who may see an opportunity. Dissenters are in every bunch. They'll have a grudge about something. Either the way I handled the Ash situation or something earlier. It could've been brewing for months. Perhaps they don't like the idea of leaving this planet behind, like Fossick. And then along comes a charismatic leader who can spot the signs. Sarka's good at rooting them out. It's his job, finding the wayward and organizing them. And when you add the followers, his numbers grow.

"No. But anything can happen."

"But he's a—" She doesn't actually say it, but her face goes through the thought process. He's a Burr. Which means his genetics are part of mine.

That's the tricky thing about Burrs. They're not only technically enhanced, scientists also manipulated their genetic structure. Burrs are faster, stronger, and more intelligent than the average person. If genetic manipulation wasn't outlawed, I imagine things would've been very different. Instead of genetic enhancements making you a pariah, it would've been a sign of affluence.

And then Ash reaches the question I've been waiting for her to arrive at since she found out I was Sarka's child. What genetic abnormalities has he passed onto me?

"It's fine," I say.

"Jordan."

"Let's go."

We don't have the time to get into this right now. It's a heavy discussion at the best of times. But I'm glad it's only Ash who knows. She may have her prejudices, but she wouldn't tell anyone. If the Union knew who my father was, I wouldn't have this command. I guess it doesn't matter now, we'll likely never see the Union again. But I'd hate to see what would happen if my crew found out. I know Sarka won't hesitate to tell them if it will benefit him.

We take the back route to engineering, down rarely used corridors. I don't want to bump into any crew and have to explain. Sarka must have told everyone that something bad happened. It's likely he's assumed command. There wouldn't be too many people willing to challenge him. We come across only one crew member. A lone aviator with his head in a tablet. I pull Ash into a cargo hold and wait for him to pass.

My heart is going triple time. It feels wrong sneaking around my own ship. This isn't the way I want to reclaim it, skulking around like I'm the thief.

Outside engineering, I pull Ash aside. We need a better plan. What if Sarka's planned for this? I know Ash and Hartley are friends, but he's smart. He may not value their friendship as highly as he regards his life.

She shakes her head. "I've learned in the short time I've known him that it's not a good idea to underestimate him. Let him surprise you, Captain."

We enter engineering. Hartley and his men hunch over one of the consoles on the far end. Hartley's explaining something. Something's gone wrong and he's not happy.

One of the engineers looks at us and drops a spanner on the ground. It clangs and echoes through the great expanse of the room. The sound pings back and forth between giant server towers.

Hartley stops mid-rant and looks up too. His jaw drops and it takes him a second before he finds his voice. "Captain. Ash." His mouth closes and opens a few times before he asks, "How?"

I wave him off and sprint forward. We don't have much time.

"I need access to a secure computer terminal." I wait for anyone to challenge me, but it doesn't happen. Instead, everyone scurries around making things happen.

"What's the plan, Captain?" Hartley asks, pointing me toward a terminal off to the side. Several eyes swivel my way with curiosity.

"Yes, Captain, what's the plan?" A deep, low voice asks.

I look and find Sarka in the doorway with a large sonic rifle pointed at us. I'm assuming it's set for a wide dispersal. Ash steps forward, angling herself in front of me. Not that it's going to do much.

"I'm curious." Sarka takes a step forward. "How were you planning to take back the ship? I have all the command codes now. And as for your ship," he spreads his arms. "Let's say I've made some improvements. A few added securities in case somehow you managed to reenact *The Great Escape*." He folds his arms across his chest, which emphases his oversized muscles. He means bombs. He's planted bombs on my ship. "So what was it? Plan a siege? Or were you planning some more sabotage?" He points at Hartley. "I suspected he staged most of our mechanical failures. Hartley assures me this ship is unable to go faster than a snail. But if the chain of command were to change, I suspect that might also change with it." He raises his eyebrows at Hartley, who doesn't look contrite in the least.

I told Hartley to keep the ship in orbit as long as possible, to sabotage it if needed. I knew from the beginning Sarka would find a way to take this ship. The last thing I wanted was to unleash him on this galaxy. Even if Sarka convinced the crew I was dead, it's nice to see my orders outlast death.

I know my father. He's been playing the long game since he got on board. He's always planning till the wake. I must have heard it a million times growing up. Plan until your wake. Always plan ahead, then plan some more. He's thought all this through with angles we haven't even considered. At least up until this point, I've been able to keep up. Sarka's been playing nice since he arrived, if not making friends, at least not creating enemies. He could've convinced them to let him help them back to the *Posterus*. And to show me how right I am, the door to engineering slides open and Yakovich walks in. The same Yakovich we left for dead in the middle of a jungle.

"Yakovich." Ash looks as surprised as I feel. "We thought you were dead."

"There's a lot of that going around." She nods in our direction, but otherwise, her face is expressionless. She plants herself between Sarka and the door. For the first time, I'm not sure whose side she's on. It's possible he's been talking her up since I posted her at his door. "Death does happen to be a side effect of leaving someone behind in a dangerous jungle."

"That's not what happened." Ash steps forward, her hands curled tight into fists.

I pull her back. This is exactly what he's hoping for, anger, confrontation, and when we're distracted, he'll make his next move. Ash looks back at me, then at my hand wrapped around her wrist. Every emotion flashes across her face, surprise, resentment, hurt, frustration.

Yakovich looks calm as always.

"I found her abandoned in the woods and helped her back to the ship before returning to rescue the rest of the crew with reinforcements," Sarka says.

"More like you were following us. You saw an opportunity to bribe your way back onto the ship and gain access to weapons." Ash is closer to the truth than anyone here realizes.

Sarka's eyes gleam. This is his moment. "Or it's possible that I'm a better captain than some people." He's almost crowing as he says it. "I'd never leave one of my defenseless crew behind to be dinner for some overgrown moss monster."

"You goddamned son of a bitch." Ash launches herself at him and in that moment, chaos erupts. I try to pull her back, but the engineers push me aside as they rush the door. Yakovich lunges for Hartley, curling her arm around his neck and bringing him to the floor. She whispers something in his ear and before I can wonder what it is, a beefy arm encircles my throat. I feel a sharp sting on the side of my neck.

"That will be enough of that."

There is silence as everyone turns toward us.

Sarka digs the knife in deeper. He smells like sweat and pears. The subtle fruit aroma reminds me of my mother. It was her favorite soap.

"You wouldn't." Ash picks up Sarka's discarded gun. Her fingers squeeze the handle. There's a quiet shuffle as everyone lines up along an invisible line, flanking each side of Ash.

"It would surprise you, Alison, what I'd do for freedom." He takes a moment, waiting for everyone's attention. I close my eyes, because I know what's coming next. "Even kill my own daughter." And then, to make sure we're all on the same page, he adds, "And she'd do the same. Wouldn't you, Jordan?"

As he planned, there's shocked silence. He's been waiting to drop that bomb since he came on board. Keeping it safe until it would do the most damage.

Ash steps toward us, gun raised, eyes pinned on Sarka.

Sarka chuckles. "Looks like a good time to be moving on." His grip tightens around my neck. It's becoming hard to breathe, and I realize he's trying to pull me back through the door.

I have two options. Dig in here, and see what happens. More than likely someone's going to get hurt. Or I can let him lead me away where I'm the only one who'll get hurt. But where could he be planning to go? I decide on the latter.

The last look on Ash's face as I disappear through the exit is total panic. If I know her, it's only a momentary setback until she comes up with her next crazy plan to rescue me. I hope it doesn't come to that.

Once we're a good twenty meters outside of engineering, Sarka stops to pull my arms into restraints.

"In all honesty, Jordan, I'm impressed. I was completely shocked to see you back here. I don't know how you did it, but that is some serious ingenuity right there."

"Don't."

"What? No, I'm serious. You should be proud of yourself. You are proving to be one hell of an adversary. Of course, I'll stop right here to take some of the credit. I am after all, the one who got you started on escaping." He tightens the cuffs. They cut into my wrists.

"What's that supposed to mean? Is this where you reenact the good father role? Tell me again how my dead mother would feel if she could see me now? Then drug me, tie me up, and leave me for dead? Or better yet, tell me how I look just like her."

"You do, you know." When I don't say anything he continues. "When I first saw you on the bridge, I thought it was her at first. It was a weird flashback moment. You looked like she did when I first saw her."

"Before you abducted her."

"I gave your mother a choice and she chose me. Was it always easy? No, but she loved me."

I turn now and glare. "Don't for a second pretend you knew her. You knew her as a woman playacting."

"I knew her better than you. You only knew her as a child knows a parent." There's a sincerity in his voice I've never heard before. "It's a shame you didn't get to know her as a woman."

"Why? Because you think that would change my opinion of her? You can pretend she loved you all you want, but we both know that's a lie." He's not going to pull me into this fantasy world. He can talk all he wants, but it won't change the facts.

"If that's what you need to believe, I'll respect that. But you don't think it strange that all our ships were out on patrol at the same time? Haven't you ever questioned how easy your escape was?"

"You're saying you knew?"

"I'm saying I helped plan it."

I shake my head. "Just like that? You let us go?" It's like watching a globe that's flipped on its axis. My whole world upends and I'm left watching trying to make sense of an inverted picture. "I don't believe you."

"The plan was to rendezvous with her once she'd gotten you to Delta. But the Union attacked your ship and I heard you'd both died. Is she really dead?" The way he asks leaves no doubt in my mind that he loved her. But I'm not convinced that she loved him back.

"We escaped in a pod. Mom took something that killed her, to conserve oxygen for me." Is that what happened? Or is it more complicated than that? Did she plan it with him with no intention of ever going back?

He pulls me along the corridor. "You still don't believe me do you?"

"No, I don't. Why would you help us? It doesn't make any sense."

"Because I knew if you were to have any sort of life, you'd need to do it on the Belt. Otherwise, you'd end up yoked to some slag and buried under a pile of brats. And you're better than that." He brushes his hand along the wall. "You made it here all on your own. Captain of your own ship."

"Such a pretty picture. Why would you even care what happened to me?"

He tugs me into a chute and points down the ladder with his knife. "I'll go first, you'll follow. No funny stuff or I cut your Achilles, yeah?" He raises his eyebrows, waiting for confirmation from me. I nod.

"Why would you care?" I ask again.

He steps on to the first rung and lowers himself until his head is poking out of the shaft. "Best not to try for two escapes in one day. I've still got my insurance policies stashed around the ship." He motions for me to step on to the ladder, which I do. It's a little awkward at first with my hands restrained in front. But eventually I find a way to climb without falling.

"I care because you're blood." He lowers himself one rung at a time. "And no matter what happens in this galaxy or the last, that still counts. Always will." His voice echoes through the chute. For the first time in my life, I wonder if he's telling the truth. Did Mom and he plan our escape? Would it matter? Would it change anything? He doesn't care about me now, or he wouldn't be doing this.

He motions to stop on deck two. The only things on this deck are the weapons locker and the escape pods. My blood drains, leaving my body cold and numb. I know what he's planning to do. I try to rush back up the ladder, but he seizes my ankle and yanks me down. I fall in a heap at his feet.

"Don't look so scared. We'll be fine. I have it all planned out."

Before I have time to argue, he pulls me to my feet and thrusts me forward. He punches a control panel with the fist holding the knife. It scrapes the wall, leaving a fine line. The door to an escape pod rushes open and I panic. The last time I was in one of these didn't end well, with Ash shooting off into the unknown. Is this what she felt? This gnawing, gut-wrenching fear? There is no way we can survive this. These pods are not meant to land on surfaces. There's no heat shield. The atmosphere would burn us up in an instant. That must be what he's planning because there aren't any ships around to rescue us. I try to tell him this, but he puts the knife to his lips and makes a shushing sound. He pulls me over to the command chair and straps me in. Without any hesitation, he initiates launch.

"This isn't going to work. We'll never make it to the surface," I say.

But instead of answering, he hums to himself as he buckles himself into the passenger seat. The door shuts with a loud whoosh and we wait in silence. And it's that moment I realize my father is a lunatic. He knows we're not going to survive. And he doesn't care. I pull at the restraints, but they're too tight. A thin line of blood drips down my wrist.

And without any more preamble, we launch, shooting straight into a stomach dropping spin. From the window I see the *Persephone*, then space. My ship, then space. Behind the *Persephone,* the planet orbits the sun. And then it all winks out of existence. Everything. The *Persephone*, the planet, they're all gone. As we spin, all I can see is stars. Far away suns with their own orbiting spheres. Beside me Sarka cackles like he arranged for this to happen. As if everything I've ever cared for were a conjurer's trick hidden under a big black cape.

Only with this trick, it's gone forever.

About the Author

CJ Birch is a video editor and digital artist based in Toronto. When not lost in a good book or working (because, you know, bills) CJ can be found writing or drinking serious coffee, or doing both at the same time. To learn more about serious coffee visit www.cjbirchwrites.com

Books Available from Bold Strokes Books

Captive by Donna K. Ford. To escape a human trafficking ring, Greyson Cooper and Olivia Danner become players in a game of deceit and violence. Will their love stand a chance? (978-1-63555-215-7)

Crossing the Line by CF Frizzell. The Mob discovers a nemesis within its ranks, and in the ultimate retaliation, draws Stick McLaughlin from anonymity by threatening everything she holds dear. (978-1-63555-161-7)

Love's Verdict by Carsen Taite. Attorneys Landon Holt and Carly Pachett want the exact same thing: the only open partnership spot at their prestigious criminal defense firm. But will they compromise their careers for love? (978-1-63555-042-9)

Precipice of Doubt by Mardi Alexander & Laurie Eichler. Can Cole Jameson resist her attraction to her boss, veterinarian Jodi Bowman, or will she risk a workplace romance and her heart? (978-1-63555-128-0)

Savage Horizons by CJ Birch. Captain Jordan Kellow's feelings for Lt. Ali Ash have her past and future colliding, setting in motion a series of events that strands her crew in an unknown galaxy thousands of light years from home. (978-1-63555-250-8)

Secrets of the Last Castle by A. Rose Mathieu. When Elizabeth Campbell represents a young man accused of murdering an elderly woman, her investigation leads to an abandoned plantation that reveals many dark Southern secrets. (978-1-63555-240-9)

Take Your Time by VK Powell. A neurotic parrot brings police officer Grace Booker and temporary veterinarian Dr. Dani Wingate together in the tiny town of Pine Cone, but their unexpected attraction keeps the sparks flying. (978-1-63555-130-3)

The Last Seduction by Ronica Black. When you allow true love to elude you once and you desperately regret it, are you brave enough to grab it when it comes around again? (978-1-63555-211-9)

The Shape of You by Georgia Beers. Rebecca McCall doesn't play it safe, but when sexy Spencer Thompson joins her workout class, their non-stop sparing forces her to face her ultimate challenge—a chance at love. (978-1-63555-217-1)

Exposed by MJ Williamz. The closet is no place to live if you want to find true love. (978-1-62639-989-1)

Force of Fire: Toujours a Vous by Ali Vali. Immortals Kendal and Piper welcome their new child and celebrate the defeat of an old enemy, but another ancient evil is about to awaken deep in the jungles of Costa Rica. (978-1-63555-047-4)

Holding Their Place by Kelly A. Wacker. Together Dr. Helen Connery and ambulance driver Julia March discover that goodness, love, and passion can be found in the most unlikely and even dangerous places during WWI. (978-1-63555-338-3)

Landing Zone by Erin Dutton. Can a career veteran finally discover a love stronger than even her pride? (978-1-63555-199-0)

Love at Last Call by M. Ullrich. Is balancing business, friendship, and love more than any willing woman can handle? (978-1-63555-197-6)

Pleasure Cruise by Yolanda Wallace. Spencer Collins and Amy Donovan have few things in common, but a Caribbean cruise offers both women an unexpected chance to face one of their greatest fears: falling in love. (978-1-63555-219-5)

Running Off Radar by MB Austin. Maji's plans to win Rose back are interrupted when work intrudes and duty calls her to help a SEAL team stop a Russian mobster from harvesting gold from the bottom of Sitka Sound. (978-1-63555-152-5)

Shadow of the Phoenix by Rebecca Harwell. In the final battle for the fate of Storm's Quarry, even Nadya's and Shay's powers may not be enough. (978-1-63555-181-5)

Take a Chance by D. Jackson Leigh. There's hardly a woman within fifty miles of Pine Cone that veterinarian Trip Beaumont can't charm, except for the irritating new cop, Jamie Grant, who keeps leaving parking tickets on her truck. (978-1-63555-118-1)

The Outcasts by Alexa Black. Spacebus driver Sue Jones is running from her past. When she crash-lands on a faraway world, the Outcast Kara might be her chance for redemption. (978-1-63555-242-3)

Alias by Cari Hunter. A car crash leaves a woman with no memory and no identity. Together with Detective Bronwen Pryce, she fights to uncover a truth that might just kill them both. (978-1-63555-221-8)

Death in Time by Robyn Nyx. Working in the past is hell on your future. (978-1-63555-053-5)

Hers to Protect by Nicole Disney. High school sweethearts Kaia and Adrienne will have to see past their differences and survive the vengeance of a brutal gang if they want to be together. (978-1-63555-229-4)

Of Echoes Born by 'Nathan Burgoine. A collection of queer fantasy short stories set in Canada from Lambda Literary Award finalist 'Nathan Burgoine. (978-1-63555-096-2)

Perfect Little Worlds by Clifford Mae Henderson. Lucy can't hold the secret any longer. Twenty-six years ago, her sister did the unthinkable. (978-1-63555-164-8)

Room Service by Fiona Riley. Interior designer Olivia likes stability, but when work brings footloose Savannah into her world and into a new city every month, Olivia must decide if what makes her comfortable is what makes her happy. (978-1-63555-120-4)

Sparks Like Ours by Melissa Brayden. Professional surfers Gia Malone and Elle Britton can't deny their chemistry on and off the beach. But only one can win… (978-1-63555-016-0)

Take My Hand by Missouri Vaun. River Hemsworth arrives in Georgia intent on escaping quickly, but when she crashes her Mercedes into the Clip 'n Curl, sexy Clay Cahill ends up rescuing more than her car. (978-1-63555-104-4)

The Last Time I Saw Her by Kathleen Knowles. Lane Hudson only has twelve days to win back Alison's heart. That is if she can gather the courage to try. (978-1-63555-067-2)

Wayworn Lovers by Gun Brooke. Will agoraphobic composer Giselle Bonnaire and Tierney Edwards, a wandering soul who can't remain in one place for long, trust in the passionate love destiny hands them? (978-1-62639-995-2)

Breakthrough by Kris Bryant. Falling for a sexy ranger is one thing, but is the possibility of love worth giving up the career Kennedy Wells has always dreamed of? (978-1-63555-179-2)

Certain Requirements by Elinor Zimmerman. Phoenix has always kept her love of kinky submission strictly behind the bedroom door and inside the bounds of romantic relationships, until she meets Kris Andersen. (978-1-63555-195-2)

Dark Euphoria by Ronica Black. When a high-profile case drops in Detective Maria Diaz's lap, she forges ahead only to discover this case, and her main suspect, aren't like any other. (978-1-63555-141-9)

Fore Play by Julie Cannon. Executive Leigh Marshall falls hard for Peyton Broader, her golf pro...and an ex-con. Will she risk sabotaging her career for love? (978-1-63555-102-0)

Love Came Calling by CA Popovich. Can a romantic looking for a long-term, committed relationship and a jaded cynic too busy for love conquer life's struggles and find their way to what matters most? (978-1-63555-205-8)

Outside the Law by Carsen Taite. Former sweethearts Tanner Cohen and Sydney Braswell must work together on a federal task force to see justice served, but will they choose to embrace their second chance at love? (978-1-63555-039-9)

The Princess Deception by Nell Stark. When journalist Missy Duke realizes Prince Sebastian is really his twin sister Viola in disguise, she plays along, but when sparks flare between them, will the double deception doom their fairy-tale romance? (978-1-62639-979-2)

The Smell of Rain by Cameron MacElvee. Reyha Arslan, a wise and elegant woman with a tragic past, shows Chrys that there's still beauty to embrace and reason to hope despite the world's cruelty. (978-1-63555-166-2)

The Talebearer by Sheri Lewis Wohl. Liz's visions show her the faces of the lost and the killers who took their lives. As one by one, the murdered are found, a stranger works to stop Liz before the serial killer is brought to justice. (978-1-635550-126-6)

White Wings Weeping by Lesley Davis. The world is full of discord and hatred, but how much of it is just human nature when an evil with sinister intent is invading people's hearts? (978-1-63555-191-4)

A Call Away by KC Richardson. Can a businesswoman from a big city find the answers she's looking for, and possibly love, on a small-town farm? (978-1-63555-025-2)

Berlin Hungers by Justine Saracen. Can the love between an RAF woman and the wife of a Luftwaffe pilot, former enemies, survive in besieged Berlin during the aftermath of World War II? (978-1-63555-116-7)

Blend by Georgia Beers. Lindsay and Piper are like night and day. Working together won't be easy, but not falling in love might prove the hardest job of all. (978-1-63555-189-1)

Hunger for You by Jenny Frame. Principe of an ancient vampire clan Byron Debrek must save her one true love from falling into the hands of her enemies and into the middle of a vampire war. (978-1-63555-168-6)

Mercy by Michelle Larkin. FBI Special Agent Mercy Parker and psychic ex-profiler Piper Vasey learn to love again as they race to stop a man with supernatural gifts who's bent on annihilating humankind. (978-1-63555-202-7)

Pride and Porters by Charlotte Greene. Will pride and prejudice prevent these modern-day lovers from living happily ever after? (978-1-63555-158-7)

Rocks and Stars by Sam Ledel. Kyle's struggle to own who she is and what she really wants may end up landing her on the bench and without the woman of her dreams. (978-1-63555-156-3)

The Boss of Her: Office Romance Novellas by Julie Cannon, Aurora Rey, and M. Ullrich. Going to work never felt so good. Three office romance novellas from talented writers Julie Cannon, Aurora Rey, and M. Ullrich. (978-1-63555-145-7)

The Deep End by Ellie Hart. When family ties become entangled in murder and deception, it's time to find a way out... (978-1-63555-288-1)